P9-CFE-553

JAN 2010

USA TODAY Bestselling Author

JENNIFER GREENE

USA TODAY Bestselling Author

MERLINE LOVELACE

CINDI MYERS

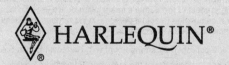

Baby, It's Cold Outside

HARLEQUIN®

TORONTO • NEW YORK • LONDON
AMSTERDAM • PARIS • SYDNEY • HAMBURG
STOCKHOLM • ATHENS • TOKYO • MILAN • MADRID
PRAGUE • WARSAW • BUDAPEST • AUCKLAND

Recycling programs
for this product may
not exist in your area.

ISBN-13: 978-0-373-83739-7

BABY, IT'S COLD OUTSIDE

Copyright © 2010 by Harlequin Books S.A.

The publisher acknowledges the copyright holders
of the individual works as follows:

BLAME IT ON THE BLIZZARD
Copyright © 2010 by Alison Hart.

DEEP FREEZE
Copyright © 2010 by Merline Lovelace.

MELTING POINT
Copyright © 2010 by Cynthia Myers.

This edition published by arrangement with Harlequin Books S.A.

® and TM are trademarks of the publisher. Trademarks indicated with ® are registered in the United States Patent and Trademark Office, the Canadian Trade Marks Office and in other countries.

www.eHarlequin.com

Printed in U.S.A.

CONTENTS

BLAME IT ON THE BLIZZARD   9
Jennifer Greene

DEEP FREEZE   107
Merline Lovelace

MELTING POINT   191
Cindi Myers

To the real Rick—
Not just a wonderful guy,
but one of the true heroes in my life

BLAME IT ON THE BLIZZARD

Jennifer Greene

Dear Reader,

Not many sane people likely head for Alaska in the dead of winter...but I have to confess that I would, anytime, any way I could get there. I adore Alaska. It's one of the most soul-renewing places on the planet. From eagles to whales, from breathtaking mountains to glaciers, every turn of the corner in Alaska is full of wonder and extraordinary life.

It seemed a perfect place to lock up Emily and Rick—two characters who think they want to hide out from life.

Actually, they were doing a pretty good job of that hiding business—until they were accidentally trapped together. Initially, of course, they could blame what happened on the blizzard....

I hope you enjoy reading the story as much as I loved writing it!

Jennifer Greene

CHAPTER ONE

WHEN EMILIE BARTLETT HEARD the battering thuds below—it sounded as if someone's fist was pounding on the front door—she burrowed under the heap of blankets without bothering to open her eyes.

She wasn't sleeping.

She hadn't slept since she could remember.

But there was no one at the front door. There couldn't be. When the seaplane brought her in two days before, the blizzard had been predicted. The pilot had argued and protested about leaving her, but Emilie knew what she was getting into.

She hadn't spent time in her family's Alaskan lodge in years, but the week before Christmas, the weather was predictable. The snow had started yesterday, silent and soft. Then the wind began—tufty and capricious at first.

By midyesterday, the view from every window was a whiteout, and the winds had turned into an orchestra of trumpet blows and percussion and high-pitched screams in every nook and cranny. No one could feel more alone than in the middle of an Alaskan blizzard, but that was exactly what Emilie wanted. To be alone where no one could reach her—at least until the holiday season was completely over.

She'd just snuggled in tight again when she heard a second round of pounding.

This time she pulled the down comforter over her head. It was one thing to be depressed, another thing to be delusional. There was no one at the door. The closest house was two miles away and probably uninhabited—few stuck out the winters around Silver Bay; the weather was just too unrelentingly rough.

The wind was ferocious enough to create all kinds of eerie, unpredictable sounds. She just had to ignore them.

The next time she opened her eyes, the bedside clock claimed it was ten the next morning. Startled at how deeply she'd slept, she stumbled out of bed, nearly tripping over her shearling slippers. The loft bedroom was dark, of course. At this time of year, it was night-dark except for a few hours a day. The wind was screaming like a howling banshee, even worse than when she'd gone to sleep.

She took five minutes in the redwood bathroom to clean up and brush her teeth, then hustled into clothes. She opted for layers, naturally, choosing a Synchilla zip-up over long wool pants and heavy socks. As an afterthought, she scooped up a couple books and some extra clothes. Probably, with a blizzard this fierce, she should conserve heat, shut off the two loft bedrooms and just live downstairs for a few days.

That was a decision she'd make after coffee, she decided, and aimed down the dim staircase.

On the third step, she faltered. Out of nowhere, the child's face popped into her mind—the scared eyes, the so-white face, the boyish shock of cowlicks, the smile she'd finally managed to coax out of him in the operating room. That smile...gone. The light in his eyes...gone.

Ruthlessly she slammed the memory from her mind. She'd deal with it. That was why she was here, holed up away from everyone over the holiday. To deal with it.

But not yet. She just wasn't ready.

The staircase led directly to the massive room below. The entire downstairs was open. Behind the staircase, the kitchen and dining area faced east. Just ahead of her was the sweep of living space, dominated by the man-tall white stone fireplace. The hearth screen darkened the already shadowed room, but she could still make out the healthy bed of golden embers. The furnace was going strong, but building up a serious fire would add a ton of warmth.

Three huge leather couches framed the hearth. She dropped the books and spare clothes on one, turned around and abruptly connected with something solid—something big and bulky and strangely warm. She tripped over the object and heard a groan—a human groan, a human *male* groan.

Her first instinct was to be scared out of her mind, but there was no time for panic to even register—she couldn't stop herself from falling, tumbling headlong, over the body.

The crash wasn't pretty. The thick hearth rug saved her head from a serious bump, but an elbow smacked against something hard enough to send shooting pains up her arm. Her ankle twisted. Her hand scrabbled into the piled logs in the cradle.

None of that remotely mattered.

"Hell," the voice repeated several times. The voice so definitely wasn't hers. It was a tenor. Sleepy. Male.

Very male.

He repeated "Hell" a few more times, making her think that possibly his vocabulary was limited. But then he seemed to remember a few more words. "I'm sorry. Damn it. Are you all right? I never meant to scare the wits out of you."

"You didn't." He most certainly had—but Emilie couldn't imagine a reason in the universe to admit it. She scrambled off him, hit her elbow again on the hearth, and still managed to push away from him fast. She hauled in a lungful of air. "Look, I get it," she said swiftly. "I have no idea why you were out in the storm, but obviously, you must have needed shelter. It's perfectly all right. I just didn't expect anyone to be here, so you startled me."

"I *did* need shelter, and I knew the lodge was here. But I didn't expect to see smoke in the chimney—and I *never* expected to find a woman here. I did knock, I swear. And kept knocking. But no one answered, and the door wasn't locked. I had to get in. I was beyond cold. Hurt."

Only the one word caught her attention. "Hurt how?"

"Burned. Wind brought a tree down, crashed through the roof, debris came down on my woodstove, started a fire. Put out the fire, but couldn't stay there, not with the hole in the roof. Couldn't secure the place, not in these conditions. So I had to get out, even if it meant negotiating with this storm. I knew the lodge was here, closest place I could get to. I—" His voice skidded to a sharp stop. His gaze homed in on her face and body as if he'd just gotten around to looking at her. "Good grief. What on earth are *you* doing here?"

Emilie blinked. Most men, on first meeting, seemed

to react to her a little differently than they did other women. She wasn't sure whether it was a major treat or a major insult that he took one gander at her tousled blond hair and blue eyes and leaped to an instant negative judgment. Granted, her normally decent figure had to look lumpy under the zillion layers of clothes—but this was still the first time a guy had responded to her with an expression akin to horror.

"Wait," he said, and swiped a hand over his face. "Wait. I didn't mean that like it sounded. Obviously you wouldn't be here if you didn't have a claim to the place. I'm the interloper, not you. It's just that…from your appearance, you don't look as if you could survive two minutes in an Alaskan winter. And for you to be here alone seems even more impossible. I just—"

Since he seemed determined to stick his foot even further into his mouth, she intervened. Only one thing he'd said so far mattered anyway. "Where were you burned? How bad?"

"Not bad. It was my place that suffered real damage. I was…"

Again, his voice trailed off. The more he looked at her, the more he seemed to be suffering from shock. Emilie hadn't felt like laughing in a blue moon…but darn it, she was the one entitled to feel shock at the intruder, not the other way around. His appearance alone should have struck her as intimidating. He had to be twice her weight and well, well over six feet in height.

Firelight accented his black Irish looks—the glossy dark hair, the striking blue eyes. His whiskers weren't quite a beard, just scruffy-looking. He had to be over thirty, but not by much. Being stranded with a stranger under these conditions was uncomfortable…but being stranded with an ultra-good-looking guy so close to her own age notched up the awkwardness a ton.

Maybe more than a ton. The way Emilie had been feeling lately, she could have been stranded with a cross between Keanu Reeves and Hugh Jackman and not cared. She only wished she could scare up some positive emotion about anything.

She glanced around the room, aware now that he'd left a trail of evidence from when he'd come in. He didn't have to tell the story for her to assess what had happened. The trail of parka and boots and gear on the floor by the door told its own tale. He'd clearly peeled off everything wet and ice-covered, then yanked a blanket from one of the couches and crashed on the fat, thick rug close to the fire.

While he kept talking, she tried to jolt herself into action. Her elbow and ankle still twinged a little from the fall, but overall, she was completely fine. The fire needed feeding, and doing something constructive gave her time to figure out who and what her interloper really was.

"It really never occurred to me that anyone would be in the lodge, until I got close enough to see the chimney smoke. It didn't matter. I didn't have any choice. I had to find shelter. But when I couldn't rouse you with knocking, I just figured you were the guy who owned the lodge, that you were sleeping hard. Truthfully I never hesitated to come in."

Her father and grandfather would have expected him to do just that. They never locked the place. Who locked a door in the middle of nowhere? The doors were latched to prevent animals from coming in, just as shutters on the windows were a protection against storm danger. But the larder was always left fully stocked. Anyone who needed supplies could use them, and then was expected to replace them. It was one of those unwritten laws in Alaska that everyone understood.

"I should have found you, woken you, I guess. But by that time, I was honestly completely wiped. Seriously cold, hurt. Just stretched beyond what I could do. In the back of my mind, I thought I'd heard a couple of doctors owned the place, but I swear, it never occurred to me there'd be a woman here—"

"Uh-huh. We've been over that." She used a fireplace fork, pushed the embers together, and then reached for the wood in the cradle. By the time she'd started with the baby-size chunks, her stranger had come up from behind to add the big suckers. The fireplace could take four-foot-long logs. Her dad used to say they could cook a bear in the hearth, if they had to—an idea that had always made her shudder.

But at that moment, her mind seemed obsessed with fire-building in an entirely different context. The stranger was close. Too close. Close enough that her body instinctively tensed in sexual awareness. He was just so obviously a strong, virile man. As soon as the fire was well loaded, she yanked the wrought-iron screen in place and quickly shifted away.

"I don't know if you need food, but I sure do. If you want to clean up, there's a bathroom behind the stairs there. I'll see what I can scare up."

Actually, she knew exactly what supplies were in the pantry, but she was hoping that if he'd get out of sight for a few minutes, she'd have a chance to catch her breath.

She turned on every light in the kitchen to start with. The whole dining area was set up institutional guy-style, all stainless steel and stone, heavy appliances, cast-iron pots and pans. Ugly. But heat piped through the floor, so her feet were warm, and besides the staples in the pantry, she'd carted in both freezer staples and fresh foods. It didn't take long to put something together. She chased up Egg Beaters, chives, fake cream cheese, pepper, frozen hash browns— not as good as a fresh omelet, but it'd have to do.

She'd whipped the ingredients together and was pouring it in a skillet when her visitor emerged from the shower. She was calmed down by then. Or so she thought.

The moment he stepped from the bathroom, her pulse jumped. Damn man. Her reaction to him was getting downright annoying. He was clean, his dark hair glossy and damp, but he was still unshaven, his clothes seriously high-tech but clearly well-worn. It wasn't his fault he was so damned striking.

He glanced at her with the same glowering blue eyes—as if he'd taken another look at her and had a similar problem. Her appearance ticked him off—for no reason she could imagine.

"If you open the cupboard to the right of the sink," she said. "You could get out a couple of plates, silverware."

"Sure. What else?"

"Nothing. This is hardly going to be fancy. How did your burns look?"

"I can't say I paid attention. There's only one that hurts. It's nothing serious." He opened the right cupboard, pulled down a couple of plates, scrounged for silverware, then turned around to see where to put them. A massive plank table took up the open south exposure, seated a dozen without half trying. He opted to set the plates on the stonework counter and pull up a stool.

Emilie didn't say, "Let me see the burns, I'm a doctor." Right now she was unsure whether she would ever be willing to put M.D. after her name again. So she just said, "I'm only asking because there's a box of first aid supplies if you need it. First shelf in the pantry."

"I bandaged up before I left."

Again, her first instinct was to press, to leap in. Instead she attacked the eggs with a spatula. "About time I asked your name. Mine's Emilie Bartlett."

"I could have guessed the Bartlett. I was told this place was called the Bartlett Lodge, that the Bartlett family had owned the property for several generations. Anyway. I'm Rick. Rick Hunter."

"Is your place going to be fixable?"

"Yeah. But I won't know when or how until after this wind and snow die down. Ideally I can fix it myself. I've got tools, roofing materials, some pretty good basic skills. But if I can't do it alone…well, then I'll radio for a plane, hole up in Anchorage until conditions are better. Unfortunately…"

She filled in the blank, as she slid the makeshift omelets onto plates. "Unfortunately, you're stuck right here until the blizzard's over."

"Afraid it looks that way." He nodded a thanks for

the plate, faced her straight. "Are you going to be okay with that?"

No, Emilie thought, she definitely wasn't. Across the long room, the fire had caught, was lapping around the logs like a hungry wolf, lightening and brightening the whole room. Illuminating him. The dark hair, the darkish beard, the shoulders that stretched his shirt, the long muscled legs. Just looking at him made her hormones vibrate like a manic tuning fork.

She could feel him continue to size her up, not obtrusively, but it was there, his gaze scouring her face, her eyes. Trying to figure her out.

She didn't want to be figured out. It wasn't personal. She hadn't left all her family and friends at Christmas—and put her whole life on hold—to disappear into the Alaskan wilderness in winter, just to be stuck with company.

But tarnation. There *was* a blizzard.

She had no choice. And neither did her stranded neighbor.

WELL, IF THIS WASN'T as comfortable as a nap in a beehive. Rick had never chosen a job in a remote area in Alaska on a whim. He had a good reason, the kind of reason he suspected an alcoholic would readily understand. If you're not exposed to your particular poison, you didn't have to worry about getting in trouble.

Rick's poison was women, and although he'd told himself a million times to get over his ex-wife's infidelity—he hadn't. He'd taken a bullet in the service. Went through broken ribs and a leg in traction after a plane crash. Overall, he knew damn well he had a high tolerance for pain; he could keep on going when others caved. But nothing hurt the way his ex-wife taking off with his best friend had. The stab in the back should have healed, but somehow there seemed no way to take the knife out.

That had nothing to do with Emilie, of course. He'd just rather be stranded with a bear than a woman, that was all.

"You don't have to do that," she said.

"You're making the meal. Only fair that I do the cleanup." He dug into the soapy water for another bowl. It was easy to see how this kitchen thing was going to go. In theory, she had a good idea, to use up the fresh food she'd brought in a stew that would last a few days. In practice, she was creating more messes than he could keep up with.

"Is there any food you're allergic to?"

Personally, he thought it was a little late to ask the question, since she'd put everything but the kitchen sink in the big pot—including some foods he couldn't identify and wasn't sure he wanted to. But she left a dripping spoon here. A bowl there. Used a couple cutting boards. Opened a can of stewed tomatoes and left the can on the counter.

"No problem," he said.

He watched her splash in some wine. Then some Russian salad dressing. She was starting to scare him.

"Do you live and work up here?" she asked.

"Yup. Started out as a civil engineer. Two years ago, took a job mapping minerals and water in certain remote areas for the state of Alaska. Can't beat the hours, the pay or the free time. My cabin's not as big as your lodge, but it's more than comfortable."

He liked her lodge, though. The loft bedrooms upstairs led to a lanai, then an open staircase down. The whole downstairs was open, with giant split-log walls. Place smelled of pine and oil. A plank floor was warmed up with thick native rugs. The dining table was long enough to sleep on, sturdy enough to do surgery. Pipes had been wired into the fireplace grate, so the fire alone could circulate at least nominal heat through the whole place. Someone had really thought through the construction.

The screaming wind drew his attention outside—not that there was anything to see from the windows but blinding white and ice. "Did you turn on a radio this morning?"

"Didn't bother," she admitted. "Hardly needed a forecaster to tell us there's a blizzard going on."

He didn't raise an eyebrow, but he thought about it. Not counting the buildup of drifts and subzero temperatures, at least another foot of snow had heaped on the landscape since last night. Normal people tended to have their ears glued to the media in conditions like this.

"You're set for firewood? Fuel?"

"My dad never left here without the woodshed completely filled. Same for the pantry. Always have to fly in freezer and fresh foods, but there's plenty to eat."

"Generator?"

She frowned. "I'm sure there is."

He was sure there was, too. But was again surprised that she didn't know—or care. He reached over her head to put away two mugs, and saw her instinctively back a few inches away from him. Not skitter. Not flinch. Just make a point of not being within touching distance.

That was okay by him. He crouched down, put away the cast-iron frying pan under the stove, felt his shoulder scream. The worst burn was there, on his back.

He ignored it, concentrated on her instead. He was still having a hard time recovering from the shock of finding a woman alone here. And even though he was allergic to women these days, it was impossible not to be curious about her.

She had an educated, well-bred look. Her hair was the color of pale wheat, all short and tousled, but still, distinctly city-styled. Even layers of warm clothes couldn't completely conceal a slim, sleek build. Her face had classic fine bones, and that incredible skin had been creamed and pampered rather than ever exposed to frostbite and bitter winds.

Her prettiness didn't really snare his attention. But her eyes did. They were bright blue. And haunted.

Not that he cared. But few women, that he could imagine, would choose to hole up over the holidays in a place as cut off from civilization as this lodge. Silver Bay was breathtaking in the summer. In the winter, it could be savagely wild. And she'd shown relatively little stress on finding a strange man sleeping in her house.

It was as if she didn't care.

That was what kept striking him.

She didn't care about the weather, about conditions, about her own safety in general. Didn't seem to care about anything.

"Hunter," she said, and then corrected herself. "Rick. I've seen you flinch a couple times. I'm going to curl up in front of the fire with a book, but I'll leave a good salve for burns on the counter here. If you need it, use it."

"May take you up on that. Thanks."

"Also, feel free to wander around. Figure out where you want to sleep, raid the closet in the upstairs bathroom for pillows, extra blankets. Just take what you need."

"Thanks. Again." He watched her put the lid on the pot and turn around to aim past him.

It was just for that instant they were in each other's breathing space.

Maybe even less than an instant when their eyes met.

A spark lit. Not in the hearth, but between them. She felt it, too, because a flush shot up her neck. And he felt it like a clutch in the groin, some stupid elemental awareness that she was one hell of an interesting woman, and his hormones knew it even if his head rejected the idea.

Out of nowhere, he said flatly, "You're safe."

As if his comment made absolute sense, she responded the same way. "I never doubted it for a second. We'll both be fine."

Maybe she believed that. He sure as hell wanted to.

Only just then, the lights went out.

CHAPTER TWO

WHEN THE LIGHTS WENT OUT, Emilie froze. The sudden crash of silence made her heart thud. Who knew the fridge and computer and furnace and clocks made so much white noise? But without it, the darkness seemed eerie and somehow menacing.

"Hey."

It was her stranger's voice, close by—Rick's eyes had to be as blinded by the sudden darkness as hers were, but he seemed to sense she was having a teensy-weensy freak-out. His hand touched her shoulder, a groping movement as if to locate exactly where she was. And once he figured that out, he swung both arms around her. It wasn't the hug of a lover, she told herself. It was more like, well, a holding.

His voice was as gruff and scratchy as his whiskery chin. "Emilie, it's all right. Just take a few steps and you'll be able to see the firelight. It'll be warm and light in there. I'll go find the generator, get it going."

"Yes," she agreed, but she didn't move. She wasn't afraid. She knew she wasn't. But that darkness was so total, for those few seconds, that it struck her like loneliness. Being alone was one thing. Feeling alone without warmth or light was a huge something else.

Ever since…the crisis…she'd steered clear of company, family, friends. Maybe it had built up. The hunger to have someone there. To be hugged. Touched. Who knew how fierce that need could be?

The stranger's arms were alien. Big, warm, strong. "Hey," he said again, but this time it was a murmur, not a greeting. "It's just the electricity. We were always going to lose power in a blizzard like this. It's annoying. But not dangerous. We'll have to do some things, to secure heat, think about food differently, water, sanitation. But it's just a storm, you know?"

"Of course I know. I'm all right." Still, she didn't move. Slowly, her lungs allowed oxygen to seep in. Slowly, her heart stopped that thud of despair. "Darn it." His skin, his voice, the feel and smell and sound of him were making her even more light-headed. It was like being held by a pirate, a stealer of hearts, a stealer of breath. A stupid image, for a woman who credited herself with being pragmatic and unrelentingly honest in every circumstance.

She stepped back, pushed back. "Well, that was my ninny move of the year. I'm sorry, Hunter, I don't know what got into me—and you're totally right. There's a lot to do. I'll get candles, a lantern…that pot of stew I made isn't going to cook on the stovetop now. There's a brick oven built into the side of the fireplace. I never used it, but I know my dad did—I've seen him. I'll figure it out."

His hand cuffed her wrist, just momentarily. "*Are* you all right?"

Emilie thought she should be the one asking him that question. He was the one stuck in a blizzard with her—

a woman who'd practically glued herself to a total stranger…and a woman who was a murderer besides.

If he knew the whole story, Emilie figured she had to be close to his worst nightmare.

THREE HOURS LATER, RICK was sore, worn-out and confused. He stomped around looking for her—not that Emilie was hard to find. No matter how big the lodge was, it was still a confined space.

And Emilie was precisely where he'd seen her last. Whoever had designed the original lodge had opted to build a brick oven into the side of the massive old fireplace. An hour ago, when he'd passed by, she was transferring the contents of the pot into a cast-iron container meant for the fireplace oven. She was still there. Still trying to figure out how to make the oven work.

The last time, he'd had a prime view of her butt, since she was leaning her whole body into the oven. It was a tight butt. A little bony. Mesmerizing, if a guy was into bony butts—which Rick definitely used to be, before he'd given up women. Now, a woman's behind was just something he noticed. He was still male, after all. That part of a woman's anatomy always had been, always would be, worth intensive study.

What she thought she would discover inside the brick oven was another question.

And now, three hours later, she was sitting back on her legs. Three lanterns had been added to the scene, obviously so she could see the oven better. Her hair looked silky white with all the ambient firelight. The style was even more mussed up, decorated with a few—he was pretty sure—cobwebs. She was staring at the oven with pursed lips. A tool kit sat at her side, gaping open.

He had no idea what she thought she was going to do with all those tools.

"Hi," she said, when she realized he was standing behind her. "When I heard the generator start, I yelled out a cheer."

"I heard the cheer. I appreciated it." He hunkered down next to her. "These are words I never thought I'd say to a woman…but I think we need to talk."

For the first time, he caught a smile. A downright perky grin. It lit up her face, her eyes, turned her from a good-looking woman to a stunner. "Those are words I don't usually like to hear from a guy, either."

He figured they should start with something easy. "Are you looking for the button to turn the oven on?"

She nodded. "I've looked *everywhere*. There's nothing here. Just this hole…"

He sighed. "You've never cooked on this before, have you?"

"No. But my dad did. I know it's a great oven. Makes fantastic bread and potatoes…sometimes pies…"

He didn't say, "There is no turn-on button, princess," because he was pretty sure that would sound condescending. He didn't want to aggravate her unnecessarily when there were so many things he had to cover that were all too likely to get her dander up. So right then, he just said, "I'll get the oven going, so you can see how it's done for the next time."

"Great."

"First, the oven either has to have a functional exhaust

fan, or a flue. You have to make sure the flue is open, right?" Immediately she sidled up next to him, stuck her head right back in the oven again. He gave her credit for being willing to listen and learn. He gave himself credit for not jumping her.

Okay. Even if he was antiwomen—a vow for life— close proximity to an attractive woman could still produce the obvious, immediate reaction. He hadn't been this hard this fast since he was around fifteen.

"Then…normally you'd use a fire-starter block. But we're going to add a cupful of coals from the real fire, add a little kindling…see? I mean *little*. Now we're going to watch to see if it takes. The coals should be hot enough to ignite the sticks without needing a match."

"Okay. Got it."

For a few minutes, there was nothing to do but wait, see if the kindling took, before they could start building the actual cooking fire. "You never use a lot of wood. Shouldn't need to. You need a bed of coals, but the whole concept of a brick oven is the concentration of heat in a small space. You don't leave it alone any different than you'd leave any other fire alone, okay?"

"I knew that," she said wryly.

Yeah, right. If she'd ever been a Girl Scout—or built a fire—he'd eat Brussels sprouts. Not a risk he had to worry about. "You mind if I ask when you came up here?"

"I flew in, or was flown in, four days ago."

"And you planned to stay how long?"

She looked at him, as she eased back on the closest couch edge, where she could watch her new oven fire.

"Until after Christmas. After the whole holiday. I didn't set an exact date, but the pilot said he'd leave January second free to come and get me. Nothing sacred about that day—particularly if there's bad weather like this. But that's the ballpark."

"The ballpark," he echoed, and hand-rubbed his eyes. "Okay. Spit it out. What's the problem."

"Look, I don't want to insult you—"

"But you're going to, huh?"

"Not out of meanness. I'm just…startled, that's all. Did you think you were well prepared to hole up for a while?"

Her eyebrows shot up in surprise. "Are you kidding? There's a full pantry of canned goods and staples. I brought bags of fresh foods with me. The shed's loaded with stacked firewood. I've got a crank radio. Enough batteries and lanterns and candles to light up the whole place," she added. "And my dad leaves a rifle here. It's locked upstairs. I can't imagine needing it, but it's just one more way I felt prepared no matter what—"

He held up a hand, to shut her down.

"What?" She was starting to sound cross.

"Okay. To start with. That very pretty, very expensive generator has probably never been maintained. She started up, but she's only got enough fuel for three or four days. And I don't see any oil or lubricant around."

"Oh." Her voice lost some of its oomph.

"You think that's a lot of stacked wood out there? There's a huge supply of firewood, you're right. But it isn't cut. Somehow I can't believe you've got a lot of experience with an axe, splitting wood. What you've got won't last forty-eight hours."

"Oh."

"And that's real good news about the rifle. But do you know where the bullets are? Do you know how to shoot if you had to?"

She sloughed off the first question, as if it were irrelevant. "Yes, I can shoot. My dad taught me."

"When you were how old?"

"Eleven."

"And you've shot a rifle how many times since then?"

She didn't answer that question, just gave him A Look. He'd flunked the course in understanding women, but this particular look was easy to translate. He could continue to ask questions, but not if he wanted to live unscarred. He rubbed at the nape of his neck again. "That little crank radio you have is real cute. Bet you can pick up any station within ten miles."

A little less glower. "Yeah. I was told it was a good one."

"But there isn't anyone broadcasting within ten miles, sweet pea. Or twenty miles. I strongly suspect there's no possibility of your getting weather or news or information from that thing."

"Oh."

"I'm just confused. That's all I'm saying. You came here for the holiday. All by yourself. About as prepared as a lamb in wolf country."

For a moment the only sound was the crackle and spit of fire—and the howling wind outside. She looked at him, as if deciding how to respond. Rick figured she'd likely be annoyed, justifiably so, but they weren't exactly at a picnic together. He wanted to know—could even *need* to know—what she was made of.

Finally she sat back and crossed her legs. "I'm thinking about knocking your block off," she said mildly.

"You wouldn't be the first woman who felt that way."

"It's none of your business how prepared I am—or not. What my story is. Or isn't. On the other hand, I don't have a reason in the universe not to tell the truth. I thought I *was* well prepared. In fact, since I tend to be downright fanatical about thinking through every detail—and certainly I knew bad weather was automatic at this time of year—I'm mortified that I flunked the job. So if you were making the point that I don't know how to cope in the winter here, you're darn right. I get it. You're prepared. I'm not. But your being here doesn't make any sense, either."

"Say what?"

"You heard me. You're as loony as I am. You're up here all alone in the middle of a blizzard, too. So you're better prepared than I am. Big deal. It's still nuts. I mean, have you committed murder or robbery or something? Are you running from the IRS? What's the point of your living up here in complete isolation like this?"

"What's the point for you?" he asked right back.

"I asked first."

"So we're going to argue about this like kids?"

"No," she said. "We're going to have something for lunch. I'm starving."

Putting together lunch, they skirted around each other like wary pups in a cage. Except that she wasn't a pup. God knew the kitchen area was big enough to play B-ball, but every time he turned around, there she was. Those haunted soft eyes, the fluff of hair, those elegant bones, that…something of hers. Defiance. Stubbornness.

Rick figured it was better to try and label her personality rather than admit she was just plain sexy as hell.

"Well, considering we don't know how the stew's going to work out later, I guess this'll do for now." But she rolled her eyes at his choice. He'd thrown together a couple peanut butter and jelly sandwiches, added a bottle of water, heaped on some chips.

For herself, she'd put together cut wedges of some sandwich with cheese and lettuce and trimmings, added a banana, a napkin, poured her bottled water in a glass.

They were in a blizzard, for Pete's sake. There was no easy way to do dishes, no purpose in fussing. But whatever.

"What are we going to do if the fireplace oven doesn't work?" she fretted.

"Work something else out. Although I'm inclined not to use the kitchen stove and oven. We need to conserve generator use for the absolute essentials. Water, for one. But there are lots of things we can cook on the fire—starting with coffee."

"Coffee's a priority beyond food, water or sleep," she said firmly.

Damned if she didn't make him grin. "Got that right. So. Are we actually going to finish that awkward conversation about how we ended up in Alaska?"

"Yeah. But I want to hear your story first."

"Fine." It was too hot to sit directly on the hearth, but the couches were body-swallowers, so he plunked down on the thick carpet, Indian-style. He had a clear view of her face by firelight from that angle. "I moved here almost two years ago, like I said. Used to be a civil engineer. Got out of school, MIT, made a great friend, and we teamed up, went into business together. Built bridges around the world. Loved it. Traveled to some godforsaken places, worked impossibly long hours in impossibly awful climates, saw a lot of life. Loved it."

"Hmm. So far I'm not hearing any criminal history or connections to the Mafia."

"Nope. Straight as an arrow. Oh. I got married en route. My partner was my best man. Angie was another dream come true. I worshipped the ground she walked on, and she felt the same way about me. I thought. She traveled with me. Was a teacher. Always found ways to help out, do stuff, wherever we were."

"Kids?"

"No kids. Both of us wanted them. But at first, we were busy seeing the world, not in a good place to have kids. And after that, well, seems she decided she loved Brad more than me."

"Brad? Your partner?"

"Yeah." He finished the second sandwich, dusted off his hands. "So that's the deal. I started out hurt. Destroyed-hurt. Then I got mad, as well. I'm still mad. I intend to stay mad until kingdom come. Got a job mapping minerals and water, employed by the kindly state of Alaska, do the hermit thing in the hardcore winter months, trek to some really outback places in the summer. They pay me a fortune."

"That's the whole story?"

"Basically. Family, friends, kept telling me I had to get over her. Over them. If one more person told me to 'move on,' I figured I was going to lose it in a real serious way.

I needed and wanted to be alone." His eyes met hers. "I'm not looking for trouble. From anyone. And for damn sure, I don't want sympathy or advice or a listening ear. I've had enough of that kind of hounding to last me a lifetime."

"Gotcha." She was still on her first triangle wedge. If she took any smaller bites, she'd still be eating that tiny sandwich at midnight. "Well, my story's a lot more dramatic. I killed someone."

He dropped his water bottle. "Say what?"

"I come from a family of doctors. A dad, a brother, two uncles, my grandfather. Lost my mom when I was little—car crash. Anyway. The deal in my family was that you knew, from grade school on, that you were going into medicine. Oh. And rule number two was that you'd spend at least two weeks every year at the lodge in Alaska. When I was a kid, I came with all my guys. They hunted and fished, and I holed up upstairs with my dolls." She pointed at him. "But…I was doing surgery on my dolls even then. So don't be thinking I was a girlie girl."

His mouth twitched. "Don't shoot me, but maybe I did have a passing thought that you weren't a natural tomboy."

"All right, all right. So maybe I was a *little* on the girlie side. Maybe I still am. Anyway, I didn't go the surgeon route like my dad and gramps. I went to school, Chicago, became an anesthesiologist. Graduated top of my class, as was expected. Got a job at a terrific hospital—Boston—as was expected. I just turned twenty-nine. Been at the job less than two years."

"And…"

"And there was a little boy. Nine. Big trauma, fell off a trampoline. Going to be a long surgery. Neurosurgeon asked for me specifically, because I'm good. Seriously good. It was going to take a miracle, everyone knew it. It was going to take all of us to bring him through."

Something in him stilled. It was unfortunately easy to guess where this was going, no matter how tough she was trying to look. "But the kid didn't make it?"

"Yeah. He died." She put down the second wedge. When it was obvious she wasn't going to eat it, he reached for it.

"And this was your fault somehow?"

"That's not really a yes or no answer. It wasn't about *fault*. He was too little, too damaged to fix. Putting him through seven hours of surgery—there was no way to keep him under that long. He had other health issues. So it was this balance, of keeping him under enough that he didn't feel anything, but not depress his system so far that he'd quit breathing." She said quietly, easily, "I did my job. Everything I could. Everything I knew how to do. But he died."

"But you were blamed?" He got the haunted eyes now. Got the wounded fragility. But still couldn't quite put it all together.

"No. No one blamed me. I'm not a hundred percent positive that anyone could have saved the child. The best surgeon, the best anesthesiologist, though, were the critical parts of the equation. My family, they've all had deaths. It's just the way it is. You can't save every patient. They were all on me to buck up, put it behind me, get over it, move on."

"Okay."

"That was...like two and a half weeks ago. The problem...isn't about blaming myself. It's about being in the position of God. I don't know that I want that power, of life and death. I hated it. *Hated* losing that boy. It's as if he were mine. As if I were the one grieving as much as his mother."

He said nothing, because he was afraid to. Her heart was in her eyes.

"I never wanted that power. I went into medicine because I was raised to be an obedient daughter who fulfills expectations. I never...made a choice. I just took the ride I was supposed to take. Maybe...I'd rather be a clerk in a clothing store. Or drive a truck. Or sell cosmetics or jewelry or something."

Again, he said nothing, but had to bite his tongue. She shut up when he was talking, so now, even if it was killing him, he had to stay shut up for her.

"The point is...I'm not sure I'm going back to doctoring. And facing the family and friends over the holidays, I just couldn't do it." She shook her head. "I'm not depressed. I'm not crazy. I just need some time to think. I want to be left *alone.* No hounding. No advice. No sympathy. I'm not looking for anything from anyone."

"Neither am I."

"There's nothing wrong with being alone."

"I totally agree."

"I'm tired of people interfering. Telling me what's right for me. I love my family and friends. But I have to live my own life."

"You're singing my song."

"I don't need anyone. Much less anyone telling me what I should do."

"Damn right."

She hesitated with a sudden frown. "What's going on here?"

He hesitated, too. "We're getting along?"

She let out a short laugh. "Who'd have thought it?"

If she was confounded, Rick figured she didn't know the half of it. He ran from women faster than skunks. No offense to skunks—or women. He just wasn't going to volunteer to be stabbed in the gut again. Realizing that he felt drawn to Emilie, not just interested but darn well *pulled*…was enough to make him want to run for the hills.

As far as Rick could tell, she had the same reaction to their storytelling. Just too much personal sharing, too quickly. Both of them ran around for a while, not specifically avoiding each other, so much as easily finding things to do that required no contact or conversation. She brought clothes and books and personal things down from the upstairs, so they could completely close up the loft rooms and conserve heat. He scouted around for the location of batteries, emergency supplies, food stock, then did chore stuff like closing doors, blocking air leaks in windows and door edges.

Eventually, though, he found her standing at a north window at the same time he was standing at a west one. There was nothing outside to see but snow and more snow. Truth to tell, it was downright breathtaking. Treacherous, but breathtaking. The view was an ever-changing dance of swirls and heaps and spangles of snow shapes...but the relentlessly screaming wind could drive anyone crazy.

"You got a deck of cards around here?" he asked.

She came through. He volunteered to play Crazy Eights, but she was the one who suggested poker, so he figured hey, whatever happened after that wasn't his fault. She'd chosen the game.

First hand, he drew a pair of aces. Still, he kept the betting down to five toothpicks, because he didn't want to discourage her right off the bat—it was going to be a long afternoon.

She showed him three tens, scooped up the toothpicks.

He searched her face, looking for signs of guile or cunning. Found nothing but delighted surprise at winning in her expression.

He hunkered down and dealt the cards. Because he was good at the game—downright great, if he said so himself—he had ample time to reflect on all the stuff she'd told him.

Man, she was so wrong.

So much about her made sense, now that he knew she was a doctor. The sharp intelligence in her eyes, yet the survival naïveté. Her believing herself to be so prepared, because she was, in her life; she just didn't have skills that were relevant in this environment. Still, the truth of her situation was obvious, would have been obvious to a stone.

She needed to be what she was. A healer. A doctor. He was sorry about the kid that died, but Emilie wasn't dumb. She should get it. The death wasn't on her. Bad stuff happened, to everyone and everything.

His sympathy for her slowly, methodically decreased—exponentially the longer they played cards.

"What," he said, "do you always have luck like this?"

"Luck?" she hooted. "Luck! This is skill, boy. Either put your bet in the pot or fold, youngster."

"This time," he said patiently, "you have to be bluffing."

"You'll have to pay to find out."

His eyes narrowed. "I'll pay. But since I'm running out of toothpicks, I think we should make the stakes just a little more interesting."

CHAPTER THREE

"STRIP," EMILIE ORDERED HIM, and had to chuckle when his jaw dropped in shock. Who'd have thought she'd have the feminine power to make him feel off balance? Or that her big-guy pirate could suddenly clear his throat because of nerves.

"Now just hold your horses. I'm not out of toothpicks yet. Close, yeah. But this time I've got a good hand."

"I'm not talking about the poker game. I'm talking about the way you wince every time you twist your left arm and shoulder a certain way."

There. His nerve level immediately simmered down. His expression changed from sudden sexual awareness— to plain old annoyance. "It's nothing. Play your cards."

"Fine. But that's my bet. If I win, you take off your shirt."

"Don't hold your breath, counting on winning," he grumped, and held his cards closer than diamonds.

Emilie wanted to chuckle again…yet felt her smile softening. The whole time they'd been playing poker, she kept recalling the story he'd told her. What a stupid wife he'd had. The woman had thrown out a man who loved her—loved, trusted, bared his soul with, appreciated, the whole serious ball of wax. Good men, men who really knew how to love, were darned hard to find. And yeah, he was scruffy-looking. But now it made more sense, why he chose to go around looking like a disreputable, dangerous pirate.

He'd felt betrayed.

He'd *been* betrayed.

He wasn't encouraging anyone—man, woman or child—to get too close again.

Calmly she laid down her hand. Three sixes. Two twos.

He stared at it in disbelief. But he didn't move.

"Now come on," she said teasingly. "This is no big deal. I just want to see the burn on your shoulder, that's all. I told you I'm a doctor. You don't need to be modest around me—"

"*Modest?* Of course I'm not *modest!*"

You'd think she'd accused him of kicking a puppy; he sounded that outraged. "I'm just asking you to take off the top layers around your left shoulder for a couple minutes. Even if you were modest, it's no big thing, you know? I promise I won't look at anything embarrassing—"

"Oh, for Pete's sake." With a disgusted look, he started peeling.

Which, of course, was precisely what she wanted him to do. Before he could balk again, she hustled into the kitchen to wash her hands and fetch the first aid supplies.

Even with the tall, bright fire, there wasn't enough light, so she added a lantern on the mantel.

"It's not worth all this fuss," he said. "It's a burn. Burns hurt. That's life. It's nothing."

It wasn't "nothing." He'd told her what happened, but now she could see it. Something burning had fallen on his shoulder—a branch, part of the roof or ceiling, whatever. The spot was a couple inches wide and several inches long. A spattering of burn "freckles" sprayed along his arm, as well, but the only sore likely to cause him trouble was the one burn. "You took good care of it," she said seriously. "It's clean. Not infected."

"What? Did you think I was an idiot?"

"Rick."

"What?"

"Shut up. I'm looking right at it. I know it hurts like hell. And it's in a spot that has to be almost impossible for you to reach. So quit being a jerk. You're right, it's fine, likely to heal with no sweat as long as you keep taking care of it. But I can put something on it, to both protect it and make it hurt less. And it's easier for me to reach it than it is for you, so it's pretty darn ridiculous for you to keep arguing."

He shut up, just like that.

She finished the job, in less than five minutes. Switched off the lantern, carted the first aid kit back to the kitchen, washed her hands again. By the time she ambled back into the living area, he'd pulled on both his tech layer and flannel shirt.

It struck her as funny...how right then, out of the complete blue, she felt a sexual pull with the power of a bullet. It didn't make sense. Moments before, she'd had her hands on his bare skin. Seen the golden orbs of his shoulders by firelight. Felt the warmth of his flesh, felt the sinew and muscle in his back and arms, felt him tense under her gentlest touch.

But she'd been a doctor, looking at the wound. And now she wasn't a doctor.

She was just walking into a firelit room with a stranger whose eyes met hers. This time, though, their connection packed a wallop. His gaze distinctly conveyed a man's experience, a man's sexual awareness, a man's blunt way of communicating that touching between them could have repercussions. Interesting repercussions. Frightening repercussions. Explosive repercussions.

"So," she said, and then completely forgot what she'd been about to say. There seemed to be nothing in her mind but froth.

"I forgot to say thanks," he said. "You really did something. I can't even feel the burn on my back now."

"Good."

"You still want to play poker?"

"Maybe after a while. For right now...to be honest, I just feel beat. I'm inclined to read, just crash early."

Her voice was casual, she was sure, the way friendly strangers would naturally talk together. That was the thing. All she had to do was ignore this unexpected awareness of him, treat him just as she would an acquaintance or neighbor.

That was the plan—and it worked that way. Eventually they tested her oven stew, which wasn't going to win any culinary contests, but at least it didn't poison them. He didn't know about her lack of skills in a kitchen. She did. They shared the cleanup, paid attention to the generator, the fire, discussed how they were going to set up sleeping, took turns in the bathroom.

She didn't know how much time passed after that. Minutes. Hours.

He'd taken the cushions off one couch, plopped them on the carpet on one side of the hearth, apparently felt more comfortable sleeping on ground level. She'd layered blankets on the far couch. Although he couldn't be farther than seven feet away, she could barely see him. The firelight was bright enough, but both of them were so completely heaped in covers that their best friends likely couldn't identify them, she thought humorously.

But her humor was fake.

He was sleeping, she believed, but somehow she just couldn't seem to drop off. The hiss and spit of fire created warm, friendly sounds...but without him talking, without their moving around, all she really heard was the blizzard.

The wind was relentless. It howled and howled and kept on howling. An animal in pain couldn't sound that mournful. That menacing. That lonely.

Troubles magnified in the darkness. The little boy's face kept flashing in her mind...and then the faces of her family, her dad and brothers and uncles. Her putty and white apartment, that had seemed so contemporary and clean to her when she'd signed the lease, now struck her as sterile. There was no personality in the place. She wasn't sure she even *had* a personality, beyond the roles she regularly played—the dutiful daughter and the excellent student and the anesthesiologist who, right from the start, got a reputation for being unshakable.

Every label she could apply to herself was relatively nice. There was nothing bad, nothing terrible. For ages she'd told herself to be proud of what she'd accomplished, for being well liked and respected and exactly the daughter her dad wanted.

It was just…that howling wind.

It made her feel…alone. As if she'd disappeared somewhere in all those obedient roles. As if she had no life, no meaning outside what other people wanted her to be.

The only thing that seemed to define her was the loss of that little boy. She knew perfectly well that she wasn't legally at fault. Or morally. Or ethically. It wasn't about that kind of fault. It was about her choice—that she'd chosen a career where she had life-and-death power over others.

She wasn't good enough.

She wasn't a good enough human being to just… take…that power.

A scream of wind, angry, shrieking, seemed to circle the house in a fresh fury. She didn't think she'd moved or made any sound, but out of nowhere the baritone on the floor said, "Oh, for heaven's sake. C'mere."

She blinked. He sounded wide-awake. And annoyed— the way he was so excellent at sounding annoyed. Even when he wasn't.

"I'm a big girl," she said. "It's stupid, letting myself react to that wind. It's just…it's the eeriest, scariest sound. I've never heard anything like it before. And it just never seems to *stop*."

"C'mere," he repeated impatiently.

Well, obviously, she wasn't getting out of her nice, warm couch-nest and going any nearer to a stranger.

It was another woman, whose feet gingerly hit the floor. Who tugged the top blanket around her and silently trod over to the big lunk's body on the carpet.

He lifted his blanket, said brusquely, "Don't let the cold air in, goose."

And she crouched down.

Smooth as a lion, his big paw came out, scooped her inside the warmth of blankets and against his long, lean body. He was covered. Just as she was. But, as if they'd slept together forever, he spooned her against him, just so, tucking the blanket protectively around her neck.

He eased back with a sigh, the weight of his arm against her waist.

The feeling of his erection sent trumpet warnings to her nerves. And of course she felt it. Even with double layers of clothes, he'd responded to her closeness the way...well, the way men did.

"Just so you know," he said sleepily, "I don't sleep with women."

"Hell's bells, neither do I."

After a moment's silence, he erupted in an earthy chuckle. "I didn't mean—"

"I know what you meant. Just sleeping together doesn't mean anything...personal." She added, "Thanks. I was scared. It was stupid. But I was. So thanks."

"On that safe business..."

She tensed faster than lightning.

"You're not," he said.

She twisted her head. "And that means...?"

"That means, don't make me out to be a saint. I can't think of a reason in hell why we shouldn't share the warmth. No one will ever know. There's no possible harm. But the thing is, we're trapped in this house together."

"Yes."

"I can't jump you. It'd be taking advantage—you know it and so do I. But that doesn't mean I don't want to. Or that I'm not thinking about it. Or that I haven't noticed you've got a really great butt."

"You think I haven't noticed that you have a really great butt, too?"

Another short silence. Then a dry, "Are you trying to suggest that I'm not safe with you, either?"

"I'm just saying…I've been a saint, most of my life, and I'm awfully sick of the halo. That's all I'm saying."

"Emilie."

"What?"

"Go to sleep. I know we're in trouble if you're starting to make sense to me." Then, "Maybe the storm'll be over by tomorrow. How long can that damn wind blow?"

She closed her eyes, feeling oddly reassured. The wind was getting to him, too. She wasn't the only one freaked out by it.

Still, she suspected she wouldn't sleep. It was too unnerving, this whole body contact. His long thighs were more unyielding than rope. The man was made of taut muscle, no give to him. The heat of his chest against her back kindled an unexpected furnace in her mind, her heart, her hormones.

It had been so long since she'd slept next to a man. There'd been a boy in college. Thom. She'd been crazy about him. He'd been crazy about her. The relationship had been hot and fast and wonderful…but then she'd gone off to med school and he'd gone off to his life. Both were on the same good-person track. They had goals.

They had ambitions and responsibilities and family expectations to fulfill.

She'd called that relationship *love*, still thought it was. But it wasn't the kind of love that actually eased loneliness. She'd never expected him to give up anything for her.

She'd never expected *anyone* to give up anything for her.

Neither did the man curled around her, she mused. Rick expected nothing from anyone but himself.

Yet he molded around her, as if valuing her warmth. His lungs released a long, slow sigh. His erection didn't fade, which should have worked like a three-alarm fire between them. But it was so odd…Emilie had the strangest feeling that Rick needed this closeness even more than she did.

She didn't know how tightly he'd been holding himself…until his whole body suddenly relaxed. As if for the first time in a long time, he felt safe.

With her.

That crazy thought was the last one she remembered.

RICK WOKE FROM A DEEP SLEEP with a sharp sense of alarm.

The soft body of sleeping beauty draped around him should have aroused that sense of alarm—for damn sure—but it wasn't that.

It was the silence.

In the dim light, the fire had burned low—too damned low; he should have wakened long before this. But the intense silence emanated from beyond. Outside.

He didn't want to ease away from Ms. Sleepy Glue. Given any encouragement at all, he'd touch what he shouldn't touch, slip inside her, let the natural heat take them both. His hormones were whining big-time over the deprivation. In fact, his hormones were downright nuts about that lean, compact body, the smell of her, the sleepy lure of her, the texture of her silky hair under his chin.

But a man didn't take advantage of a vulnerable woman.

It was one of those stupid cardinal rules he'd never shaken.

So he slipped out of the covers, and immediately felt the burst of cold startle his skin. He fed the fire first, then hit the bathroom, and after a quick cleanup, unshuttered a window to get a good look outside.

It was a uniquely Alaskan morning. Didn't look much like Christmas Eve. There was no tinsel, no red ribbons, no fancy lights. There was just an ocean of white snow, still as stone.

The sky, to the north, was a fistfight of clouds, knuckling together, circling in dark shadows, portending the next wave of storm. This blizzard wasn't even close to over yet.

But there was a chance, for a few minutes, to get out. As he geared up, he checked on Emilie—but she slept and kept on sleeping. He suspected she hadn't rested well in a blue moon.

His first step outside delivered both magic and menace. Nothing more beautiful than an Alaskan winter, no question. But you couldn't breathe ice, and no amount of clothing totally protected from the cold. Rick knew he couldn't last long, but a couple things had to be done.

The first was making sure he had access to the

woodshed—which didn't take more than shoveling out the door under the overhang. That only took a few minutes, but the second problem—the biggest priority—was the lodge roof on the west side.

The lodge had been built right, with a high slant to the roof, and material that reflected sun. But this particular storm had been unusual, started up after a rare stretch of warmish temperatures. So the first layer on the roof was ice. Thick ice. Heavy ice. Followed by at least three, maybe four feet of snow on top of that.

It was the overall weight that worried him.

If the blizzard were over, it probably wouldn't matter—but it wasn't over, and there was no guessing how much more weight the roof could take. He looked at the massive job, shook his head, doubted he could make a dent before the next pounding blast of storm hit—assuming the cold didn't wipe him out first. But he had to try, at least get as far as he could.

Time passed. Who knew how much? He wasn't an idiot, kept a sharp eye on the sky, stayed conscious of how cold he was getting. It was the sudden sound of a voice that distracted him.

"What on earth are you *doing?*"

He turned around, looked down, and for the first time in a blue moon wanted to let loose a plain old silly belly laugh. Emilie had the sense to search for her dad's winter gear, rather than wear her own city-girl jacket, but damn, she looked like a robot. Her head was covered with an ear-flapping fur cap. Both her parka and leggings were way too long. Her mittens would have fit a mountain man, and the boots were almost bigger than she was.

When she tried to walk, she resembled the abominable snowman.

She said something else, but it was hard to understand, because her mouth was completely covered by a woolen muffler.

"Yeah," he said, "I'm really shoveling the roof."

She pushed down the scarf. "Just tell me straight, Hunter. Did you start out the morning *drinking?*"

"Don't I wish." Damn. She made him want to laugh all over again. "Head back inside the house, Doc. You don't need to be out here."

"That's what I thought, too. But now I realize you've turned into a complete lunatic on me, I can hardly leave you out here alone."

He got serious fast. "Emilie, this is the deal. We got a ton of snow, too much snow, from one direction. I was afraid the roof could cave under the weight. I just want to shovel off the first layers. We'd be okay, except that there's even more snow coming. The roof's in good shape, it's just that this blizzard is in the humdinger class."

She said something. He couldn't understand her, so she shifted the scarf again. "My roof. My problem, too. Not just yours."

"You can't do this. It's all right. Just go back inside."

He should have known better than to suggest she couldn't do something. Might as well have waved a red flag in front of a bull.

She started toward him, but even to take a few steps, she had to extend her arms for balance, like a child stuffed in a snowsuit. In spite of himself, in spite of aching arms and a biting-hurt shoulder and exhaustion starting to beat at him, he sat down in a heap of snow and laughed.

"*Erl!*" she said through the scarf.

"I'm not making fun of you, I swear. I appreciate your willingness to help, honest to Pete, but there's no way you could hold a shovel, much less navigate with one."

She responded with more garbled swearwords—or the equivalent of swearwords. Her attitude was clear enough, even if she couldn't be clearly understood. At least she didn't attempt to shovel. She just scrambled up the mountain of snow to the roof, and started scooping up heaps of snow with her mittens.

He was going to object again...but then didn't. She crawled up with the agility of a monkey, in spite of all her oversize clothes, and managed to climb higher than he had or could. He'd been using a shovel, haphazardly loosening any snow he could, heaving it off the roof, just hoping to make a difference before the next storm hit. Her method of attack showed her doctor personality, all fastidious perfection. She'd scoop off snow, but then tidy it all up, make each section look neat and even.

They tangoed. It didn't matter how or who was doing what. They were making a difference.

Only then he heard it. The wind waking up. The first sound started out like an ogre's innocent yawn, but it was enough to snap his head up immediately. He looked back, saw the ominous black sky coming toward them like a tsunami.

"*Emilie!* That's enough. We're going back in the house. *Now.*"

But she wasn't done. She wanted her part of the roof cleaned off just so, no uneven ends or heaps left hanging. She was doing her damnedest to make scalpel-straight edges, wanting everything exactly right.

He heard it again. The ogre waking up. For a few more seconds, there was complete silence, but then out of nowhere came a slow, slow, slow roar that built and built....

"Emilie." He scooched up, grabbed her arm. "*Now.* In the house. *Now.*"

"But I'm almost—"

The snow hit like the slam of a door—fierce, hard, sharp. That fast, he couldn't breathe, literally couldn't take air that cold into his lungs. Even trying to move a few feet, he got sick-headed, dizzy, made tougher because of needing to pull Emilie with him.

She hadn't initially understood—but she did now.

Her instinct seemed to be to curl up in a ball.

Anyone's instinct would be the same. The slug of wind, the slap of snow, the punch of icy air could have beat up a prizefighter. Within seconds, visibility changed to a complete whiteout and the temperature dropped. Although he knew they were still on the roof, he couldn't actually see any part of the lodge—or anything else. Everything was a blinding, slashing white.

Fear could be paralyzing, Rick knew. But the worst threat right then was the debilitating cold. He wasn't certain how long it took to move them two feet. Then three.

He was losing sensation in his hands and feet, but he was far more worried about Emilie. She'd swaddled up good, but in clothes too big for her, snow and cold could easily have sneaked under the layers. Even minutes mattered, but he was literally blind, groping through nothing but white to find purchase, balance, something, anything solid that he could recognize.

Finally he felt the drop—they both tumbled off the roof. He pulled Emilie up and glued her against his side.

He found the door, battled with it. It took forever—*forever*—for him to get the damned thing open. He pushed her inside first, not meaning to be rough, but out of breath and out of strength both. Then he shut out the wind, secured the door and slumped against it, heaving in a lungful of oxygen.

He couldn't move. Not for a while yet. When he realized how hard he was shaking, he mentally swore at himself for allowing Emilie to stay out so long. He'd known the storm was picking up again. Known she was an Alaska rookie, no matter how many times she'd stayed at the family lodge. She hadn't lived here. Didn't know danger or blizzards.

As soon as he got some wind back, he started peeling off gloves, then boots. His snowsuit was crusted with heavy ice and snow, making it harder and heavier to negotiate. He seemed to be moving slower than a slug. His hands were just too frozen, but the stinging tingles meant there was no real harm; he was getting his circulation back. Even his eyebrows seemed to be shedding snow, which would probably tickle his sense of humor. Later.

Right then, as soon as he regained his mobility—and his senses—he tracked down his doc. He found her on the floor in the big room, crawling on all fours toward the fireplace, and almost there, but still in all her gear.

"Hey. You okay?"

"No," she said.

For a man who hadn't laughed since he could remember, she seemed to provoke him into smiling in spite of himself. She was talking. So she was all right.

She stopped in her tracks when he hunched down beside her.

"I'm too cold to walk, too cold to talk. Too cold to think," she said.

"I know."

"I changed my mind about coming to Alaska for Christmas."

"I know."

"It was fun. On the roof. For a while."

"Shh," he said. The silly hat with the flapping fur ears, he threw a distance. Slowly, then, he started peeling off the layers, the mittens past frozen fingers, the scarf so stiff it didn't want to bend.

"Don't take anything off! I'm freezing now!"

"Shh. We'll get you warm." The boots didn't want to tug off. He tugged them. Then the first layer of socks, then the second. It was bare feet and bare fingers that were the most endangered. The extremities. Toes. Fingers. Nose. Ears.

She was clearly shiver-cold. White-cold. Miserable-cold. But there was color slowly shooting back to her skin. He couldn't move fast, not when his own fingers still felt as if each were five inches thick. And he was too damned worried to smile yet, but by the time he'd tugged off the peripheral gear, she'd crashed on the hearth rug like an immobile zombie. He tugged off the giant-man snow pants, the parka.

"Are you getting feeling back in your hands and feet?"

"More feeling than I ever wanted to."

"Is there any body part you can't feel?"

"My nose."

He loomed over her, checked out the pink nose. Her eyes shone softly in the firelight, and her hair was a glistening tousle around her face. "Rick?"

Her voice was still thicker than molasses.

"Don't worry about talking. You'll feel stronger in a bit. Just go with it. Rest."

"It's just...I didn't know. That blizzard could kill us."

He sobered. "But it's not going to."

"We could die."

"But we're not going to."

"I've always thought of rough weather as...a nuisance. A serious nuisance sometimes, but nothing more than that. It never occurred to me to be afraid before. But that storm, Rick. That blizzard. It's alive."

CHAPTER FOUR

EMILIE COULDN'T GET OVER IT—how fast the storm had come back. How completely blinded they'd been by snow and wind; how they'd been laughing at the impossible job of shoveling the roof—and yeah, it had been physically taxing and freezing, but they'd still had fun. She'd been laughing, the way she hadn't laughed in weeks. Then...

That sudden paralyzing cold.

The wind screaming in her ears.

The fear so huge that she couldn't move, couldn't breathe.

"It was like a demon, that wind. It sounded as if it were alive, personally attacking us...." Abruptly Emilie realized that she was the only one talking. She still didn't have the strength of a pansy. When Rick started peeling off her wet, heavy outer clothes, she'd just let him.

It really hurt when he first pulled off boots and socks, and her bare feet suddenly started to get sensation back. Her nose, cheeks and chin were all stingingly coming back to life again, too. As Rick yanked off her dad's old snow pants, then unzipped her ice-crusted parka...she couldn't have stopped him, didn't want to.

He was shedding her clothes.

She was still shedding her fear.

Nothing suddenly changed, exactly. She just seemed to notice a tiny detail. All her outer layers had now been peeled off, and yet he was still shedding her clothes.

Although she'd been looking at Rick the whole time they'd been talking...now she quietly, carefully, really looked at him. The firelight crackled beside them, shimmery, warm, golden. His eyes had that same golden warmth, focused intensely on her face.

Maybe he wasn't talking, but his hands were masterfully communicating. His fingers unfastened the last button on her cardigan, then peeled off the sweater as carefully and competently as he'd gotten rid of her jacket and scarf. Only this wasn't an outer layer. This was a lot closer to her bare skin. To her bare heartbeat.

Her lips parted. She thought she was going to say something else about the weather, but somehow disasters like blizzards and near dying of cold now seemed insignificant.

His hands reaching for the snap of her corduroy pants...now that was significant.

She felt danger of an entirely new kind.

So much for the silly blizzard. So much for the life-altering decisions facing her. So much for everything else.

Her heart stopped, then started again, beating wildly fast, worried fast. It was the look in his eyes. The slow, steady, intense look. She could stop him; she knew it absolutely.

But he wasn't going to stop unless she pulled the halt card.

A log fell in the grate, shooting stars and sparks against the screen. The constant growl of the generator echoed in the distance. Yet nothing seemed to distract her from the look in his eyes, the expression on his face.

Moments later, her shirt seemed to have disappeared. Her pants seemed to have formed a heap under the coffee table, another magical impossibility. It was perfectly obvious to Emilie that this wasn't really happening. In real life, she never slept around casually, never slept with strangers, couldn't be doing it now. She barely knew this man…but she knew enough to believe there was about zero chance they'd ever meet again once the blizzard was over.

She thought, maybe he was bored.

She looked in those deep, intense eyes, and shivered. Nope, he wasn't bored.

She thought, who knew he'd even been attracted to her?

But she looked again, at the hard-boned hunger in his expression, and swallowed. She'd known. She'd felt it. It just never occurred to her that either of them would conceivably do anything about it.

When he finished stripping her down, he stretched next to her, balancing on an elbow, and lifted a hand to her face. A fingertip whisked a strand of hair from her forehead, then whispered across her chin. His hands were rough, yet somehow his touch and tenderness made her feel softer than satin.

"Still afraid of the blizzard?" he asked.

"No."

"Still cold?"

Seconds before, she had been. Now, she felt as if a

furnace of heat was licking up her veins, igniting crazy thoughts in her head.

She knew what he was inviting. Didn't care. The more she looked in those eyes, the more she felt the sneaky intoxication of temptation. Chopping thoughts kept zooming through her mind. The stupid man, alone up here in this wilderness. Wounded from the inside out. Letting one woman's betrayal isolate him from all life's choices.

And he wasn't the only stupid one.

She'd strived to meet everyone's expectations for as long as she could remember, always done what she had to do, let others define what was right and wrong, define who she was.

But right now, this second, held all the promise of possibilities. This second…this could be for her. This man could be for her. This moment could be totally for her.

And without her even knowing it, without ever saying a word aloud, a decision was suddenly made. She leaned over, closed her eyes and kissed him.

His lips were firm, thin, yielding. She tasted recklessness, the silk of risk, and went back for more.

He didn't need any further invitation. His fingers sieved through her hair, anchoring her for a second kiss, a deeper, darker kiss involving tongues and teeth. She sank back. Her hands chased up his arms, careful of his shoulder, but needing to touch, to stroke, to experience the feel of him.

He responded like lightning to dry tinder. He'd seemed so patient before, so clearly willing to let her make the decision, no push, no pressure. Now…it seemed as if he were a powder keg of pressure, had been storing up an arsenal of emotion and need and hunger for months.

He tugged off her long-sleeved silk tee and found her mouth again before the shirt was even over her head. Fingers fumbled at her cinnamon-colored lace bra, seeking the hooks in back…finding the hooks in front. There was a moment's laughter…and then another chuckle, when his bare foot brushed hers and she let out a short shriek—his toes were still cold. Ice cold.

Those cold feet of his inspired her to warm him up, the way he'd warmed her. She rubbed, tugged, smoothed. Used the heels of her hands. Her mouth. Her breasts and abdomen. And while she explored sensations on him, with him, she stealthily went after his clothes.

He'd started out with more layers on than she had— sweater, shirt, then a tech top beneath that. And his pants didn't want to come off those long, lean legs. He was such an alien species, so different from the manicured city men she knew. He was all calluses and hard edges, all muscle and brawn. In so many ways he struck her as a pirate, a stealer of virtue and senses, a man who pillaged a woman's common sense, who took and took and gave her back…

Everything.

At one point, they both seemed to rear back, gasping for breath. He stared at her as if trying to comprehend where all the fire was coming from…. Her? Him? Whatever the source, they seemed to be compounding it with every touch, every sound, every taste. By the time she had him completely naked, his skin had been sheened by the fire, gold and damp.

And she wasn't waiting any longer. Her heart seemed

to think she'd waited her whole life for this, for the chance to experience making love with no pretenses, no agenda, no worrisome expectations. She knew him somehow. He wasn't a friend or a neighbor or a medical community person or any of the other people she saw every day of her life.

But she knew Rick in some unexpected basic, primal way. His heart—she sensed how to reach it. His emotions—she sensed how to touch them. His naked vulnerability—and yeah, they were both naked by then. It was more than bare skin against bare skin. It was her mouth, confessing loneliness and need. It was his hands, expressing tenderness and wonder. It was both of them, coming together in fear and fire, not alone for the first time in so, so long....

Emilie realized, for herself, that it was the first time in forever.

RICK FELT AS SAPPED AS a beached whale. He'd yanked a cover over her. Got up, because he had to, couldn't let the fire go down...but after feeding the monster fresh logs, he sank back against her as if he couldn't hold himself up a second longer.

Her eyes were closed. He thought she was napping. She *should* need a week of solid rest after all the energy she'd just vented, luxuriously, on him. His gaze roamed her face, the tangle of hair, the golden shoulder in the firelight. Where had all that passion come from? Who'd have guessed so much explosive power could be contained in such a compact little body?

Abruptly he realized she was awake. Her eyes were

sleepily looking right back at him. "Pretty serious look on your face, fella," she murmured.

"Just trying to figure it. How the two of us could have moved heaven and earth, yet if we had that kind of power, how come we haven't been able to shut down the blizzard?"

A shy smile turned into a chuckle and made her face softly radiant. "I was hoping I wasn't the only one who heard the earth move."

"Oh, no. You weren't alone." He wanted to see that radiant smile again, couldn't believe how it transformed her from a damned pretty woman into…breathtaking. It seemed a measure of how unhappy she'd been, how long since she'd just let loose a natural, simple, easy smile. "I told you I tended to be suspicious of women, didn't I?"

"You did," she affirmed.

"And I told you I'd kind of turned into a…well, basically a misogynist."

"You definitely implied you were allergic to women these days, yes." She lifted a hand, knuckled his scrubby cheek. "Listen. If you go around hating women like this, I'm surprised you haven't collected a harem over at your place."

Darn woman warmed his heart. Nobody warmed his heart. His heart had atrophied into stone a long time ago. Or so he'd thought. "Hey."

"Uh-oh. That sounded like a serious 'hey.'"

"It was." He clutched in a breath. "I didn't plan this, I swear, Emilie."

"I doubt either of us dreamed there was any possibility of this happening," she agreed.

"The point is—I didn't use anything. I didn't have anything on me."

Her expression turned pensive. "I'm on the pill. Not because I've been sexually active or because there's anyone in my life right now. But because I was raised to be the Ultra Girl Scout."

"Always prepared."

"That's the theory. But I can't say I was remotely prepared...for you."

Silence seemed to fall. The fire, the generator, the storm—the same sources of background din were just as prevalent...yet somehow all he heard at that moment was the intense, intimate silence between them.

"Are you going to regret this?" he asked her.

"Never. I will *never* regret this," she said fiercely. "You? Are you regretting we did this?"

"Are you kidding? Not in this life." He lifted a gruff hand, pushed a tangled curl from her brow, aware she was still touching him...aware he couldn't seem to stop touching her. "But..."

She froze the minute she heard that "but," jumped in before he could possibly finish the comment. "But, of course, this was all just a moment's craziness. No one has to know. Neither of us are going to make too much of it. Why would we?"

"Why would we," he echoed, and couldn't fathom why his pulse suddenly clunked. "It's not as if you had any interest in staying in Alaska."

"Or as if you had any interest in moving back to the lower forty-eight. Good grief. I don't even know where your home used to be."

"Used to be Denver."

"Whew. A long way from Boston."

She was still smiling, but his pulse kept skidding down a long, dark luge run. She seemed in a major hurry to shut down the possibilities for them. He should have been in an even bigger hurry.

Pretty damned ridiculous to imagine how they could be a couple when this was all over.

God knew how the idea had even popped in his mind.

"Is your back okay?" she asked suddenly.

"My back?"

"The burns. I think I should look at it again—"

"I think you caretake more than enough people without adding me to the list." Damned if he wanted to be another responsibility in her life. "I've got an idea."

"What?"

"Steak. Cooked on the fire—"

"We still have stew left over from yesterday."

Yeah, they did. He'd tasted her stew. "Doesn't steak sound good? Smothered in onions and mushrooms? Maybe see what else we can conjure up from that huge pantry? Make a real feast?"

FOR A WOMAN WHO'D NEVER HAD a silly side, Emilie couldn't remember laughing so much. The steaks were juicy and sizzling and fabulous, slathered with onions and mushrooms and some kind of sauce he'd concocted. Dessert was some kind of bread pudding he threw together—took a lot of rum—that he served with a flourish and a candle on top.

The lodge had a major liquor stash, but usually no

wine. He'd scrounged around, though, found a bottle for her in the back of a cupboard, and after wiping off a couple inches of dust, opened it. She took one sip and sputtered it all over the floor. Apparently it had turned into vinegar.

She could drink some of her father's whiskey—aged thirty years, the good stuff—but only by holding her nose.

He made Irish coffee to top off the meal, although by then, he was lying on the carpet, with his feet up on a log, watching—as he put it—her eating bird bites.

"I'll bet you'll be done by midnight," he said with awe.

"Would you quit teasing? I was starving. I practically ate like a wolf, shoveling it in."

"Ah, yeah. That's you. Uncouth. No manners. Just a pig at the table."

"Thanks." She lifted a napkin and delicately dabbed a corner of her mouth. "People have always teased me for being fastidious."

"You?"

"That's the thing. I'm free to let out my closet pig with you."

She thought he'd be ill. He started choking, and then laughing, and couldn't seem to stop.

She sank back against a couch cushion, delighted. Beyond delighted. Laughter lit up his face, his eyes, took away the shadows. He was wearing bulky layers, as she was. Double wool socks, as she was. Their picnic feast was on the gnarled coffee table, as casual as she'd eaten since she could remember. And she'd made him laugh.

She couldn't get over how...smug she felt.

She didn't make men laugh. Most men she knew liked her. Respected her. A few had been scared off by her IQ, but no guy, since she could remember, thought she was funny. Or just...*had* fun with her.

"*What* are you looking at?" he demanded.

"I can't believe how hard you're laughing at me."

"Of course I'm laughing at you. At your letting out your closet pig. Sounding so happy about it. Honey, I don't think you've got a messy bone in your entire body. I hate to be the one to tell you, but you'd flunk the pig course."

"I certainly would not. I..." Her voice dropped off. She frowned, without having a clue why.

Something was different. Completely different. Startlingly different.

His head shot up at the same time hers did. "The storm," he said, and leaped to his feet.

She got it then, too. The wind had stopped. Except for the short lull when they'd worked on the roof, there hadn't been a moment without that incessant, screaming wind in days now.

The sudden crash of silence was the most peaceful thing she'd ever heard.

She scrambled to her feet as quickly as Rick, beat him to the closest window, fumbled with the catch on the shutter. The generator and fire were still making background noises, but outside...

Her breath caught. After all that awful wind, all that sharp, mean snow and slashing, bitter, killer-cold...outside, there was a sea of diamonds. The white landscape rolled and tucked in waves and more waves, all lit by a full silver moon and sky full of stars. The reflections were so brilliant that the snow glittered brighter than jewels.

She looked at Rick.

He looked back. "Are you thinking what I'm thinking?"

Simultaneously they scrambled to their feet. Although their outside clothes were still damp from before, it didn't matter. The lodge had a closet full of serious parkas and boots—although most of them were sized for the men of the family. But getting suited up in fresh, warm gear was easy enough.

They tussled like puppies at the door, Rick chuckling as he let her go first—although he also stopped her long enough to retie a long woolen scarf around her nose and mouth. The moment they stepped out, he tugged her in front of him, pulling her back against the warmth of his body.

It was beyond cold. So cold her lungs felt as if they were trying to breathe ice, even tucked against Rick, with his arms wrapped around the front of her for extra warmth. But the cold didn't matter anyway. She didn't need to breathe, didn't want to breathe.

She'd never seen anything more magical, never imagined it. The whole landscape was diamonds and crystals and sky. It was like music, a world so soft and pure that it hummed wonder in her heart. As fearsome and frightening as the blizzard had been, now she felt engulfed by an extraordinary feeling of peace.

She felt Rick's chin tuck on top of her head. "I just realized what day it is."

She hadn't. But his mentioning it made her swallow fast. "Christmas," she said.

"Might just be the most special Christmas I can remember."

She lifted her face. "For me, too."

"We can't stay out, Doc. It really is too cold to breathe."

"Just a couple more minutes," she pleaded.

He catered to her. By the time they'd both turned into icicles, she caved and admitted it was time to head inside. Realizing it was Christmas turned her quiet for a while. She puttered around, cleaning up, straightening up. Rick did the same, checking the generator for fuel, stacking enough firewood for another day.

By accident more than attention, she found herself standing at the west window at the same time he was. The lodge was shadowed in that corner, firelight blocked from their view, but the darkness enabled them to see clearly outside. The medieval table was right there, with a dozen chairs around it, but neither seemed ready to sit. They both couldn't seem to stop looking out at the beauty and silence of the landscape.

He reached over to cuff her close to him, but it wasn't a lover's invitation, more just…affection, she thought. "Afraid our problems aren't over just because the storm is, Doc. Can't imagine that we'll have power for days. No way to get out of here yet. Tomorrow morning, I'll start splitting logs for more firewood."

She hadn't planned on getting out for several more days, anyway. But she suspected both of them would suffer cabin fever if trapped inside forever. She wondered if they'd make love again. He'd touched her, been touching her, as protectively as a lover, but his gaze had turned distant, his mood quiet. She didn't know what that meant...but it seemed obvious that once they realized what the day was, their thoughts had turned inward.

"What did you do when you were a kid at Christmas?" she asked.

He leaned back against the window. "Had heaps of relatives over. There was always lots of noise, lots of food, lots of kids running around. When the women were getting serious about holiday doings, they'd kick out all the kids and guys to cross-country ski. When we got back, there'd be piles of presents under the tree. Families packed in together, stayed overnight usually. The kids would be three in a bed, the floor littered with sleeping bags."

"Sounds like enormous fun."

"Yup. Great fun, great family. Things started changing over time, of course. By the time the parents retired, the extended family seemed to be scattered all over the place. Everyone who can still gets together." He hesitated. "Initially, when I got married, that was a serious part of the dream for me. I wanted to create more family like that. Cousins and brothers and sisters close enough to play together. Heaps of noise. Always a baby crying, a baby being rocked. Always so much food the table could hardly hold it all."

Emilie felt a thick lump in her throat, thinking again of all the repercussions of his ex-wife's betrayal. The woman had not only destroyed a marriage, but a whole dream of a life—for what, just some selfish affair with another guy? How easy it was for her, to go out and create her brand of Christmas and family…but she'd left Rick as shrapnel.

"How about you?" he asked gruffly. "How was the holiday at your house?"

She didn't mind answering, but she had to move, couldn't just stand idle to talk. Not about this. "Right now, at this very moment, my dad and uncle will both be asleep in their chairs, probably with Jimmy Stewart on the tube. Christmas Eve, my brothers' and uncle's family will all have come over. They'd open the family presents, do the church thing. But Christmas morning, the single people would all congregate at my dad's house…my dad and uncle are both widowers, and I'm not married, nor is my one older brother…."

She ambled past the kitchen, with Rick ambling beside her, stopping to grab a cookie from the counter. She aimed back toward the warmth of the fireplace. "My dad will have made breakfast this morning. He's not a cook, but he has one dish he makes. They're a special kind of crepe, made with rum. They're so rich, they're to die for. We would have had an early-afternoon dinner—pretty much leftovers from the day before. Dad's always had it catered. We could have any from five to twenty at the table, depending on everyone's schedules. But it would be an awfully rare Christmas we made it through both days without one of us being called to the hospital."

"You're missing it," he said.

She perched on the end of a couch, but as soon as he sat down, he scooped her next to him. His warmth, his strength, made her aware how tense she'd suddenly become. "Your traditions sound more fun than mine…but I also suspect everybody tends to remember the funny goofs rather than the perfect holidays. I remember one Christmas dinner where the turkey slid off the plate. Another, where all the food was served, and four of us got paged at once to head for the hospital. And another one, when we sat down and realized my oldest brother was AWOL. We found him outside, a little too much scotch before dinner, I suspect, lying in the snow making snow angels and singing. Oh, he was in such disgrace with my dad."

"Sounds like your family are 'good people.'"

"So do yours."

He leaned his head back, slouching down the same way she was, using the coffee table for a footrest. "But you're here, instead of with your family."

She closed her eyes. "I had all my presents for everyone under the tree before I left. They know I love them. Know I'll miss them. But if I were there…I'd be hearing an endless round of heavy-duty advice. I've heard it all before. I have to get back in the saddle. When you're a doctor, you have to deal with life and death. You can't always win those battles. It's not on you. You still do what you can. And you've been moping enough."

"From everyone?"

She nodded. "I've already heard the same thing, over and over. Christmas would have amounted to a lynching with the whole group ganging up on me. I'm happy *not* to be there. Happy to have made the choice to come here, blizzard or no blizzard. I needed the time. That's no crime, darn it."

"No, it isn't."

"And I found you. Even if it's only for a few days," she said, "I found you."

Abruptly she twisted in his arms, hooked an arm around his neck, and kissed him. His mouth was familiar now, the taste and texture, the mesh and melt he created for her and with her, and her eyes were already closed. She didn't want to talk about herself anymore, was tired to bits of thinking about her life, herself, her reality right then.

She wanted her lover.

She wanted the only man who'd ever spun her out of herself, who gave as aggressively as he took, who made her forget who she was and everything she didn't want to be. With him, when his arms were around her, she was nothing more, nothing less, than a woman in love.

Whether this was the kind of love that lasted…she didn't give a damn.

Her mouth took his. Her arms enfolded his. Her body took him in. That was all she knew, all she wanted to know.

CHAPTER FIVE

EMILIE WOKE UP IN THE MIDDLE of the night to a familiar dream. It wasn't the kind of nightmare that made her shake, but the opposite. It was the kind of nightmare that made her ache.

It was just that little boy's face in her head. The so-long eyelashes. The two untamable tufts of hair, boyish cowlicks. The pinched fear in his face when she'd first walked in. The trusting smile she'd worked so hard to win from him before surgery…now gone. The light in his eyes…gone.

The loss of that child…aching in her heart like an insidious piranha.

Rick's voice came from the darkness. "Try talking about it."

She didn't know she'd wakened him. Didn't remember exactly how they'd gotten from the couch to their make-shift bed by the fire. She remembered making love—exquisitely well—but now she seemed to be spooned against him, her back to his chest, his arm around her side. Maybe because she wasn't looking at him, maybe because it was the darkest time of the night and she was exhausted from wrestling the problem on her own, she started to spill.

He responded in a deep, sleepy voice, and offered her all the empathy she could conceivably want. "Why should you?" He echoed her own words. "Why should you feel you have to take on the responsibility of life and death?"

"Exactly. I'm not God. I never wanted to be God."

"You could make a mistake. Everyone does. Nobody can avoid making an occasional mistake, but when you do it, someone could die. Not this kid. He wasn't your fault, of course. But someone else. And then that mistake would be on your conscience forever."

"Yes. Exactly. You understand." It was such an enormous relief, to have someone listen to her, someone agree with her.

"Someone else can take that responsibility. Why should it be you? There are lots of other doctors. Lots of people who love that power over life and death. And there are lots of people who really don't give that much of a damn, because they just don't feel things that deeply. They won't go through what you've been going through."

She frowned. "Exactly," she said again, but somehow not as strongly.

"The job is probably done better by someone who doesn't care. They don't get hurt that way."

Abruptly she shifted in his arms. It was too dark to see his face clearly, but his eyes met hers, clear and calm. He'd sounded so sympathetic. He looked so sympathetic. But now she got it. He was being manipulative, saying between the lines that she had to go back to work— because she did care. Because she did hurt.

"Hey," she said, "I thought you were on my side."

"I am. Aren't I saying the right things?"

She narrowed her eyes. "I don't think I love you anymore."

"I didn't know you loved me before this." He sounded more amused than hurt by that revelation.

"Well, I did. I was wildly in love with you yesterday. Wildly in love, stupidly in love, totally in love for the first time. But no more. You threw that away. So don't try being smarter than me ever again."

"Did I say I was smarter than you?"

Under the covers, she poked his bare chest. "And another thing. You're up here for the same reason I am, cookie. Because you don't want to get hurt again. Pretty idiotic, for someone of your talents and skills and experience, to play out your life as a hermit."

"I'll be darned. Did I ask for your opinion?"

"Yeah, well, I probably wouldn't have given it, if we hadn't made love. You're an extraordinary lover. How can you think it's a good idea to live alone forever, the rest of your life, without sex? When you're so fabulous at it?"

"Was that a slap or a compliment?"

"It was a slap, you jerk. Can't you tell when you're being insulted?"

"Apparently not with you."

"And another thing—"

He shuddered. "Oh, God. Not that. Anything but that. Every time a woman says 'and another thing'...nothing ever follows that a guy wants to hear."

Even though he retucked the covers around her neck, she poked him in the chest again. "And another thing," she said firmly. "I don't know why she cheated, but it's not on you. It's nothing you failed to do or did."

His voice dropped the teasing tone. "You don't know that."

"Yes, I do."

"You couldn't possibly know that." He was starting to sound just a wee bit outraged.

She sighed. "She was shallow. And stupid."

"For Pete's sake. You don't know that at all."

"Yes, I do. A bright woman would never leave a great guy because of a momentary click for another man. First off, she wouldn't open that door. And second off, she'd fight for what she had. Love. A good man. The vows and commitment she made. And third off, if she was that unhappy with you, then she should have gotten out of the relationship, before cheating. Because that's ethics."

"And you think you're the final word on this, because you've had so much experience with relationships?"

"Oh, quit giving me a hard time. You know what I'm saying is true. She hurt you. Maybe it was such a bad hurt that you'll never forget it. But if you think her cheating is somehow your fault, that's just dumb. She had a major fault line in her ethics. In her values. Frankly, you can do better."

"Is it because we had sex that you suddenly decided I needed this major lecture on stuff that's none of your business?"

"We didn't have sex. We made love," she corrected him.

"Damn right we did." He loomed over her. "And we'd better do it again, right now and fast. Before this fight goes to a place that neither of us wants to travel."

"We shouldn't fight on Christmas," she agreed, even as she was reaching for him.

"How about if we don't fight at all. We may not get out of here for a couple of days...but that's not much time left."

She hadn't forgotten. The real world was waiting for her out there—her world. She had decisions that had to be made, a career to decide on, a life to put back together. This was just a short oasis of time. That was all it was, all it could be.

Suddenly she was kissing him for all she was worth. She wasn't denying or evading. She was just in an uninhibited hustle to be with him, to cleave, to shore up memories. Who knew if love that sprang up this fast could possibly last? But the bond was real. Her connection to him, with him, was potent and wonderful and infuriatingly real. In her heart, she knew irrevocably that she'd never feel this way about anyone else.

WHEN RICK WOKE THE NEXT morning, she was curled around him like a petal on a rose, soft and sweet—and completely unnerving. Emilie was unlike him in every way, had a life that couldn't possibly mesh with his. Yet he woke up, thinking of stuff he wanted to tell her about. Thinking he already wanted to make love with her again. Thinking that he was already so attached that separating was going to feel like cutting off a limb.

He didn't trust women. How had he forgotten that so fast?

He edged out of the covers, tried to quietly do the obvious first round of activities—a fast shower, feeding the fire, checking the generator. He figured she'd be awake by then, but she was curled up under all those blankets, just the tip of her blond head showing.

Didn't look as though she was missing him.

He started suiting up. The wood supply had gotten them through so far, but it was a good thing the storm had quit, because he could get out to the woodshed, start splitting more. He wasn't positive how much physical exertion the shoulder burn could take, but he knew darn well his brain needed the exercise.

Hard work was always a good way to kick some sense into a man. He pulled on gloves, checked on her one last time.

She was still sleeping. Sound as a baby. Clearly didn't miss him.

He stepped out, felt the slap of icy air and told himself it felt good. A slap upside the head was exactly what he deserved. Trudging the distance to the shed took all the wind out of his sails—it was only fourteen feet off the back door, but the snow was deep and heavy.

Inside the dim shed, at least he was out of the wind. Cords of wood were already neatly stacked, but he wasn't about to touch that. No one in this neck of the woods took advantage of shelter without leaving the place stocked as he found it. A few cords in back were clearly still aging, too wet, would smoke if they were used too soon. He prowled around until he found what he wanted—some good seasoned wood and a sharp axe. He left the door open for light, yanked off his hat, took off the top parka layer, and started in.

A half hour passed. Then an hour and more. By then, he was starving for breakfast, starving for Emilie, and he'd split three-quarters of a cord.

When he stood up and wiped his brow, his heart

slammed to a stop. He smelled something dark and ripe even before he turned around and saw the big, hulking shadow blocking the shed doorway.

It wasn't the first time he'd seen a brown bear. Alaska was their stomping grounds, after all, not humans'. Rick loved the big beasts, had never done anything to invite bear trouble, never had trouble with one. Before.

The big guy didn't look good. His cinnamon-brown fur was ashy; his body too lean. Standing up, he stretched maybe nine feet. He'd probably been sleeping most of the last month, but brown bears didn't hibernate all winter. When they did wake up, it was because they were hungry. If the bear had been trapped for the whole last week of storm, he wouldn't have had a chance to get out and find food.

He had that look.

Hungry.

Angry-hungry.

Rick told his heart to quit slamming, because he had to think—damn quick and damn well. The bear blocked the only exit to the shed.

He had no way out. He had the axe, so he wasn't completely without a weapon. But the bear spotted the glint from the axe, and suddenly let out a roar worthy of Tarzan.

Maybe Rick had the axe, but fear shot through his pulse faster than bullets. This wasn't just a bad situation. It was downright ugly.

EMILIE WASN'T SURE WHAT woke her—but she lurched to a sitting position from a dead sleep. She thought for a second a patient was in trouble—a ridiculous thought, of course—but she'd always had a strange sixth sense, sometimes knowing when a patient was in trouble before there was an ounce of evidence to make her worry.

Obviously that wasn't the issue here. The only rotten-wrong thing was obvious. Rick was gone.

Not just gone from the pillow next to her. There was an emptiness in the place, a lack of sound and life. A lack of *him.*

She pushed off the covers. It didn't take two minutes to know he was outside—his parka and winter gear were gone. So he was cutting wood, she guessed. Maybe she wasn't up to wielding an axe, but she could help haul in the firewood.

She hit the bathroom, cleaned up, brushed up and started heaping on fresh layers—silk long underwear, flannel pants, thick socks, a tech shirt, then a wool sweater layer. In principle, she wanted coffee and a hot breakfast, couldn't think of a single reason why she should charge outside in that blistering cold. Their making love had been terrific, but she hadn't forgotten their fight before that.

It hadn't been a clean fight. It'd been a go-for-the-sore-spots fight. He'd said what she didn't want to hear. She'd told him some home truths he definitely didn't want to listen to.

She yanked on boots, thinking it was crazy. *She* was crazy. Because she'd rather be fighting with him—even if it meant being downright miserable—than not be with him. Even for a second.

Because that really *was* nuts, she parked on a crabby frown before opening the back door.

And immediately froze.

So did the bear.

She took in the nightmare scene in a snapshot. Logs and pieces of wood were scattered everywhere in the snow. The bear was on all fours, at the door of the woodshed, but the moment he heard her, he whipped around and stood up on two feet. Crouched down, he looked huge. Standing up, he looked menacing and terrifying.

"*Rick!*" Rick had to be trapped in there. Maybe hurt. Maybe worse.

"I'm here."

"Are you—?" She couldn't get a question out before the bear bared his teeth and lumbered straight for her. She heard Rick shout something about locking herself in, staying inside, but it wasn't as if she had a choice at that instant. She slammed the door, shaking so hard she could hardly manage the dead bolts—and immediately felt a thunderous pound as the bear pushed at the door. The critter scratched to get in, making long, angry scratching sounds, then tried another pounding ram.

She'd have hurled if she had time.

She yanked off her hat, spun around, headed for the stairs. She couldn't guess how long Rick had been trapped in the shed, but the logs strewn all over the yard told the story. The bear was trying to get to Rick. The bear was winning. Rick wasn't.

She charged upstairs, feeling the unwieldy weight of outdoor clothes slowing her down, not willing to stop. She jogged through the dark hall, fumbled with the closed door to the master bedroom—her dad's room, when he stayed here.

Naturally, she immediately crashed her knee into the bed board—the master bed was practically big enough to sleep five—ignored the shot of pain, whisked into her dad's closet and scrabbled for the push-button battery light. She spotted the gun cabinet at the same instant she remembered that—of *course*—it was locked.

She backtracked into the bathroom, yanked open the medicine chest. Her dad kept the cabinet key in an empty bottle of Midol—which he called theft protection. Her dad's brand of humor. She shook out the key, dropped the open vial in the sink, ran back to the cabinet.

Inside were two rifle-type guns, both long, and to her, both ugly. Her dad had forced her to learn how to shoot, always saying that you couldn't visit a place like this without being able to protect yourself. She got it, always had, just couldn't scare up a liking for guns. Now, though, she chafed at how long it'd been since her dad had made her exercise the how-to of putting in ammo and shooting them. Years, for sure.

The first try, she put the wrong ammo in the wrong gun, swore at herself in a scream, got it right the second time. She hurled back downstairs, thinking Rick had to be all right. He *had* to be.

She had a moment's panic when her fingers touched the dead bolt. It wasn't quite that simple, being willing to go outside, face the bear again. So she gave her heart three seconds to quit its stupid slamming, pushed the dead bolt loose and opened the door. Immediately the bear smell assaulted her nostrils—it was so distinctively rank and feral. Accelerating adrenaline far more was the immediate rush of sounds—the growls and roars of the bear, the sounds of wood being heaved. The snowy yard between the shed and house was almost completely littered with debris now.

"Rick?"

There was no response—except from the bear, whose head showed up in the shed doorway. He'd been in there. With Rick.

"Just tell me—are you hurt?"

It was a stupid question, she knew. Whether he answered or not didn't alter what she had to do—which was get rid of the bear. Whatever it took. There was no other option, no other choice, nothing to think about. The only way she could get to Rick was by getting rid of the damned bear.

The critter appeared no happier than when he'd last spotted her. He heaved up on two feet, rolled his head and growled, loud enough to shake her inside and out. She could see blood coming from his shoulder—not a lot—but enough to guess Rick had managed to cut him with the axe, not enough to maim the bear, not enough to stop him. Apparently just deep enough to infuriate him.

Even more worrisome, Emilie realized, was that Rick might no longer have the axe. If he'd thrown it at the bear, it was his only weapon—and she couldn't imagine him using the axe unless it was absolutely his only option.

She flicked off the safety and hefted the repeater rifle to her shoulder—the monster weighed a *ton*. The bear had just plopped on all fours and was coming toward her, fast. Who could imagine how fast the huge animal could be? So she just shot.

And shot.

And shot.

Tears blistered her eyes. It hurt. Every pull of the trigger sent a bruising kickback to her shoulder. She vaguely remembered her dad instructing her on how to hold the gun, but it just wasn't a moment when she could access those old lessons. This was about doing it. Getting it done. Whatever it took to get to Rick.

When her vision cleared—could it only have been seconds?—the rifle was empty. The strong smell of cordite choked the air. *"Rick."*

She couldn't see the bear. Didn't know if she'd hit it, hurt it or scared it—and didn't care. Her first impulse was to run to the shed, to Rick, but the more rational decision was to run back in the house and get more ammunition, until she knew exactly what had happened.

But then she heard him. "Is anything on the continent still alive out there, Doc?"

He probably thought he was being funny. Not. She galloped into the shed, leaping and tripping over logs all over the Sam Hill place. Rick was on the ground, half-buried in a makeshift shelter of logs, covered with wood chips and bark and debris.

"You're hurt." She didn't see specific blood or injury, but she saw his eyes.

"Not bad."

"Hurt from the bear? Or from a fall? Exactly what kind of—"

"Emilie. I'm fine. I admit, I might need a little help getting to my feet. But first things first—where's the bear?"

"I don't know."

"Is he lying in the yard?"

"He should be. It was one of those repeater guns. I shot the whole load right at him."

"I think you should go back in the house until we know where he is...."

Yeah, right. If the dimwit thought she was leaving him out there, in the cold and hurt, after that kind of battering, he needed his head examined.

Actually she intended to do just that—examine his head—among other body parts. But somehow, once she heaved off all the firewood and finally got to him, she wrapped her arms around him tight and couldn't seem to let go. Not for that second. Not for that minute.

"Hey," he murmured. "I'm okay."

Maybe he was. Maybe he wasn't. But she was shaking like a leaf in a tornado, and her head was thick with tears and fear. "Let's not ever do this again. The bear thing. Talk about *not* fun."

"Okay. But, Em...we're not sure where he is right now."

"I know."

"We need to get up. To get in the house. To figure out where he is and what's going on."

"I know. I know."

Still she couldn't seem to move. She just wasn't ready to stop shaking quite yet. She'd been afraid of a ton of things in her life. Wasn't everyone? But not like this. Not like a wild animal, face-to-face.

When she still didn't let him go, Rick said casually, "I'm hurt. Not seriously, but he did get one good swipe at me. Claws went through my—"

That fast, the shaking stopped. The word *hurt* galvanized her like nothing else could have. She shut down the residual panic, twisted around, took a fast look at his eyes and face color. "We're getting you inside. Right now," she said briskly.

"Think that'd be a good idea. I'm pretty weak."

He didn't look weak, but a serious assessment of his injuries couldn't be done until she got him inside. "Come on. I'll get you up...."

She hooked his arm over her shoulder, already thinking ahead. He'd been exposed to the cold for too long, had to be pretty bruised up, but the worst and most immediate problem, of course, was if the bear's claws had broken skin. She was thinking antibiotics, not guns, when halfway to the house, Rick said, "You want to bring in the rifle."

"It's out of ammunition." How irrelevant could a stupid gun be, anyway?

"Doc. Trust me. There's more ammo. And other bears. You know what a pretty repeater like that costs?"

"Do you see anyone in the near vicinity who cares?" Twice more en route to the door, she glanced around frantically—worried the bear had come back.

Rick apparently had the wherewithal not just to pick up the gun but to glance around a couple times, too, because at the door, he noted, "You did an amazing job of tearing up the roof on the woodshed."

"Huh?"

"I was afraid we were going to have to track down an injured bear. But I don't see any sign of blood, and it's pretty obvious you were aiming at the sky. I see a branch off the top of that pine, and that has to be eighty feet up. Not counting what you did to the roof—"

"That's more conversation than I need right now. In you go…"

She got him in, locked the door, made him put down the stupid rifle and herded him into the kitchen. The fire was low. She didn't care. She had him stripped down and sitting on a stool in the kitchen before he could even try giving her excuses.

"Hey. I thought you were an anesthesiologist."

"I am. But there's a wee bit more training involved than just how to put people to sleep—"

"Yeah. That's the part I was interested in. The drugs. Couldn't we skip all this poking and prodding and go straight to some painkillers?"

She didn't answer. She was too busy. The burn on his shoulder was still big, still sore-looking, but in spite of the day's acrobatics, it didn't look worse, just needed fresh attention. He had blood and scrapes on his hands, needed cleaning, sliver removing. Bruises—my God. They were forming all over his arms and body.

And he hadn't lied about the "bear swipe." The huge claw had broken through the parka fabric, through his flannel shirt, through his tech shirt. Thankfully those multiple layers had protected him from any worse injury, but the claws were big and sharp, and had left him with some scratches, and some puncture wounds. "The thing is," she muttered, "it's not that bad. But it'd be better if it were in a location where I could soak it. And better yet if I had some tetracycline around…"

"How about morphine? Jack Daniel's?"

"The thing is, tetracycline's a lot better than penicillin for problems like animal bites. They're just different germ and bacteria threats altogether…."

"You're not listening to me."

"All right," she said briskly. "This is going to sting a little—"

"Wait—"

"Hey, big guy. Almost done. Then you can take your wasted body in by the fire and I'll bring you something to eat and you can tell me all about it."

"I'm suffering *now*."

"Uh-huh. Just stay real still for the count of twenty…."

"*Yeoch*. You're killing me. Give me back to the bear. He was nicer."

She rolled her eyes. "You know, when I first met you…"

"The morning when you fell over me?"

"I wasn't thinking about that specific moment. I was just reflecting that originally I thought you were the toughest, most macho, truly *male* guy I'd ever met. You put shivers down my spine. And now, what a letdown, to find out after all this time that you're really a wimp."

"Does that mean I don't still put shivers down your spine?"

She cut the last strip of tape, sealed it over the sanitized cut and carted the supplies to the sink—which meant he was finally free to get up. Only he didn't move. He still sat on that stool, looking at her, clearly determined to wait for an answer.

CHAPTER SIX

"ALL RIGHT, ALL RIGHT, I admit it, you still put shivers down my spine." Her voice sounded testy for good reason. She *was* testy. They'd been attacked by a bear, for Pete's sake. She had every right to be riled, every right to go into a coma of panic if she wanted to. She put her hands on her hips to illustrate that opinion.

He eased off the stool, as if he hadn't been remotely hurting all this time—in spite of his complaining—and looped his arms around her waist. "Good. Because you put shivers down my spine. Thanks for cleaning me up, Doc."

"You scared me half to death."

"You think you were scared? You should have been out in the shed. I've been trying to think through what incited that bear…."

"What?" He'd leaned forward and pressed his forehead to hers. Every thought in her head turned smooshy. If there'd been music, they'd be dancing…slow dancing, the kind where you just swayed a little, touched, teased, hearing music only the two of them heard within the circle of each other's arms.

"Yeah. I think he woke up before the blizzard, hungry,

getting hungrier when he couldn't get out. And then he smelled our smoke—you know how much we've been cooking on the fire. Nothing as good as raw fish to him. But still, the hungrier he got, the crankier. And then when he found me, saw me, he probably thought my throwing wood around was an aggressive move. So the poor guy was just being who he is."

"A bear."

"Yup. Three things I have to tell you, Em."

"Okay." She thought, this was really an insane time to be dancing. They should be doing practical things, like feeding the fire, getting something to eat. Both of them needed to unwind after that incredible ordeal. Her heart had been pounding panic for ages now…although at this specific moment, with his lips brushing her cheek, possibly her heart was pounding for an entirely different reason.

"The first thing is—remind me to be in the next county when you decide to aim a gun again."

"That's okay. I don't intend aiming a gun again. I really hate them."

"I kind of noticed that. And that was the second thing. Because you hate guns, it means all the more that you came out to save me. I'd have had to shoot myself if something had happened to you. But all the same. Thanks."

She could feel a smile forming, a silly, soft smile. Funny, how all that stress was just disappearing, like fog on a soft morning. "So what's the third thing?"

"Okay. I don't know what you're going to end up doing for a living, Em. Whatever you want. But I'm telling you straight, you're a doctor. You're a natural. You may not want to stand up for life-and-death stuff, but you do. It's who you are. It's how you think. You can do something else, but that doctor thing is always going to be there under the surface."

Her smile faded like wind. "There went the shiver down the spine."

"Annoyed with me, are you?" Something in his expression made her think he was studying her, waiting or watching…for something.

"I just think that we've both been through a seriously traumatic time together. And I don't need another stressor at this very second."

Still, he didn't move. "But that's just the thing, Em," he said quietly. "We're running out of seconds. If you flew up here to make up your mind about what really matters to you…your time for thinking's almost over. Have you made a decision about what you're going to do?"

What she was going to do, she decided, was make herself a sandwich, curl up on the couch in a nest of blankets and read in absolute silence for a while. She didn't have to speak to her temporary roommate. She could be ticked at him if she wanted to be.

He seemed to opt for exactly the same program. He fed the fire, made himself a sandwich, and then fell into a crash-nap on the other couch. As a doctor, she knew the best thing for him was rest. But as a woman, she was all churned up. He just didn't seem remotely upset by the blizzard or the bear…or the idea of her leaving. He slept like the dead no matter what.

Or so she thought.

Out of the blue, she heard a voice from the other couch. "Are we talking again yet?"

Her face was hidden behind a book. "Not unless you're willing to consider the possibility that you've lived up here like a hermit long enough."

"Hmm. I think we both take advice really well, don't you?"

She smiled behind the book, because darn it, she couldn't help it. They really were equally awful at hearing advice. "Maybe…*maybe*…I appreciate your perspective. When I get an opinion from family, it's always slanted toward what they want me to be, what they want me to do. At least when you offer advice, at least you're looking at…well…me."

"Well, that's easy. Looking at you has been the best part of the past few days."

Damn him. Now he was giving her a warm-fuzzy. And he wasn't a warm-fuzzy kind of guy. For that matter, she'd never been a warm-fuzzy kind of woman…at least until she met him.

"Rick?"

"What?"

"What's your next move?"

He didn't pretend to misunderstand the question. "When the weather clears enough for a copter to pick you up, I'll hitch a ride, if you don't mind. I can't shut down my place for long, Doc. The place needs repairs and things done. But I can start setting things in motion from Anchorage. I don't know how long those projects and problems will take to resolve. If the weather stays decent, I can get back here, and get the cabin repaired to the point where I can leave it."

"And then?"

"And then, if I can get my ducks in a row, I might consider looking for work back in the lower forty-eight."

"Like…back in Denver?" she asked casually.

Silence. When he didn't answer, she turned a page in her book. She hadn't read a word since lying down and still didn't have a clue what the book was about.

Abruptly, he broke the silence. "I think we've done enough talking, don't you?"

"Darned right," she murmured, heaved off all the warm covers and stalked toward him.

He lifted his blankets. She climbed in. A snuggle was all she wanted. He was bruised and hurt, his body traumatized. Her heart was just as traumatized. Never mind if he was aggravating and frustrating. She just wanted the closeness of his body, of him. He folded her into the tuck of his body, covered them both. It was a big couch, but even so, two grown-up bodies were cramped for space. Or would have been, if they'd been taking up the space for two.

"You need rest," she said. "You were really beaten up, have to feel both physically and emotionally exhausted. You need some recoup time."

"Right," he said.

"So," she murmured, "can you try another nap?"

"Not in this life," he said, scooping her around so they were face-to-face. The kiss began on her brow, moved to her cheek, then homed in on her mouth, on her senses…on her heart.

All these years, she kept thinking, she'd never lost it. Now and then she'd lost her mind, her common sense, her keys. But she'd never lost her heart.

Not like this.

She'd never imagined love like this. A man like this. Not for her.

But just like her, Rick had been pushed and prodded into recovering from a heart-shaking problem before he was ready. No one could force someone else to feel. Or to *want* to feel.

She was going to have to leave him. And it already hurt.

EMILIE WALKED INTO THE LAST room in the pediatrics ward. Outside, it was pouring rain, an April shower with lightning and thunder, unfortunately making the late afternoon gloomy and dark. She strode in with a smile, but the boy in the far bed tugged fast and fierce on her heart.

Billy was eight, according to his chart. She'd read all the medical and physical facts about him, but the surprise was seeing the Irish-white skin, the shock of cowlicks, the lover-blue eyes.

He wasn't the boy from her old, sad nightmares, but he pushed all her loving buttons exactly the same way.

"Go away," he said, fear in his voice and his eyes rapidly filling up. "I want my mom."

"I'll bet your mom just stepped out to use the restroom, Billy. I know she's close by. My name is Dr. Emilie."

"I don't want any more needles. I want to go home. I want my mom."

"Well, that's amazing," Emilie said gently, and perched closer. "Because I want exactly those things. I want your mom here for you. I want you to go home as fast as possible. And I want you not to need any more needles for a long, long time."

The tears stopped falling, but he gave a long shuddering breath, still looked at her suspiciously. "My leg hurts."

"I know it does. But we're going to fix that."

"My dad said I can have anything I want when it's all fixed. You know what I told him?"

"What?"

"I told him I wanted to go to Alaska. He was su'prised. He thought I'd say Disney World. But Alaska has bears and whales."

If there was a child in the universe made to give her more heart pangs, this one took the cake. "I've been to Alaska," she told him. "And you're darned right. Alaska is full of bears and whales. And eagles. And all kinds of other wonderful things."

"You went there?"

"Yup."

"Did you see a bear?"

"I saw a great big giant brown bear. Way bigger than me." Now that he wasn't so fearful, she checked his pulse, the readings over his head, did her own cursory examination of his general state of health.

"Were you scared?" Billy wanted to know.

"I was petrified. I shot a gun at it."

"Wow. A big gun?"

"Yup. A kind of rifle called a repeater."

"Did you kill the bear?"

"No. To be honest, I never wanted to kill him, but I thought I might have to because he was a very mean bear, and he was close enough to really hurt me. So I shot. But because I'm a terrible, terrible shot, he just ran off. So nobody got hurt and everybody ended up happy."

"Tell me again how big he was."

Emilie suspected he'd try to distract her by retelling that story forever, but there was an operating room being prepared. "I will in just a minute. But as soon as your mom gets here, I'm going to take you for a ride. We're both going to stay with you until you go to sleep."

"No. Wait." Worry pinched his face again. "Are you my doctor now?"

"I'm one of your doctors, Billy. But I have a really lucky doctor job."

"'Cause why? Why do you have a lucky job?"

"Because it's my job to make sure you don't hurt. How could there possibly be a luckier job than that?" She'd already hooked the sedative into the IV. Billy's mom showed up in the doorway, looking—naturally— exhausted. A nurse showed up to wheel him into the prep room with her, but Emilie motioned them back for a moment. "Are you looking at me, Mr. B?"

"Yeah."

"So look in my eyes, and you'll know I'm telling you the truth. We're going for a ride. Then we're going into a room with a lot of lights. The doctor will be there who's going to fix your leg. But I'm going to be there, too. I'm going to give you some medicine so you'll go to sleep, and I'll stay with you the whole time you're sleeping. And I can't promise this, but I think there's a good chance you might dream about whales and bears if you concentrate."

"I'm not going to sleep." The IV was starting to kick in. His eyelids were starting to droop, his speech starting to slur.

"Okay."

"I'm too old to take naps."

"Of course you are."

"And I want to hear about the bear again."

"The great big fuzzy brown bear?"

"Yeah, that one…"

Emilie winked at the tired mom, as they wheeled the youngster out of the room. She kept up with the story for as long as he stayed awake, although she changed some details to accommodate the circumstances. The bear turned out to be a good bear with soft fur and soft eyes, who was lost and scared. But then the bear's mom showed up…

She changed a few other parts of the story, too, to protect the innocent. She never mentioned the pirate of a man who'd stolen her heart—the way he felt, the way he'd made her feel. The way she'd cleaved to a stranger the way she'd never cleaved to anyone.

She put Rick out of her mind, though. She had to. She went in, and did her job, and since Billy was her last patient for the day, she waited until he was out of surgery, and then sat with him and his mom in the recovery room.

"You're sure he's all right?" Billy's mom kept asking, even though the surgeon had reassured her right after the surgery.

"He's going to be just fine. He won't be jumping out of trees for a while, but I'm sure he'll think up other mischief to keep you busy." When she glanced at that child again, his eyelids were starting to flutter open.

"Hey," he said groggily.

"Hey right back."

"I've been dreaming. About the bear."

"Was it a good dream?"

"It was a *great* dream. We were running in circles, around and around, until I got silly dizzy." He added, "I'm still dizzy. But my leg doesn't hurt anymore."

"We gave you some strong medicine, short stuff. You won't be dizzy once it wears off. And your leg won't be perfect for a while, but it won't ever hurt like it did before. And you'll be going home pretty soon."

Ten minutes later, Emilie left them, yawning as she pulled off her cap and shook out her hair. It'd been a long day. A good one, but still, she'd been on her feet since before seven that morning. It was time to throw off her scrubs, climb into street clothes and curl up with a good book. Maybe pick up Chinese on the way to her apartment.

As she walked down the corridor, she pulled out her cell phone. Naturally, it couldn't be used in the hospital, but as expected, she found messages from her dad and oldest brother. There was a birthday coming up this weekend. Because she was the lone female in the family, she was expected to bring the cake—which, of course, she would.

For the past few months, there hadn't been a single day without voice mail from family. They were still unsure what they had with her. She'd come back to her work—which was what her family all wanted. But they still didn't understand why she'd left at Christmas, or what was different about her since she'd returned.

She'd tried to tell them that she was fine. Because she was.

She was changed, that was all. Forever. No way around it.

She dropped the cell phone back in her pocket and rounded the corner—almost bumping into a tall, dark-haired man. She laughed, said, "I'm sorry. I wasn't paying a lick of attention...."

And then frowned. The man was wearing an old leather aviator jacket over old jeans. His dark hair glistened with rain, and he had strong, square features, eyes bluer than the sky.

The beard was gone. That was the thing. The scruffiness, the wild hair, the lost eyes had all disappeared.

Damn, but he was handsome. Who knew?

"Well, would you look at what the storm dragged in." She tried to sound casually amazed—instead of stunned out of her tree.

"You were supposed to call," he said.

"You didn't ask me to call." She was positive she'd have remembered if he had.

"Yeah, well that was because it took months to get all my life-stuff taken care of. The whole time, I was hoping you were pining for me."

She parted her lips, but her heart had leaped so high in her throat that she had to swallow. And because she didn't immediately respond, he jumped back in.

"So this is what you're wearing when you're dressed to impress, huh?" He motioned to her wrinkled scrubs, the booties, the messed-up hair and soap-clean face.

"Hey, if I'd known my best guy was going to show up, I'd have put on the hair cap, too. It really adds to a girl's allure."

"You don't need anything to add to your allure, Doc."

She couldn't leave him hanging out alone there any

longer. "I'm getting the impression that maybe, just maybe, you pined for me as much as I pined for you."

"Maybe," he admitted.

"So...do I get a hug or do we have to stand around in this hall talking nonsense forever?"

And finally, there it was. Those long, strong arms. The familiar thump of his heart, the warmth of his body, the strength of him. The vulnerability.

"It seems," Rick mentioned, "that there's a lot of infrastructure rebuilding going on in your city."

"Lots of needs. But no funds, the last I knew."

"Yeah, that's what I was afraid of. But I asked. Sent in my credentials. And it seems that as long as I work harder than two men, and do brilliant work, I've got a job."

She reached up, to touch his cheek. "You actually moved for me?"

He shifted on his feet—even though he never moved even an inch of distance. "I moved...because you were exasperating enough to get on my case about the hermit business. And then because your Boston has a ton of seriously interesting infrastructure problems."

She wasn't fooled by those details. "You moved for me," she repeated.

"I couldn't have," he assured her. "That would have been stupid. I had no idea whether you'd even be willing to see me again. Or if you'd forgotten all about me. What we shared...you know darn well we could have blamed it on the blizzard."

"I never blamed it on the blizzard," she whispered. "I blamed it on you. For forcing my eyes open. For forcing my heart open."

"I blame you for doing the same darn thing to me, Doc," he murmured right back.

And then she lifted up, making it easier to kiss him. Making it easy for him to kiss her right back.

Tucked around each other, they headed out into the warm spring night.

To my handsome, debonair hubby—
we've crisscrossed the world together,
each mile filled with the wonder of discovery.
Here's to many more such journeys!

DEEP FREEZE
Merline Lovelace

Dear Reader,

My husband and I were getting ready for a cruise to South America and Antarctica when I was offered a chance to write a novella set "somewhere cold." Was that fate or what? I'd done so much research in preparation for our trip that I couldn't wait to dive in to a tale set on the White Continent.

My research came nowhere *close* to the awesome reality of Antarctica, however! I've traveled to many places over the years but that vast, stupendously beautiful, constantly changing continent blew me away. I saw penguins of all shapes and sizes, whales, seals and ice. Lots of ice. Small, drifting floes. Big, fat bergs. Glaciers thousands of feet high. It was truly a once-in-a-lifetime experience—one I hope you'll get a taste of in "Deep Freeze."

Check out pictures from our trip as well as information on other upcoming releases on my Web site at www.merlinelovelace.com.

Merline Lovelace

CHAPTER ONE

"IT'LL BE FUN, MIA. A real adventure, Mia."

Shoulders hunched against a cold so vicious it bit into her bones, Mia Harrelson shot her sister an evil glare. Either Beth's teeth were clattering too loudly to hear the snide comments or she chose to ignore them.

That didn't stop Mia. Now that they were safely inside the covered lifeboat and dry land was—hopefully!—only moments away, the nerve-grinding tension of the past six hours was slowly loosening its grip.

"It's summer in the Southern Hemisphere," she said sarcastically, pressing closer to her shivering sister. "Much warmer than Rhode Island in January. All we'll need to pack are bikinis for Rio. Shorts for Montevideo. A light jacket for Antarctica. Ha!"

"Gimme a break." Her nostrils pinched with cold, Beth dug her chin into the collar of her inflatable life vest. "You can't hold me responsible for a freak storm."

The heck Mia couldn't! Someone had to take the blame for this disaster, and her sister was the closet target—right after the idiot captain who'd run their cruise ship aground.

In a more generous frame of mind, Mia might have

accepted a little of the responsibility for their present predicament herself. Okay, most of it.

After all, *she* was the dope who'd gone all gooey-eyed over a drop-dead gorgeous lawyer with a come-hither smile. *She* was the fool who'd tumbled into bed with him on their second date. *She* was the naive twit who'd never imagined someone so charming and urbane was into hidden cameras and kinky Web sites.

And *she* was now out there for the whole world to see, wearing nothing but a red lace thong and star-shaped cutouts over her nipples.

A groan worked its way through her numb lips. Among her friends and coworkers she was now and would probably forever be known as Number 112. The latest in a string of conquests by the man who labeled himself Don Juan. The same international Don Juan, Mia had discovered to her utter mortification, whose Web site got something like three thousand hits a day from those wanting to check the progress of his one-man campaign to seduce every gullible female who came into his orbit.

Mia's dismay had quickly morphed to anger, then to a furious determination to force the bastard to remove her picture from his rogue's gallery. She should have known a lawyer would cover his ass. Not only did she *not* get the photo off his Web site, she was threatened with a lawsuit if she revealed Don Juan's real identity. As he'd so callously explained, he hadn't posted her name or any other identifying personal data. There were lots of women out there with coal-black hair, green eyes and a dimple in one rear cheek.

Yeah, right! That stupid dimple had made her the recipient of so many sly winks and waggling brows at work that Mia had jumped at Beth's travel suggestion. Why not take advantage of midwinter cruise sales to get out of town for a few weeks and let the sniggering die down?

She'd driven in from snowy Newport, Rhode Island, and met Beth at the airport in Boston. Together they'd flown down to Rio to soak up the sun for three glorious days. Then, to Mia's profound regret, they'd boarded the ultra-luxurious *Adventurer II* for a twelve-day cruise that included stops in Argentina, Uruguay, the Falkland Islands and Chile. And several days cruising the Antarctic Peninsula.

Looking back, Mia was forced to admit their first day in Antarctica hadn't been so bad. Daytime temperatures had hovered around fifty degrees. She and Beth had dressed in light layers—cotton turtlenecks, wool sweaters, waterproof windbreakers—and hung over the rails with the other passengers to ooh and ahh at spouting whales and penguins cavorting on the ice floes that drifted by.

This morning had started off sunny, too. Then a gray cloud rolled over the top of the glacier-skirted mountains off the port side of the ship. With it came plummeting temperatures and knifing winds. The next thing the more than three hundred passengers knew, visibility had dropped to near zero, the wind was screeching along the decks and the *Adventurer* was wallowing like a drunken sailor.

Some extremely nauseous hours later, the ship hit a submerged ice shelf. Everyone was looking extremely scared and replaying *Titanic*'s last moments in their heads when an announcement came over the intercom instructing all personnel to dress in their warmest clothes and report to their muster stations.

Now here they were, plowing through vicious seas while the storm still raged outside their covered lifeboat. Ice pellets pinged against the roof and windows. The wind howled like a mortally wounded dragon. Waves smashed against the hull. All that kept Mia from giving in to a healthy bout of hysteria was the fact that they were about to dock at a U.S. research station. Or so the white-lipped ship's officer commanding the lifeboat had assured his moaning, miserable passengers just moments ago.

When a sudden thump set the boat shuddering, terror speared through Mia's heart. She reached over to clutch her sister's hands but the elderly woman on Beth's other side preempted her.

"We hit a floe!" the woman cried, ashen-faced. "We're going to drown!"

Beth, bless her sensible, substitute-teacher's heart, had plenty of experience dealing with incipient panic.

"No, we're not. Didn't you feel the engine slowing? We must be at the research station."

Mia clutched that straw with the same desperate eagerness as the other woman. Still, her heart stayed in the middle of her throat while the crewman at the helm reversed thrust and backed off, then nudged the throttle forward again.

"Prepare to disembark," the officer in charge shouted over the shrieking wind.

The passengers waited anxiously until another crew member put his shoulder to the hatch. Wind and sleet instantly poured in. Eyes watered. Smiles froze in place. Yet nothing could dampen their ecstatic relief as they inched toward the steps.

"Careful," the ship's officer cautioned. "Wait for the next swell!"

Ski-masked and goggled faces loomed above the open hatch. Gloved hands reached down. One by one, rescuers grabbed the passengers' upraised arms and hauled them bodily from the wildly heaving lifeboat.

Beth and Mia helped the other passengers to the hatch. They were younger than most of their fellow travelers by several decades. When they'd booked the cruise, they hadn't known they'd chosen a line that catered mostly to retirees. In retrospect they should have realized most people their own age would have to beg or cajole or threaten to quit to get two weeks' vacation time so soon after the Christmas holidays.

Not that Mia had minded the age disparity on board the *Adventurer*. She'd sworn off men anywhere near her own age for the foreseeable future.

Refusing to think about the jerk who'd propelled her into this insane outing, she and Beth helped the others up the steps to the hatch until—finally!—it was their turn. A pair of gloved hands reached down for Beth. Her legs flailed, scissoring in the frigid air. When she swooped upward and disappeared into the gray sleet, the harried ship's officer beckoned Mia forward.

"Your turn."

Braced by two of the *Adventurer*'s crew, blinded by the stinging sleet, she groped for another pair of outstretched arms. An iron grip banded her wrists.

"I've got you."

He'd better have her!

Mia had time for that one, wild thought before she was hauled up and onto an icy dock. Staggering, she would have fallen back through the hatch if not for the brutal grip on her wrists.

"Hold on."

Her rescuer yanked her forward and anchored her with an arm around her waist. Gulping, she breathed in needle-sharp ice crystals and the rubbery tang of his orange parka.

"That's the last of them," the ship's officer shouted behind her. "We'll secure the boat."

"Roger that! I'll take this one to the station."

Head down, her body angled against the waterproofed parka, Mia stumbled along the slippery pier with her rescuer. A gasp of relief rose in her throat when she touched solid rock, only to spiral into a yelp when her sneakers almost went out from under her.

"Careful," a deep voice growled in her ear. The arm around her waist tightened, cutting off what little breath she had left. "The lichen's slippery."

"What was your first clue, Sherlock?"

Oh, crap! The wind *had* to die for a second or two at that precise moment. She tipped her head, hoping her rescuer hadn't picked up her sarcasm.

No such luck. She was almost certain she caught a smile in a pair of seriously blue eyes shielded behind ice-encrusted goggles.

"Actually," he replied, bending close to her ear, "the name's Walker. Brent Walker."

"Nice to…meet…you," she got out through teeth that clattered like marbles in a tin can.

Walker-Brent-Walker yanked at the zipper on his parka, whipped open one flap and tucked Mia under his arm. Warmth flooded her. The sensation was instant and so welcome she decided to ignore his distinctly uncomplimentary editorial about tourists who traipse down to the end of the world in tennis shoes and lightweight windbreakers.

Nested against him like a penguin chick tucked under its parent's wing, she scrabbled over the slippery rocks to a set of wooden stairs. At the top of the stairs he steered her toward a narrow walkway.

"Welcome to Palmer Station."

She peeked out from under the flap of his parka, eager for a glimpse of shelter. She'd done some reading on Antarctica prior to boarding the *Adventurer.* Not much, admittedly. Like Beth, she'd been far more interested in the portion of the cruise itinerary that included Rio's fabulous beaches and Buenos Aires' sultry tango bars.

Still, she'd read enough to know at least ten or fifteen countries maintained permanent research stations on the White Continent. One of those stations housed over a thousand people during the polar summer.

This obviously wasn't it!

Her stomach plunging, Mia saw only a handful of blue metal buildings huddled together on the rocky shoreline. Two were midsize structures, the rest hardly more than sheds or shacks.

"How…? How many…people live here?" she stuttered through numb lips.

"Forty-two this summer. About ten of us will winter over."

Forty-two plus three hundred stranded tourists plus another hundred or so crew members? Mia lurched along the wooden pathway with Walker-Brent-Walker, wondering how in the world they'd pack everyone inside.

Very closely, she discovered when he steered her into the closest of the two large buildings. She found herself in a foyer facing a solid rack of orange. Waterproof parkas and pants like the one Walker wore jammed the rack and dripped onto the linoleum. While her rescuer shrugged out of his goggles, gloves and parka, Mia scanned the jam-packed hallway beyond the foyer.

Still-shaken tourists huddled in the corridor and in the labs and offices leading off it. Officers and crew members from the *Adventurer* roamed among them. Clipboards in hand, they checked names against passenger lists. People Mia assumed were station regulars also circulated, passing out mugs of steaming coffee and chocolate.

The scent of hot, foamy chocolate almost made her weep. But another glance around the hall drove everything except Beth from her mind.

"My sister," she said worriedly. "She came off the lifeboat right before I did, but I don't see her here."

"She may be in one of the labs," Walker replied, dragging off the black knit watch cap he'd worn under his parka hood. "Or upstairs, in the dining room or berthing area."

Mia nodded, taking her first good look at the man. Her initial thought was that no male should be allowed such a dangerous combination of tawny hair, electric-blue eyes and strong, square chin. Her second, that she'd been taken in once by a man who ranked several notches higher on the stud scale than this one. Smarmy, smut-sucking Don Juan had totally immunized her against world-class hotties like Brent Walker.

Which didn't explain the frisson that raced over her thawing skin when he took her elbow and steered her into the hall.

"We'll find your sister. But first…" He raised his free hand and caught the attention of a fellow station member toting a tray of steaming mugs. "Hey, Jill! We could use a couple of those."

"You got 'em."

The woman passed over two mugs of hot chocolate. She looked to be in her late thirties with an easy smile and a headful of curly red hair. Walker introduced her as Dr. Jill Anderson, a marine biologist who'd racked up more than two hundred dives during her three Antarctic summers and one winter.

"That's how we categorize folks here on the ice," the biologist said as Mia gulped down a swallow of the life-restoring chocolate. "You've got your fingees. Loosely translated those are, ah, friggin' new guys. Then those with one summer under their belt. Then multiple sum-mers. First winter-over. Multiple winter-overs. First trip to the pole. And… Well, you get the picture."

"I think so."

With a friendly nod, the biologist moved to supply another stranded tourist, and Walker steered Mia down the crowded corridor.

"So which category do you fall into?" she asked, peering into each office and lab they passed in search of Beth.

"This is my second summer. Also my second winter. Normally we rotate off the ice after each season, but I'm staying over this time."

One taste of Antarctica—winter *or* summer—was more than enough for Mia. She couldn't imagine volunteering to stay through a long, perpetually dark winter on this isolated outcropping of rock and ice.

"What do you do here?" she asked as they approached a flight of stairs.

Before he could answer, the radio clipped to his belt crackled.

"This is Janie, Brent."

Walker unclipped the radio and keyed the mike. "Go ahead, Janie."

"We just completed a head count. We've got one hundred two pax, seventeen crew over here in GWR."

"Roger that. I'll get a count here at the BioLab and get back to you."

He hooked the radio back on his belt just as a glad shout rang out from above their heads.

"Hey, sis! Up here!"

Mia tilted her head back and spotted her sister leaning over a railing two stories above.

"They've got showers," Beth called down joyously. "Hot showers! Hurry up before the line gets too long."

She swung toward Walker, who nodded. "Go ahead."

When he accompanied the nod with a smile that crinkled the weathered skin at the corners of his eyes, Mia swallowed. Hard.

Oh, boy! Ohboyohboyohboy! Good thing she'd sworn off the male of the species. This particular specimen packed more firepower into a grin than any other she'd come across in a long time. Including jerk-off Don Juan.

"You'd better grab a shower while you can," he told her. "I have to get to the communications room to check on the ships diverting to Palmer to pick you all up."

"Hang on a sec."

That came from the heavy-set male descending the stairs directly ahead of them. A faded University of Wisconsin sweatshirt encased his bulky torso and a bushy brown beard covered his cheeks and chin.

"I need your name for our station log," he told Mia, his pen poised over a clipboard.

"Mia Harrelson."

He scribbled the information and nodded. "Harrelson. Got it."

She started past him. Head cocked, he stopped her.

"You sure look familiar. Have we met? Maybe at a conference or something?"

"I don't think so."

"You're not in the biospheric measurement field, are you?"

"Not even close. I edit middle school history and social sciences textbooks."

"Hmm." He leaned closer, scrutinizing her face. "I could swear we've bumped into each other somewhere. Did you go to UW?"

Dread settled like an icy lump in Mia's stomach and chilled the insides barely thawed out by the hot chocolate. Praying her all-too-recent past hadn't caught up with her, she shook her head.

"Nope. The University of Rhode Island. 'Scuse me."

Walker added his voice to hers. "Stand aside, Allen. The lady needs out of those damp clothes."

"Oh. Sure. Sorry."

Mia brushed past him and hurried up the stairs. Just as she hit the second-floor landing she caught the tail end of a startled exclamation.

"Omigod! Brent, that's her!"

"Her who?"

"Number 112!"

CHAPTER TWO

"NO WAY!"

Brent's gaze flew to the woman on the second-floor landing. The dismayed glance she zinged over her shoulder confirmed her ID even before Allen did.

"It's her," the meteorologist insisted as the passenger disappeared around the corner. "Same green eyes. Same jet-black hair."

He lowered his voice so it wouldn't carry to the cruise passengers milling nearby and waggled his brows.

"Whatdaya wanna bet Ms. Harrelson's got a sweet little dimple on her left butt cheek?"

That produced several immediate reactions in Brent. Not the least of which was the memory of Ms. Harrelson's left butt cheek pressed against his thigh all the way up from the dock.

"Number 112," Allen chortled gleefully. "Here at Palmer, of all places. Who wudda thunk it?"

Certainly not Brent.

He hadn't followed Don Juan's salacious blog all that closely. He didn't have to. Allen and a couple of other guys at the station checked the Web site regularly for updates. Their hooting and whooping when a new entry went online alerted anyone who might be interested to saunter by for a look.

Brent was no monk. He'd done his share of sauntering. But Don Juan's gallery of good-time girls just didn't do it for him.

Probably because his ex-fiancée fit right into that category. She'd explained all in her e-mail just weeks before Brent was due home after his first summer on the ice. She'd gotten bored sitting around waiting for him. So she'd gone out. Had a little fun. Met someone else. Several someones, he'd learned later.

Ironic really, since Linda was the one who'd pushed him to resign his air force commission and take a job with the civilian agency that managed all U.S. facilities in the Antarctic. Once he got some polar experience under his belt, she'd argued, he could work a management position with the company right there in Denver.

Thankfully, the thrill of living and working where few others had ever ventured and the close camaraderie of the scientists and support personnel on the ice helped ease the sting of Linda's defection. So much so that Brent had come back for a second summer when offered the job as station manager.

A Colorado native, he'd grown up on skis and snowmobiles. After earning his USAF pilot's wings, he'd breezed through the Arctic portion of SERE—Survival, Evasion, Resistance, Escape—training conducted at Eielson AFB, Alaska. Designed to help downed aircrew members survive in an arctic environment, the course taught lifesaving techniques that included methods of constructing thermal shelters and ways to build fires from unlikely materials.

But nothing in Colorado *or* Alaska could compare to Antarctica. Like so many others before him, Brent had fallen under the spell of the sometimes harsh, often unforgiving, but always fascinating White Continent. He also thoroughly enjoyed the challenges of his job.

As operations manager, he was responsible for the safety and welfare of every person at Palmer. That involved direct supervision of the support staff and close coordination with the senior scientist on station to ride herd on the other researchers. No easy task given the diversity of their research projects and often unique support requirements. The scientists kept Brent's carpentry, power plant, materials, medical, communications, food service and boat dock personnel jumping.

Now he had a station full of stranded tourists to add to the mix…including Number 112.

Shoving the mental image of a seductive, nearly nude Mia Harrelson to the back of his mind, he told Allen, "I talked to Janie in GWR a few moments ago. She gave me her count."

"Yeah, she contacted me, too. With her tally and mine, I make the total at two hundred eight passengers, thirty-five crew."

That tracked with Brent's mental count. He knew from monitoring the *Adventurer*'s distress calls that a Ukrainian resupply ship en route to Vernadsky Station had picked up the remaining passengers and crew.

Now all he had to do was engineer the return to civilization of those stranded at Palmer. Just their luck the reinforced-hull scientific research vessel that supplied the station had already made its January run and was back at its home port in Argentina. They'd have to rely on the other ships in the area to pick them up. With that in mind, Brent mounted the stairs to the second floor and made for the communications room.

His comm tech sat surrounded by the racks of equipment that included both low and high frequency radios for short- and long-range communications, as well as a full spectrum of satellite voice and data uplinks. Hovering at his side was an anxious officer from the *Adventurer.* After introducing himself to the officer, Brent peered at the satellite monitor.

"What's the latest, Jack?"

The thin, wiry comm tech tapped a yellow blip on the monitor. "This is the Chilean navy cruiser that was out on a training mission. They've diverted to Palmer and can take seventy souls on board."

"ETA?"

"Three hours, twenty minutes." He tapped a second yellow blip. "Next closest is the *Sea Lion.*"

Brent smothered a curse. Another cruise ship. Too big to dock at the station. They'd have to ferry the remaining passengers out to her.

"She was down peninsula at Trump Island. She's coming about but her skipper radioed that he's worried about the ice buildup."

So was Brent.

He watched it carefully while he coordinated relief activities between the station's two main buildings. As its name implied, the BioLab housed biological laboratories on the first floor. The comm center, admin offices, storage areas, kitchen and dining room were on the second. The third provided coed living areas.

A wooden walkway connected the BioLab to the Garage/Warehouse/Recreation Building. The GWR contained the power plant, additional storage, the library, a workout room, a lounge and additional, open-bay berthing.

Both buildings were now full to overflowing with stranded tourists. They took turns using the station's communications media to let folks at home know they were safe, then lined up for hot showers and wrapped themselves in blankets or borrowed gear while their wet clothes tumbled in the dryers. The doc kept a close eye on several individuals with known heart conditions, and the station's two cooks were scrambling to prepare hot meals.

When Brent swung by the kitchen for an infusion of hot coffee before going back outside, he discovered Mia Harrelson and her sister had volunteered to bus tables between waves of hungry diners. Mia glanced over at his entrance and immediately colored up. Red staining her cheeks, she bent to attack a table with a damp cloth.

Well, Brent thought wryly, that reconfirmed her alter ego as Number 112. He found her reaction interesting, though. He would have thought a fun-loving party girl who let herself become the subject of those kind of photos would enjoy the notoriety they brought her.

While she blushed and swiped furiously, he introduced himself to her sister. "You must be Beth Harrelson. I'm Brent Walker, station manager here at Palmer."

"Hi, Brent. Thanks for taking us in."

She was shorter than her sister. Maybe five-four to Mia's willowy five-six or -seven. Both women had shoulder-length black hair, but Beth's was a wild mass of curls while Mia's was smooth and slick from her shower. Almost begging for a man to run his fingers through it.

Well, hell! He was as bad as Allen. Slamming the door on that thought, Brent smiled at Beth.

"I see you've been introduced to gash."

"Gash? I don't... Oh, you mean cleanup duty. Yes, one of your people explained that you all take turns cleaning up the dining area and kitchen after meals. My sister and I figured that was the least we could do in exchange for your hospitality."

"Do either of you need anything?" he asked.

"No, thanks. Everyone's been terrific about raiding their closets and supply store. Haven't they, Mia?"

Her sister had to raise her head and look at Brent then. "Uh-huh."

Yep. No doubt about it. She was definitely 112.

And if the punch to Brent's gut was any indication, it was a good thing she would be departing Palmer in a few hours.

OR NOT.

The situation looked decidedly grim when he bundled up and fought his way down to the boathouse. Neither he nor his boat manager liked the look of the ice piling up against the dock. Known as grease ice, the soupy layer could coagulate quickly to form a barrier impenetrable by anything other than ships with reinforced hulls.

Brent kept a wary eye on buildup until the Chilean navy cruiser arrived. He and his crew helped hustle the allotted seventy passengers aboard. They then held their collective breath until the *Sea Lion* radioed it was standing off shore and awaiting transfer of the rest.

Working with the crew of the *Adventurer,* they shepherded the next group of distinctly nervous passengers into a lifeboat. A second lifeboat followed shortly after the first, and both returned for another load. By then the ice had thickened so much the coxswains could barely bring their craft alongside the dock.

When the boats headed out to the *Sea Lion* again, Brent had to make a tough decision. Freezing temperatures. Knifing winds. Gray ice. Visibility down to less than a hundred feet. The lethal combination left him no choice.

Reluctantly, he radioed the *Sea Lion* and informed them he was halting transfer operations. The cruise ship captain agreed with the decision. He also indicated he would weigh anchor immediately to avoid becoming caught in the ice.

That left Brent with the unenviable task of breaking the news to the last seventeen passengers and three crew members still awaiting transfer. Trudging back up to the boathouse, he faced the group that had bundled up in anticipation of their imminent departure.

"Sorry, folks. We've had to discontinue transfer operations. You'll have to wait out the storm here at Palmer."

After a chorus of groans, one of the older passengers asked the sixty-four-thousand-dollar question.

"What's your best guess at to how long the storm will last?"

"Our weather gurus think it might blow through tomorrow. But…"

If his time on the ice had taught Brent anything, it was that Antarctica was like no other place on earth.

"Polar storms are pretty unpredictable. Depending on the ice buildup, you could be here another day." His glance skimmed the group, snagged on a pair of emerald eyes. "Or week."

Mia swallowed another groan.

Great! Just great! She'd heard the bearded scientist blurt out her notorious alter ego. Caught the subsequent, speculative glances from a number of his coworkers. And now she was stuck here with this crew. Indefinitely.

So much for getting away while the buzz over her entry into Don Juan's hall of infamy died down!

Dismayed, she trudged back up to the main building with Beth. As she shed her borrowed parka, dismay segued into indignation, and indignation into determination.

Enough was enough. She'd taken a ration of crap from her *own* coworkers. No reason she had to take it from the crew here, too. Jaw tight, she waylaid Walker in the first floor corridor of the BioLab.

"I need to speak to you. Privately."

He hooked a brow at her tone but gestured to one of the labs leading off the main corridor.

Once inside Mia skimmed a glance over the impressive array of equipment. She edited primarily history and social studies textbooks, but she'd attended enough meetings with the science editors to know they would salivate at the sight of all these ultra-high-tech microscopes and fluoroscopes. She let her gaze roam the lab, collecting her thoughts before she turned to face Walker.

He'd leaned a hip against the lab counter. He still wore his watch cap. Only a few strands of dark blond hair showed beneath the rim.

"About your friend in the University of Wisconsin sweatshirt..." she began.

"Right. Dr. Allen Barclay. He probably knows more about electromagnetic phenomenon in the ionosphere than anyone else on earth."

Unimpressed, Mia crossed her arms. "Apparently he also knows quite a bit about the contents of a Web site maintained by a total scuzz-bag who calls himself Don Juan."

"Scuzz-bag?"

"I have other, more descriptive labels for the guy. I won't bore you with them, but I *would* appreciate it if you would ask your people to refrain from mentioning him or the number 112 anywhere in my vicinity."

Walker studied her for several moments. Mia refused to squirm but could guess what he was thinking. An exhibitionist who posed for pictures had no right to complain about being ogled. He didn't say so, however, he merely dipped his head in a brief nod.

"I'll put out the word."

"Thanks. And just for the record," she added, hating that she had to defend herself, "Scuzz-bag took those pictures without my knowledge or consent."

Walker didn't let her off the hook that easily. His tone cool, he laid the blame right where it belonged.

"That is you, though?"

"Yes."

"In his hotel room?"

"Yes."

"Wearing only a black lace thong?"

She ground her teeth. "It was red."

The thoroughly disgusted reply lightened Walker's expression. A smile crept into his eyes, along with a hint of sympathy.

"I'm guessing you'll conduct a room-to-room search for recording devices the next time you accompany anyone to a hotel room."

Mia's shudder wasn't exaggerated. Neither was her fervent vow.

"There won't be a next time! Not for the next ten years or so, anyway. One complete and utter humiliation per decade is my limit."

His smile eased into a wry grin. "I hear you. That's pretty much how I felt when my fiancée dumped me a couple of weeks before our wedding."

The confession cut through Mia's antagonism and embarrassment. She felt herself relaxing for the first time since she'd heard his buddy utter her number.

"When did that happen?"

"Three years ago."

"So you've only got seven more years to go before you get back in the game?"

"About that."

So he'd been inoculated, too. Good to know he was as immune to her as she was to him.

"Well, I guess I'd better go upstairs and find a place to bed down for the night. Or week."

THE FOLKS AT THE RESEARCH station went all out to accommodate their unexpected guests. After opening the small store on-site to provide them with necessary sundries like toothbrushes and combs, Palmer's residents rearranged their living quarters. Married couples squeezed in with other couples while singles doubled and tripled up.

As station manager, Brent Walker rated a private room. So did Jill Anderson and her husband, Doug, also a marine biologist and the senior scientist at Palmer. They vacated their sanctuaries, though, and made them available to older couples off the cruise ship.

Amid all this relocating, the on-site personnel took time to explain essential matters like mealtimes and protecting Antarctica's eco-environment by carefully managing waste, human and otherwise. Mia and Beth got a quick briefing from the two women they were to bunk with.

Mary O'Neil had received a National Science Foundation grant to measure glacier flow rates. Tiki Fujiyoshi, a PhD candidate in seismology from the University of Hawaii, was almost as new to Antarctica as the passengers off the *Adventurer.*

"I flew into McMurdo two weeks ago and choppered up here," she confided as she wedged her bed against a wall to make room for the sleeping bags they'd procured from supply.

"McMurdo's the main U.S. research station in Antarctica," Mary explained. "Their summer population can get up as high as twelve hundred. Two to three hundred winter-over."

Mia was more interested in a possible alternate route of escape than the station's census.

"You say it has an airstrip?"

"It does," Mary confirmed. "They have regular flights during the summer, but about the only planes that can get in during the winter are ski-equipped military transports."

Thoughtfully, Mia helped Tiki stash the bedroll. There had to be some way she and Beth could hitch a ride back to civilization on a nice, fast transport. If it was up to her, she would never set foot on another ship. Any ship. Large, small or in-between.

CHAPTER THREE

MIA'S SECOND DAY ON PALMER Station was pretty much a repeat of the first.

Vicious winds continued to lash the peninsula. Sleet pinged down, gusted up and whipped around. Both the windchill temperature and the visibility deteriorated to the point that Brent announced via an intercom system that he'd declared a Condition Two.

"That means everyone has to travel in pairs to do any work or research away from the station," Jill explained at breakfast. "If it worsens to Condition One, you stay in whatever building you're in and don't go out at all until visibility improves and the windchill temperature rises above minus a hundred degrees Fahrenheit."

"*Minus* a hundred degrees," Mia squeaked, almost choking on her eggs Florentine. "It was in the high forties yesterday, before the storm hit."

"That's Antarctica for you," the marine biologist said cheerfully.

Mia shared an incredulous glance with her sister and went back to her eggs. The breakfast buffet put out by the station's two cooks lacked the visual artistry of the cruise ship's lavish spread but more than matched it in flavor.

When Mia and Beth complimented the cooks and once again volunteered for cleanup duty, they were treated to a tour of the spotless, fabulously equipped kitchen. Afterward, Jill offered a visit to the science labs and a look at ongoing research projects for anyone who was interested.

"Can I take pictures?"

That came from Beth, who'd stuffed her digital camera in her jacket pocket before abandoning ship. Mia had been more concerned with saving their asses than the hundreds of photos they'd snapped in South America.

"I substitute teach at an elementary school," Beth explained. "I'd love to show the kids pictures of an Antarctic research station when I get home."

"We can do you better than that," Jill said. "If you like, you can use one of our computers to set up a blog and send real-time pix back to the kids."

"Omigosh! That would be fantastic."

"Let me hook you up with Allen Barclay. He's really into blogging and online videos and such."

As Mia knew all too well!

When Jill called the stocky scientist over to their table, Mia braced herself. She hadn't received a single snigger or knowing look so far this morning, but...

To her relief, the bearded scientist merely gave the group a friendly nod. Obviously, Walker had put the word out as promised.

Mia got a chance to thank him for that after Beth peeled off with Allen and Jill shepherded her laboratory tour group toward the stairs. When they passed the corridor leading to the administrative wing, Mia caught a glimpse of the station manager entering his office.

"I'll catch up with you," she told Jill and detoured in the other direction.

Interesting place, she thought as she passed the open doors. One office was decorated in early aviary. Ostrich and peacock plumage vied for wall space with seagull feathers crossed like swords and what looked like streamers of fuzzy penguin chick down. The office next to it contained a remarkable collection of Elvis memorabilia. Posters, DVD covers, bobble figures—even a guitar-strumming teddy bear in a spangled, flare-legged outfit.

Mia guessed the decorations were probably one of the few ways folks at Palmer had to express their personal tastes. With communal living, working and recreational areas, these small offices represented islands of individuality.

If so, Brent's individuality ran along more retro lines. His office was maybe eight by ten and boasted a doublepaned, frost-rimmed window with a view of the boathouse and dock. The furnishings were strictly functional—file cabinets, a row of reports in neat binders, a large whiteboard stickered with notes and schedules, a workstation topped by a sleek computer.

Hung on the wall next to the whiteboard was a photo of the Palmer Station crew gathered together and waving at the camera. Right below it was another picture of the crew, looking wet and cold as they huddled under gray blankets. Wondering what that was all about, Mia rapped lightly on the door.

Brent was at the computer, his back to her, the ever-present radio clipped to his waist. At the sound of her knock, he swiveled around.

"'Morning, Mia."

Damn! There it was again! That crinkly-eyed smile. Good thing she was completely immune to all things masculine right now.

"'Morning, Brent. I didn't mean to disturb you."

"No problem. I was just checking the weather."

"How does it look?"

"Not good. Please, come in."

He got up to sweep a stack of papers off the chair next to his desk. When he turned to deposit them on the file cabinet, Mia got a view of muscular thighs and a tight, trim rear encased in well-worn jeans. With the jeans he wore a blue plaid flannel shirt and black turtleneck.

Sternly, she repressed the traitorous thought that the blue in the plaid seriously deepened the blue in his eyes.

"How'd you sleep?" he asked as she took the chair he'd cleaned off.

"Fine. Better than fine, actually. It's been a while since I bedded down in a sleeping bag. I think Beth and I were at Camp Winihaha last time. But this bedroll was really comfortable."

"It should be. The National Science Foundation designed those bags specifically for folks at the South Pole. You don't want to know how much they cost you as a taxpayer."

"Probably not. Listen, I just… Uh…" The photo beside the whiteboard drew her fascinated gaze again. "Okay, I have to ask. What's with the wet hair and gray blankets?"

"It's a tradition. Those of us who are up for it take a ritual plunge into the sea when our last supply ship of the year leaves the dock."

"Weird. Very weird."

Grinning, he laced his hands across his belly. His very flat belly, Mia couldn't help but note.

"That's only one of many rituals we practice down here at the bottom of the world."

"Like gash?"

"Like gash," Brent confirmed. "And mouse house, our Saturday morning station cleanup. If you come to the lounge after dinner tonight, you'll get to participate in another ritual."

"It doesn't involve ice baths, does it?" she asked with another glance at the photo of the stripped-down plungers. "Or taking off my clothes in front of a camera? Been there, done that, don't plan to do it again."

He had a nice laugh. Deep and rich and resonant. Mia found herself smiling in response.

"None of the above," he assured her, chuckling.

"Actually, that's why I stopped by your office," she explained. "To thank you for putting out the word about the pictures on Don Juan's Web site. I haven't been on the receiving end of a double take or elevated eyebrow all morning."

"Good to hear. If it helps any, no one meant to embarrass you. Living in such close quarters, we're all usually pretty careful about respecting each other's boundaries. It's just that it caught folks by surprise to have, ah, a celebrity in our midst."

"Right," Mia drawled. "That kind of celebrity status I can do without."

He cocked his head. "You couldn't get Don Juan to take your picture off his site?"

"I tried. Believe me, I tried. Unfortunately, the bastard's an attorney. He covered every legal angle. Even threatened me with a lawsuit if I exposed *him* to the world."

"Bastard is right."

"Ugh. Just talking about him leaves a bad taste in my mouth." Grimacing, she pushed to her feet. "Guess I'd better let you get back to the weather."

He flicked a glance at the screen. "I've seen what I need to. How about I show you around the station instead?"

The invitation surprised Brent as much as it did the woman facing him. He'd been so busy making sure the stranded passengers were fed, provided whatever clothing they needed and bedded down that he'd caught only sporadic glimpses of Mia last night. Once he'd hit the rack himself, though, he'd thought about her. Hard not to with Don Juan's vivid imagery floating around inside his head. Although…

He'd had to work to reconcile that sultry sex kitten with the shivering wreck he'd hauled out of the lifeboat. And both of those women bore only a superficial resemblance to the one here in his office.

The eyes were the same vibrant green. And the lips every bit as kissable. But this Mia was fresh-faced and well-rested and minus the chip she'd carried on her shoulder last night. With her hair caught back in a loose ponytail and her slender figure enveloped in baggy red sweats, she could have passed for one of the eager young grad students who came down to Palmer as research assistants.

And left again. Just as Mia and her sister would leave once the weather cleared.

Suppressing the insidious wish that the sleet and wind would hang around for a few more days, Brent dragged a down-filled vest off the back of his chair.

"Let's find you a parka and I'll give you the three-dollar tour."

SEVERAL HOURS LATER a rosy-cheeked and windblown Mia reported for lunchtime kitchen duty. Patrick, the senior station cook, had put Beth and one of the other stranded passengers to work preparing ingredients for a shredded carrot salad.

"Where did you disappear to?" Beth asked when Mia had grabbed a paring knife and joined them at the stainless steel counter.

"Brent showed me around the station."

"He did, huh?" Her sister paused in the act of scraping her blade along a fat carrot. "And how is it you rate a private tour?"

Mia didn't have an answer for that. Or for the niggling little question about the *real* motive for her detour to his office this morning.

Yes, she'd wanted to thank Brent. And yes, she'd intended to make her visit casual and quick. That didn't explain why she'd jumped at the chance to spend several hours in his company.

She and Beth would be out of here soon. Tomorrow, hopefully. Hadn't she learned her lesson, for God's sake? Spending a few hours or days with a man didn't mean she could trust her judgment concerning him.

So Walker had an easy air of competence and authority? So everyone here at this small, isolated community seemed to hold him in high regard? That didn't mean squat when it came to the man-woman thing…as she knew all too well.

"How did the blogging go?" she asked her sister in a deliberate change of subject. "Did Allen get you all set up and online?"

"Yes, he did." Enthusiasm and excitement leaped into Beth's face. "I've already posted my first blog about the marine aquarium, complete with pictures. This afternoon he's going to take me through the Terra Lab."

"What's that?"

"Beats me. Guess I'll find out this afternoon. You know—" Beth gave her sister a speculative glance "—you ought to be taking notes and pictures, too. You've always talked about writing a children's book. Palmer Station would make a great setting for one."

"I'm sure there are plenty of children's books out there about Antarctica."

"So? Do another one."

Lips pursed, Mia considered the suggestion. She enjoyed her work as an editor but did harbor a not-so-secret urge to try her hand at writing.

"This is the chance of a lifetime," Beth insisted, wagging a half-scraped carrot. "I bet Jill and Brent and the others would be glad to let you interview them about their work."

Brent had given Mia a pretty good fix on the scope of his responsibilities this morning. But…

She *would* need considerably more detail for a book. "You know," she said slowly, "I might just take a few notes."

WORD THAT MIA WAS CONSIDERING writing a book about Palmer Station spread through the permanent residents with the same speed her alter ego had the day before. Both scientists and support personnel were more than willing to show her how they passed their time.

As a result, Mia spent a mind-blowing hour with Doug Anderson, Jill's husband and the senior scientist presently at Palmer. She left his lab with pages full of notes on equipment and experiments ranging from sampling the DNA of algae that lived in the frigid waters hundreds of feet under the ice to implanting microscopic transmitters in Adelaide penguin chicks to track their migration.

When she exited the lab, Beth caught her and suggested she join the excursion to the Terra Lab. The bushy-bearded Allen Barclay seconded the invitation after offering a sincere apology.

"I'm really sorry, Mia. I shouldn't have blurted out that business about Don... Er... You know."

"Apology accepted." More than ready to put that whole sorry business behind her, she gave the meteorologist a breezy smile. "Now where is this Terra Lab of yours?"

"About fifty yards behind the BioLab."

"Behind, like in outside?"

"Like in outside," he confirmed.

Despite being wrapped in a borrowed parka, Mia seriously questioned her need for this level of detail in her book as she and Beth and Allen trudged up to the building set atop a short rise behind the BioLab. They had to lean into the wind at almost a ninety-degree angle and slit their eyes against the wind-whipped sleet.

And this was just January! The middle of their supposed summer! She couldn't imagine what conditions must be like in winter.

They made it to the lab with considerable slipping and sliding but no real mishaps. Tiki was already there and eager to give them a layman's explanation of the research she was doing for the Global Seismographic Network's long-term seismic survey.

Allen took center stage next. He did his best to go easy on the technical jargon as he explained the various experiments in progress, but he lost Mia long before he did Beth. For a substitute teacher who worked primarily with grade-schoolers, she had sure developed a sudden interest in PhD-level meteorology. Or was her interest due to a certain PhD meteorologist? Mia hung back, observing the give-and-take between her sister and the pudgy scientist.

Actually, now that she had time for a closer look, she realized most of his bulk came from his layers of clothing. His thick beard added to the illusion, as well. Beneath that hairy mask he wasn't bad.

"NOT BAD AT ALL," BETH confirmed when the sisters returned to the BioLab.

They'd detoured to their third-floor room to clean up and drag a comb through their hair before dinner. The fact that Allen had offered to wait for Beth outside the dining room hadn't been lost on Mia.

"So what's the deal with the furry doc?" she teased. "Are you two working on more than a blog?"

"Not yet. I'm thinking about it, though. He's not as hunky as your station manager, but he's really sweet under all that facial hair."

Startled, Mia halted her comb in mid-drag. "Brent isn't 'my' station manager."

"If you say so."

"C'mon, Beth. You of all people know there's no way I'm going to jump into another brief, mindless and potentially disastrous affair."

"Who says this one has to be disastrous?"

"Get real, sis. We're outta here as soon as the weather clears. Neither one of us should start something we can't finish. Besides," she added, attacking her hair again, "in case you haven't noticed, there's a distinct shortage of privacy here at the station."

"What I *have* noticed is that the Palmer crew is a pretty resourceful bunch. Where there's a will, I suspect they could find a way." Grinning, Beth stuffed her comb in the little cubbyhole beside the mirror. "Let's go eat. Allen says they're having some kind of ritual movie showing afterward."

"Uh-oh. Another ritual."

She told Beth about the ice plunge on the way to the dining room. Once there, Allen and Tiki filled them in on several other traditions during a luscious dinner of baked ziti, salad and homemade bread. One such tradition involved a green-ice sculpture competition on St. Patrick's

Day. Another required a hike to the top of the glacier behind the station before officially shedding fingee status.

The sisters got to participate in another time-honored tradition when they made the dash to the GWR building for movie night. The lounge could barely accommodate everyone. Folks perched on bar stools, on scattered chairs, on top of the pool table, on the floor. Jill Anderson manned the tabletop popcorn machine at one end of the bar while her husband poured soft drinks and wine for their guests from bottles purchased at the station store for the occasion.

"Beth! Mia! Over here."

Allen beckoned them over to a tiny wedge of floor space he'd saved. The sisters had just settled cross-legged when Brent made a late appearance.

"Got room for me?"

"Sure." Beth sent Mia a smug, I-told-you-so look. "Scoot over, sis."

With everyone crammed in hip to hip and knee to knee, the small lounge heated up fast. And with Brent's muscled thigh nudging hers, Mia heated up, as well. Calling herself ten kinds of an idiot, she forced her attention to the big-screen TV.

"Brace yourself," Brent warned, snitching from her bag of popcorn. "We show this same movie every January. Usually not until the last day of the month, but we moved it up on the schedule in honor of our unexpected guests."

"Why?"

"You'll see."

She did, less than two minutes after the opening credits began to roll for *The Thing*. A science fiction horror flick starring Kurt Russell, the movie featured a shape-shifting alien that infiltrated an Antarctic scientific research station. Palmer's regulars had memorized most of the dialogue. In thrilling, hyperdramatic voices, they chorused each line along with the actors.

Privately Mia thought *The Thing* did a darn good job of depicting Antarctica's hostile environment, but by the end of the movie she was laughing so hard her sides hurt. Some of the guests and a number of station residents lingered afterward for another glass of wine.

Gradually, the lounge emptied except for the overflow crowd bunking down there. Beth and Allen departed together, Mia and Brent following a few moments later. Once outside, they discovered the wooden walkway connecting the buildings had acquired another slippery coat during the movie.

"Careful," Brent warned. "You'd better hang on to me."

She hooked her arm in his and kept her head down against the wind until they hit the BioLab's double doors. When the door whooshed shut behind them, she shook off the sleet and smiled up at him.

"Palmer Station is really taking me back to my childhood. First sleeping bags, à la Camp Winihaha. Now having someone walk me home from the movies. It's junior high school all over again."

"Not quite," he returned with a grin. "If this was junior high, I'd be all in a sweat trying to figure out how to wrangle a kiss on your front porch."

He said it lightly, making a joke out of it. Yet as soon as the words were out, his gaze dropped to her mouth and his eyes darkened to cobalt.

All of a sudden Mia forgot how to breathe. "Do you…uh…want a kiss?"

In answer, he pulled off his glove and ran his thumb along her lower lip. Once. Twice. His skin was warm on hers, his voice low and husky.

"Oh, yeah."

CHAPTER FOUR

THE KISS STARTED OFF LIGHT. Easy. Brent's lips brushing hers. His fingers threading through her hair.

Mia tried to ignore the slow sizzle his mouth generated. Sternly, she reminded herself why she was stuck down here at the bottom of the earth. And that she'd sworn to tread carefully where men were concerned. Very carefully.

Yet his mouth felt so good on hers, darn it! So warm and sensual and right. That thought was front and center in her mind when Brent pulled back.

"You okay with this?" he asked, searching her face.

She was, she realized. The mere fact that he'd asked, that he understood her instinctive need for caution after the fiasco of Don Juan, bridged the gap.

"Yes. You?"

His grin slipped out, quick and sexy and all male.

"Absolutely."

The kiss was deeper this time, greedier. Their mouths locked. Their tongues mated. Mia gave in to the need to slide her hands up and over his shoulders. He reciprocated by hooking an arm around her waist and tugging her against him.

They had on too many layers for direct contact but she

could feel his strength and heat. She reveled in both…and in the cleansing joy of just letting herself go again.

When he raised his head once more, his breath came as fast and hard as hers. He stared down at her, so close she could see herself in his eyes.

"Wow," he said softly.

She drew in a gulp of air. "Wow is right."

Brent leaned his free arm against the door, caging her in while he tried to decide what the heck to do next.

Unfortunately, he didn't have many options. The station was bursting at the seams with almost double its maximum capacity. Privacy was nonexistent, except maybe in one of the labs or offices.

As quickly as that thought surfaced, Brent squelched it. No way he was hustling Mia into a lab and backing her against a spectrophotometer or algae tank. That would put him in almost the same class as that jerk, Don Juan. Yet he wasn't ready to say good-night. Or let her out of his arms.

Inspiration hit a moment later. "You up for a late-night dip?"

"In the icy sea? No way!"

"Actually, I was thinking of the hot tub."

She blinked up at him. "Are you serious? You guys really have a hot tub?"

"We do. It's more of a necessity than a luxury. Divers use it to soak the chill out of their bones after going under the ice. We keep it bubbling 24/7 so the water doesn't freeze."

"It's *outside?*"

"It is," he admitted ruefully. "But sheltered from the wind."

She wavered a moment or two before shaking her head. "My bathing suit is still aboard the *Adventurer II*."

With noble restraint, Brent refrained from suggesting they go *au naturel*. "Not a problem. You have a T-shirt on under your sweats, don't you?"

"Yes."

"That's what most of us wear."

Mia had her doubts. Serious doubts. But, as advertised, the small hot tub tucked behind the BioLab building was protected from the worst of the weather. Still, she hung back while Brent slid off the cover and adjusted the water temperature.

He made quick work of stripping down to a black T-shirt and a pair of thick, thigh-hugging trunks obviously designed for warmth. He stepped into the tub and quickly sank up to his neck.

"Come on in," he teased when she hesitated with her hand on her jacket zipper. "The water's fine."

With great reluctance, she shed her outer layer. Her red sweats came off next, her borrowed boots last. The arctic night air raised instant goose bumps over every inch of her exposed flesh. Shivering, Mia almost jumped into the tub.

"Ahhhhh."

Steam curled upward from the surface of the bubbling water. Encased in the warm fog, she felt her way along the built-in seat. Brent negated the need to find a perch by the simple expedient of tugging her onto his lap.

"Now," he murmured, threading a hand through her hair. "Where were we?"

Mia's internal temperature shot up to match the

water's. Brushing her lips against his, she punctuated her reply with kisses.

"Right...about...here."

God, he tasted good! Felt good, too. Her eager hands explored the chest molded by his wet T-shirt while her mouth and tongue played with his. Brent reciprocated by sliding his free hand down her rib cage and over her hip.

It couldn't go beyond kissing. And touching. She knew that. Despite the late hour, someone else could hit on the same idea and mosey on out to the hot tub. Or Beth could come looking for them.

Nor did Mia intend to take things beyond this slow, sensual exploration. If nothing else, Don Juan had taught her to look hard and long before baring herself. But man-oh-man, what Brent could do with his mouth and hands and tongue! The bubbling water and wet steam couldn't compete with the heat searing Mia from the inside out.

Wiggling around, she hooked a leg over his and straddled his thighs. They sat face-to-face, breath to breath, belly to belly.

"We got the ends of your hair wet." Smiling, he combed his fingers through the limp strands. "You have tiny icicles forming."

"Only on the outside."

Inside, she was having major hot flashes. Especially when he planed his hands down her hips and slid them under the hem of her wet T-shirt. She could feel the callouses on his palms against her slick skin. Feel, too, the sudden hardening under her thigh.

She was playing with fire. Mia acknowledged the

danger even as she locked her arms around his neck and brought her mouth down on his.

The hard ridge jerked under her thigh. Brent gave a small grunt and moved his hands down to cup her bottom. He eased her over an inch or two. Positioning her. Stoking her. Exploring the small indentation in her left cheek.

It was the damned dimple that brought her to her senses. With a ferocious effort of will, Mia wiggled back and put some distance between them.

"We'd better stop," she got out on a husky note. "I'm, uh, not certified for deep water dives."

The joke was corny but conveyed her message. Brent blew out a long breath.

"Guess we'd better get you certified before we take to the water again," he said ruefully.

"Guess so. Ready to go back inside?"

His mouth tipped into a wry grin. "Give me a minute."

THAT GRIN WAS THE FIRST THING Mia remembered when she woke the next morning. Beth and Tiki lay curled up in their sleeping bags on either side of her, Mary in the bed. To the rhythm of their soft, even breathing Mia replayed every moment of that steamy hot tub session in her mind.

Her heart thumped as she remembered the crazy sensation of having her body engulfed in swirling heat while wind and sleet knifed through the frigid air.

Speaking of which…

Belatedly, Mia translated the soft hum of her roommates' breathing into an absence of other sounds. Like a screeching wind and sleet dancing off the roof. She raised her head and saw the faint glimmer of hazy dawn outlined in the frost-rimmed window.

"Oh, no!"

The dismayed murmur slipped out, surprising her. She wanted to go home. She really did. Getting plucked from icy waters after being forced to abandon ship was *not* her idea of a fun vacation. And camping out on the floor of a crowded dorm room was okay for a night or two, but this sleeping bag didn't compare to the bed in her nice, cozy Newport condo.

On the other hand...

She'd let herself get all hyped up about the possibility of writing a book about Antarctica. She now had pages and pages of notes and had planned to take more today. Then, of course, there was Brent.

Brought back full circle, Mia sighed. No point in wishing they would have more time to explore this undeniable attraction. If the cessation of wind and sleet was any indication, she and Beth would soon be on their way home.

Trying to work up some enthusiasm for their imminent departure, she wiggled out of the sleeping bag and headed for the bathroom. She was washed and tooth-brushed and dressed in her jeans and wool sweater before Beth or the other two women so much as stirred.

She left them to their snoozing and followed the yeasty scent of fresh-baked rolls to the second-floor dining room. A scattering of Palmer residents and their stranded guests had beat her down. Including, she saw with a quick intake of breath, the station manager.

When he looked up at her entrance and did the crinkly-eye smile thing, Mia felt a sharp stab of regret. Departing Palmer Station now seemed more like a punishment than a reward for keeping a stiff upper lip during those scary hours in the lifeboat.

When she grabbed a cup of coffee and joined him at his table, he confirmed her guess that she and the others would soon be on their way home.

"The storm's blown itself out."

"I noticed."

"I've been down in the comm center for the past half hour. Your cruise line is diverting an Argentinean ice-breaker with a reinforced hull to pick up its stranded passengers and crew. With luck, you'll be on your way back to Punta Arenas this time tomorrow morning."

"Not till tomorrow? Good!"

She covered her involuntary exclamation with a breezy smile.

"That'll give me more time to take notes. I might just get a book out of this experience yet."

"You might at that. But you can't give your readers a real feel for Antarctica unless you walk on ice."

"Wasn't that ice we were slipping and sliding around for the past two days?"

"Ice-coated rocks and walkways don't come close to the real thing. Tell you what. I need to get with my key staff at eight and have a meeting with Jill to go over some modifications she needs for the outside aquarium tank at ten-fifteen. If the weather holds I could walk you up onto the glacier after lunch. It's about a half-mile trek. An easy climb, if you're up for it."

"I'm up for it. I think."

He grinned at her dubious expression. "If you need more incentive, climbing Big Blue will qualify you to graduate from fingee status."

Climbing anything with Brent was incentive enough but Mia made a show of giving in reluctantly.

"If you say so. Okay, Walker, I'm in."

"Good. Meet me in the lounge after lunch. I need to give you a safety briefing before we go up on the glacier."

WORD OF THE PENDING expedition spread during the morning. When 1:00 p.m. rolled around, a weak but determined sun had burned through the soupy haze outside and a group of six enthusiastic hikers had gathered in the lounge. Tiki was among them, excited about her chance to shed her fingee designation. Beth had planned to participate, as well, but got a better offer from Allen.

"He's checking me out to see how I handle a snowmobile," she confided to Mia. "Then we're going to a penguin rookery on the other side of the island. I should get some terrific pictures for my blog. You can use them in your book, too. With due credit to the photographer, of course."

"Of course. Have fun."

"You, too."

Beth departed with a cheerful wave and her camera zipped inside her jacket pocket. Mia then turned her attention to the slide show Brent projected onto the big-screen TV. If she'd harbored any foolish illusions that a stroll on the ice might not be all that difficult, he soon set her straight.

Two other station regulars besides Tiki had joined the

expedition. Like Brent, they were experienced ice climbers and members of the Palmer Glacier Search and Rescue Team. They helped him explain basic safety precautions and demonstrate the required communications equipment. Then Brent showed detailed satellite imagery of the trail up to the glacier. Marked by flags flying from tall poles stuck in the ice, it looked to be about fifteen or twenty feet across.

"It's absolutely essential everyone stays on the trail," Brent warned. "We test it for crevasses regularly. The path is safe, or we wouldn't take you up there. But it's late in the summer and the glacier is melting under the snow, so we all need to exercise caution."

Mia did a mental ooooooh-kay and seriously considered wimping out. The fact that this was her last day at the station—and with Brent—kept her in the mix.

The experienced hikers made sure everyone slathered on plenty of sunscreen to protect against ice glare before rechecking cold-weather gear and walkie-talkies. Only after Brent was satisfied that everyone knew how to operate the communications equipment did he lead the way to the exit.

Mia squared her shoulders and braced for the wind and bone-biting cold of the past few days. Instead she stepped out into absolutely still air and a temperature that had already nudged up to a toasty thirty-three degrees.

"Whoa!" she breathed. "What a difference a day makes."

Nodding, Brent made a sweep of the glacier behind the station. It gleamed a dull aqua in the slowly strengthening sunlight.

"This is the Antarctica that keeps bringing us back."

Him, maybe. She wouldn't put Palmer at the top of her list for vacation spots. Although…

As she followed him toward the sloping path, she had to admit the place had an eerie beauty all its own. The jagged mountains in the distance speared straight into the sky. They were skirted by glaciers that moved with imponderable slowness toward the sea.

As Mia trudged up the wide path, the only sound she heard apart from her own labored breathing was the rumble of the surf sweeping into the coves and inlets below. Just like along Rhode Island's coast, she thought. Only instead of washing against a shore lined with expensive condos and the "cottages" of the superrich, this ocean encircled a continent almost untouched by human habitation.

She was listening to the tide's restless ebb and flow when a thunderous boom split the air. With a startled shriek, she ducked and threw her hands over her head. She wasn't the only one freaked out by the cannonlike boom. Tiki almost nose-dived into the snow at Mia's feet.

"Look!" Brent shouted, pointing to an ice-bound cove some distance down the coast. "The glacier's calving."

Both women spun around just as a massive chunk of ice broke away from the main body. Transfixed, Mia watched the house-size piece crash into the sea. Tiki snatched off her gloves and fumbled for the camera in her pocket. She got off only a couple of shots before the grinding, howling noise died and the churning sea subsided.

"Oh, man!" she exclaimed, checking her shots in the

viewfinder. "We just watched an iceberg being born. Is that cool, or what?"

Actually, it was pretty darn awesome! Mia had never witnessed a display of such raw, elemental power before. Moved in a way she didn't quite understand, she fell back into line for the rest of the trek.

Standing on top of the glacier turned out to be another incredible experience. Palmer's handful of blue metal buildings were the only man-made structures anywhere in a seeming endless vista of sea, sky and ice. When Mia made a half turn, the station disappeared from her line of sight. She could have been alone on the ice. Alone in the universe. The stillness was profound, the view so incredibly humbling and uplifting.

Brent stood back while Mia took in the primal essence of Antarctica. Her expression mirrored the same stunned amazement he'd seen on the faces of so many other first-timers. But he'd never felt the same jolt while observing those fingees as he did while watching her. Or the same raw hunger. It was there, deep in his belly, when he moved to her side.

"Spectacular, isn't it?"

"And then some. I understand now what pulls you back here."

"You should think about spending more time here. The National Science Foundation funds programs for artists and writers, you know."

She swiveled to face him. "Really?"

"Really. We had a professional photographer on station last summer. He got a NSF grant to do a black-and-white photo study of the various ice forms."

Her emerald eyes filled with speculation. Just as quickly, it faded away. "I doubt NSF would give me a grant. I'm not an established author."

"True, but you're an established editor. Seems like a logical jump for me."

Was he pushing too hard? Sounding too eager? Probably, but Brent didn't care. All he knew was that he didn't want this woman to drift into his life for such a short time, then drift right out again.

"Stop by my office when we get back to the station. I'll show you the links so you can apply online."

"You really think I should?"

Smiling, he gave the same answer he'd returned last night. "Oh, yeah."

Then, of course, he had to follow up with another kiss. Something to cap her glacier walk. Something for him to think about after she'd gone.

"Got it."

The amused comment brought both their heads around. Tiki had her camera aimed at them and clicked off another couple shots.

"I'll e-mail the pictures to you, Mia. And to you, Brent," she added with a wink.

THE DESCENT TOOK MUCH LESS time than the climb. Beth hadn't yet returned from her excursion to the penguin rookery, so Mia detoured to the kitchen for some hot chocolate and fresh-baked cookies.

Several of her fellow cruise passengers were in the galley. She shared a table with them and echoed their excitement over the projected departure for home in the morning. All the while she was mentally marshaling pros and cons regarding a much longer stay at Palmer.

Three or four months here at the station wouldn't be so bad. If she got a grant, she could take a leave of absence from her job. Or even edit textbooks online while down here at the station. Either way, she would have plenty of time to work on her own book.

Uh-huh. Sure. Like that was the driving factor behind her sudden desire to check out this grant business.

She was still listing arguments for and against the idea when she headed for the administrative wing. Was she making a mistake? Jumping in feetfirst again? She'd known Brent Walker for what? All of three days? Less time than she'd known Don Juan before she let him make a complete fool of her. Yet here she was, thinking about rearranging her entire life so she could spend a few months down here at the bottom of the world with the man.

This time was different, though. Her instincts had been flawed regarding Don Juan, but everything in her said she could trust Brent. She believed that with all of her heart…until she was a few steps from his office and caught the exchange inside.

"This is her?" an unfamiliar voice asked. "Number 112?"

"That's her," Brent confirmed.

Mia's insides cramped. Oh, no! Not again. Not *him,* too.

Her feet dragging, she took another step. A third. Saw Brent and another man hunched in front of his computer. While she writhed inside, the younger one let out a long, low whistle.

"Wow. That's some sweet dimple on her…"

"Skip the editorial, Monroe. Just mark the Web site."

Mia didn't wait to hear more. Slowly, she backed down the hall and retreated to the dining room again.

Mercifully, the others had left. The place was empty except for the cooks at work in the kitchen. Mia nodded to them as she went to stand at the window but didn't speak. She couldn't. Raw emotion had her throat in a vise.

He'd marked the Web site. Tagged the salacious picture of her. That shouldn't have hurt so much. But it did, dammit! It did.

Arms wrapped around her waist, Mia stared at the expanse of snowcapped coast. Her thoughts churned so wildly it took a moment for her to register the two small black specs in the distance throwing up rooster tails of snow. Beth and Allen, returning from the penguin rookery. Mia watched their progress blindly while she writhed inside. How stupid could one woman be? How gullible and naive and *stupid?*

She could think of only one reason for Brent to bookmark that disgusting Web site. So he could return to it over and over again after she departed Palmer. Maybe… Maybe even boast to Allen and the others how he had almost bagged the good-time girl. Display the picture Tiki had snapped up on the glacier as proof.

Disgust ate at her insides like acid. Not with him. With herself for actually thinking he was different. For believing he'd seen beyond that disgusting photo.

Hot tears stung her eyes. Fiercely, she blinked them away. She wouldn't cry. She *wouldn't!* Instead, she fixed her gaze on the two snowmobiles.

Thank God for Beth. Mia could talk to her. Work through this hurt and…

Her thoughts stuttered to a stop while her mind tried to make sense of the sudden disappearance of one of those snowy rooster tails.

She pressed her palms to the frigid windowpane and leaned closer. Her first, horrified thought was that the snowmobile had fallen into a crevasse. She almost sobbed with relief when she spotted the machine lying on its side. Relief morphed swiftly into anxiety when the rider didn't crawl out from under the overturned vehicle.

Her heart thumped as the other snowmobile fishtailed around and halted. The rider climbed off, too far away and too bundled up to tell if it was Beth or Allen, and ran toward the other vehicle.

Mia didn't wait for more. Shoving away from the window, she raced out of the dining room and tore down the hall to the administrative wing. She was only a few feet from Brent's office when she heard the staticky cackle of a radio.

"Mayday! Mayday! Palmer Station, this is Allen Barclay. Come in please!"

CHAPTER FIVE

THE FRANTIC CALL FROZE MIA just outside Brent's office. Her heart in her throat, she watched while he whipped the radio off his belt and keyed the mike.

"This is Brent. What's the nature of your emergency, Allen?"

"Beth Harrelson's Jet Ski hit an ice spur. It rolled over on her. She's writhing in pain and can't get up."

Oh, God! Terror sliced through Mia's veins. She couldn't move, couldn't breathe. Just stood there with her heart pounding while Brent barked out a swift reply.

"Don't try to move her. I'm activating the crash team. We'll get a GPS fix on your location and respond immediately."

"You can see them!" Mia gasped. "From the dining room window!"

He jerked his chin in acknowledgment and flipped a switch on the console above his desk. His voice blared through the intercom a second later, sounding calm and in control despite his grim expression.

"Attention all personnel. The crash team should report to GWR immediately. I repeat, all members of the crash team should report immediately."

He grabbed his jacket off the back of his chair and pushed past Mia.

"We'll bring her to the clinic in the GWR. You can wait there."

"I want to go with you!"

"This is no time for amateurs on the ice," he snapped over his shoulder. "Wait at the clinic."

MIA HIT THE DINING ROOM FIRST.

Her face plastered to the window, she gnawed on her lower lip until a large tracked vehicle with *Glacier Search and Rescue* stamped on its side roared out of the GWR building. Two smaller vehicles burst out behind it.

Fear pumped acid from her roiling stomach into her throat as the three rescue vehicles raced toward the snowmobiles. Allen was down on his knees in the snow, his back to Mia. She couldn't see Beth.

When the crash team reached the scene, five people rushed over to surround Allen. Mia kept her clenched fists against the cold glass and didn't draw a full breath until she saw her sister eased onto a backboard, strapped down and lifted into the tracked vehicle. Only then did she fling away from the window. Rushing down the stairs, she hit the exit door and ran along the wooden walkway to the GWR building.

Jill Anderson's husband, Doug, was already in the GWR when Mia rushed in. As the senior scientist at Palmer, he'd maintained an open comm link with the crash team while ensuring everything was ready to receive the accident victim back at the station.

"The doc's got everything he needs here to treat most

emergencies," he assured Mia. "X-ray equipment, a lab, a full pharmacy, two trained EMTs to assist him. They'll take good care of your sister."

Mia clung to that promise until the crash team carried Beth in on the backboard. A white-faced Allen Barclay had one handle of the board, Brent another. Beth was conscious, thank God, and responded to her sister's welcome cry with what started as a smile but ended in a rictus of pain.

"I'm...okay."

"Right. Uh-huh. You look just dandy."

Mia tried to follow the stretcher into the clinic but Doug restrained her.

"There's not enough room inside. You need to wait here until the doc checks her out."

She watched anxiously from the doorway while the crash team laid Beth on the exam table, still strapped to the backboard. Three members of the team then exited the small clinic. The two trained EMTs remained inside to assist the physician. Brent was one of them. He gave Mia an encouraging nod before he shut the door in her face.

Allen paced the hall with Mia. Behind his bushy beard, his faced was twisted with worry and self-recrimination.

"I made sure I went ahead of her the whole way. Checked every foot of the track. But that damned ice spur was a few inches below the surface and I went right over it."

They swung back and forth, with Mia trying to reassure Allen and him doing the same for her. Finally, the door to the clinic opened and Brent emerged.

"She's okay," he told the anxious group. "Pretty bruised and shaken up, but no broken bones or internal injuries that the doc can detect."

"Can I see her now?" she asked, gulping back a big, fat sob of relief.

"You can. She's a little woozy," he warned. "The doc gave her some Demerol for the pain."

Woozy understated the case considerably. Beth was almost out of it but managed to greet her sister with a real smile this time.

"Some vacation, huh?"

"No kidding! How're you feeling?"

"Like I just got run over by a snowmobile."

"She was lucky," the station's doc confirmed. "Nothing worse than some nasty contusions on her stomach. We'll keep an eye on her for a while, though, just to be sure."

He rolled a stainless steel stool over for Mia, then retreated to the back of the clinic to write up his report. Mia plopped onto the stool and threaded her hand through her sister's. Beth dozed off for a while and woke with a little start.

"Sis?"

"I'm here."

Beth's lids drifted down and she dozed off again. She was still asleep when Brent returned to the clinic some hours later.

"I'll take the next watch," he said with a nod that included both Mia and the doc. "You two go get some supper."

Now that her terror for her sister had subsided, Mia

had had time to think about what Brent had been doing right before the accident. His swift action to aid Beth mitigated some of Mia's hurt and disappointment. Enough remained, however, for her to be very glad she was departing Palmer Station the next morning.

Which is exactly what she conveyed to Brent when she and the doc returned after supper. She kept it light. Breezy. No sense embarrassing herself by admitting how close she'd come to making another stupid mistake.

"Thanks for what you did for my sister this afternoon," she told him while the doc checked Beth's vitals. "Antarctica's turned out to be quite an adventure, but we'll sure be glad to get home."

He cocked his head and studied her with those penetrating blue eyes. "I hope this accident hasn't turned you off the idea of applying for an NSF grant."

She'd been turned off all right, but not by the accident.

"That book thing was a crazy idea. I'm an editor, not a writer."

"Maybe I can convince you otherwise. How about a cup of coffee later, after Beth settles in for the night?"

"I'm going to hang here with her. But thanks. Again."

Before he could reply, she turned away.

Frowning, Brent hooked his thumbs in his jeans pockets. He'd been given the brush-off before. Most notably by his fiancée just weeks before their wedding. Ironically, this one hit a helluva lot harder.

Mia Harrelson had gotten to him in their short days together. Her frankness in facing up to the mistake she'd made with that Don Juan had won Brent's respect. So had her willingness to pitch in and help here at the station.

Mixed in with that respect was a growing attraction laced heavily with desire. In the few short days they'd been together this woman had turned him and his controlled, orderly world upside down. The idea that she would leave in the morning ate at his insides.

Then again, he had to consider the very real scare the sisters had had this afternoon. If Beth had sustained serious injuries beyond the scope of their limited medical facilities, getting her to a hospital in time could have meant the difference between life and death. No surprise that Mia's budding wonder and appreciation of Antarctica's awesome beauty had fizzled and died on the spot.

Along with her interest in him, apparently.

Maybe it was for the best, Brent concluded as he left the clinic. He'd tried a long-distance romance. It didn't work. No reason to think this one would, either. Mia would depart tomorrow. Brent would remain on station until his between-tour leave in early March. And that was that.

MIA ECHOED EXACTLY THE SAME sentiments early the next morning as she and her sister gathered their few possessions and prepared to depart Palmer Station.

They were dressed in the jeans and turtlenecks they'd arrived in. Mia had topped her turtleneck with a U.S. Research Station Palmer sweatshirt purchased at the station's small store. Beth's sweatshirt came compliments of Allen Barclay and the National Science Foundation's Electromagnetic Ionospheric Research Project.

Beth was moving *very* gingerly this morning. She sported a vicious-looking bruise on her stomach from its close encounter with the skimobile's handlebar. The accident hadn't dampened her enthusiasm for Antarctica, though.

"I can't believe you're giving up the idea of a book about this place."

"This place, as you term it, is just a little bit too overwhelming. I'd rather put everything that happened here behind me."

"Including Brent?"

"Including Brent."

"Why? What's up with that? I thought you two had struck a few sparks."

Shrugging, Mia stuffed her toiletries into a ditty bag.

"Sparks can burn, especially when you jump into the fire too fast. I've learned my lesson."

She hadn't told her sister about almost walking in on Brent while he was marking Don Juan's site for future reference. What was the point?

"Come on, let's get you downstairs. The last intercom announcement said to be ready to board in twenty minutes."

DESPITE HER EAGERNESS TO PUT Palmer behind her, Mia found it harder than she'd anticipated to say goodbye to the station manager.

Brent was on the dock, directing operations. He wore an orange float parka for visibility and safety, teamed with snug jeans and a black knit watch cap covering most of his blond hair.

Behind him loomed the gray-painted hull of the icebreaker. In true Palmer tradition, Brent had invited the ship's captain and crew ashore for a tour of the facilities. The captain had reciprocated by inviting the Palmer folks aboard for a traditional Argentinean breakfast of sweet, sticky *medialunas* accompanied by black coffee and glasses of steamed milk flavored with bittersweet chocolate.

Mia got a taste of the chocolate when Brent drew her aside at the gangplank.

"I have something for you. A little souvenir of your visit to the bottom of the world."

He reached into his jacket pocket and extracted a flat box. Inside was a multifaceted, lead glass medallion in the shape of Antarctica.

"One of our guys in the machine shop makes these. If you hang it in a window, it'll refract the sun in a rainbow of colors."

"Thank you. I didn't expect a gift. You…everyone here at Palmer…have been so generous already."

"We aim to please."

Oh, crap! He had to do it. Smile down at her like that.

Wondering what the heck it was about those weathered laugh lines at the corners of his eyes that turned her insides to mush, Mia slid the box into her pocket.

"I'm sorry. I don't have a goodbye gift for you."

"I'll settle for a kiss."

She could hardly refuse without explaining why. And explanations aside, a traitorous part of her wanted one last touch, one final brush of his mouth on hers. If nothing else, it would serve as a reminder of how close she'd come to making another mistake.

Going up on tiptoe, she let her lips settle against his. He tasted of chocolate and warm, seductive male. When she ended the kiss, genuine regret for what might have been tinged her voice.

"Bye, Brent."

"Bye, Mia."

Once aboard the icebreaker, most of the rescued cruise ship passengers went below but the two sisters stayed out on deck while the ship got underway. The engine rumbled to life beneath their feet. Brent and the others on the dock loosed the mooring lines. The icebreaker's crew winched them in. Slowly, the ship gathered speed and nosed through ice that had melted into slush with the warmer temperatures.

Suddenly Beth gave a shocked gasp. "What on earth are they doing?"

She hung on the rail, her disbelieving gaze locked on Brent and Allen while they stripped off jackets, shirts, boots and hats.

"It's a Palmer ritual." Mia had to bite her lip to hold back a strangled laugh. "Brent said they do it when their resupply ship leaves. I guess… I guess they're taking a special plunge in our honor."

And plunge they did, straight off the dock. Her last sight of Brent was as he waved to her from the ice-flecked water.

CHAPTER SIX

MIA HAD DISCOVERED THE HARD way that summers in Antarctica could turn real nasty, real fast. So could winters in New England.

She and Beth felt the sting when they walked out of Boston's Logan International Airport five days later. Both sisters squinted in the bright, brittle sunshine and gasped at the breeze off the bay that drove the windchill down to a teeth-clenching minus ten.

Although the cruise line had sprung for first-class tickets home, the long flight had left them both drained. Mia dropped a still tender but much improved Beth off at her apartment then headed for home. She had to battle the usual I-93 traffic snarl until she hit the relatively open stretch of 24 South. An hour and a half later she pulled up outside her condo in Newport's north end.

After the spartan quarters at Palmer Station, her one-bedroom efficiency seemed as spacious and elegant as one of Newport's fabled mansions. Mia had stretched her savings to buy the place and had thoroughly enjoyed painting and decorating it. She'd opted for pale celery walls throughout most of the condo, with darker green accent walls in the dining alcove and bedroom. The furniture was covered in chintz sporting bright, splashy pink, red and purple spring tulips. Coordinating chintz plaids draped the windows and bed.

Grateful to be home, she shed her coat, peeled off her clothing and hit the shower. She was in bed fifteen minutes later, asleep in twenty.

THE ENTIRE NEXT DAY GOT swallowed up by necessary posttrip activity. With the remainder of her cruise derailed, Mia still had several unused vacation days left. She decided to devote one to the myriad chores waiting for her at home. She had groceries to buy, mail to sort through, bills to pay. Not much laundry to do, as her suitcases were still aboard the stranded *Adventurer II*. The cruise line had promised the passengers' personal belongings would be retrieved and forwarded, but she wasn't holding out much hope.

The line had also sent the passengers home with reams of paperwork to fill out regarding compensation and liability. She got through most of the stack but decided to ask a friend in her company's legal department to look over the documents to make sure she wasn't signing away anything essential.

Setting the paperwork aside, she booted up her laptop to check her e-mail. The four hundred-plus messages in her in-box drew a low groan.

"I *have* to tell those clowns at the office to take me off their joke forwarding lists."

As she skimmed the chronological list, she saw several from Palmer Station. Tiki had sent the first, hoping Mia had made it home safely. Attached to the e-mail were JPEGS of the photos Tiki had snapped on the glacier.

A little ache settled inside Mia's chest as she stared at the photo of Brent and her silhouetted against a seemingly endless backdrop of ice and sky. Every detail stood out in the reflected glare—including his smile just before he kissed her.

With a pang for what might have been, Mia saved the attachment, replied to Tiki's e-mail and scrolled down to one from Brent. He, too, hoped she'd made it home without further mishap. Asked about Beth. Gave her an update on the efforts to get the *Adventurer II* off the ice. He also enclosed a link to the National Science Foundation Web site…just in case she changed her mind about applying for a grant.

Mia drafted several versions of a reply before hitting what she considered just the right note. Friendly, but not too personal. Appreciative of all he'd done for her and Beth, but not too gushy. Lips pursed, she reread the reply yet again before finally hitting Send.

The e-mail on its way, she let her gaze drift upward to the cut glass medallion she'd hung in the window above her desk. The facets refracted the light and sent points of color dancing against the opposite wall. Just as Brent had promised they would.

The little ache inside Mia's chest spread. How could she have been so wrong about him? *Had* she been wrong about him?

THAT QUESTION HOVERED in the back of her mind during the weeks that followed. One of her coworkers brought it front and center again when he stopped by her workstation on his way back from the coffee machine.

"Bet you're relieved Don Juan's site is no more."

Surprised, Mia glanced up from her computer. "It's gone?"

"You didn't know?"

"I don't make a habit of checking it for the latest updates," she drawled.

The barb struck home. With a sheepish grin, the guy hiked his coffee mug in acknowledgment of the hit.

"It's been down for a while," he told her. "Since before you came home. I guess we were all so worried about that business of your ship going aground, we forgot to mention it when you returned to work."

Yeah. Uh-huh. Or no one in the office had wanted to admit they'd become Don Juan junkies.

Mia waited until she got home that evening to verify that the site was down. Sure enough, when she keyed in its URL all that came up was gray fuzz. Not even the standard message that her browser couldn't locate the site. She did a double check by Keying in "Don Juan, Number 112" on Google. The correct Web address popped up but when she clicked on it the screen filled with fuzz again.

"Good riddance."

Immensely relieved, she shut down her Web browser. It looked as though Brent would only have the picture Tiki had snapped on the glacier to remember her by. If he wanted to remember her at all.

HE DID, SHE DISCOVERED when she answered the doorbell the second weekend in March.

It was a bright Saturday afternoon, with a definite hint

of spring in the air. But Mia wasn't expecting anyone so she peered cautiously through the peephole. When she saw who stood on the other side her jaw dropped. Mixed in with her astonishment was a wild burst of joy that had her yanking the door open.

"Brent! What are you doing here?"

"I'm as surprised as you are that I had the nerve to…"

Thrown completely for a loop, Mia waited for him to continue.

"It's a little complicated," he said after a moment. "Can I come in?"

"What? Oh. Sure."

Still stunned, she led the way into her living room. As she took in his neat black slacks and suede jacket, she couldn't help wishing she'd pulled on something a little more presentable than gray sweats. And done more with her hair than just stuff it back in scrunchie. And…

"Nice place," Brent commented as his gaze roamed her celery-colored walls and splashy tulip chintz.

"Thanks." Still flustered by both his appearance and her instinctive reaction to it, she blurted out, "How did you know where I live?"

"You can find anyone on the Internet these days."

"Oh. Right."

That brought her down to earth with a thud.

"So why, exactly, are you here?"

Brent was damned if he knew. He'd told himself repeatedly that Mia had been smart to give him the brush-off, that their worlds were too different to mesh. Right up until he'd boarded the plane for the States to take his leave, he'd planned on flying back to Colorado for three weeks of doing nothing. But the moment the plane had touched down in Houston, he'd changed his ticket. Now here he was, facing a woman he'd known for all of three or four days but had thought about incessantly for the past two months.

"As I said, it's a little complicated."

He scrubbed a hand over his jaw, trying to put into words the crazy urge that had landed him on her doorstep. It didn't help that Mia looked every bit as seductive as he'd remembered. Not every woman could carry off shapeless sweats and a fresh scrubbed face the way she could.

"The thing is…"

Might as well lay it out, he decided. Worst-case scenario, she would laugh in his face and boot him out the door.

"I kept thinking about the days you were at Palmer. How rushed they were. How we didn't really have time to get to know each other. Discover each other's favorite movies. Favorite iTunes downloads. If you prefer pizza over, say, corn dogs. So I thought maybe we could fill in the gaps.

"You came all the way from Antarctica to Rhode Island to find out whether I prefer pizza or corn dogs?" she asked incredulously.

"For starters." He had to grin at her astounded expression. "I'll be honest. I'm also hoping to rekindle whatever it was that sizzled between us down at Palmer. I tried to extinguish the spark, Mia. Especially after I got your let's-be-friends e-mail. Damned embers just wouldn't die."

Her mouth opened, snapped shut, opened again. "I...
Uh..."

"I know," he acknowledged ruefully. "I'm as surprised
I had the nerve to show up unannounced as you are."

He knew he was out on a limb here. Way out. But he'd
let the fiancée he thought he'd loved go without a fight. He
couldn't let Mia go, too, without making *some* push to
discover what it was about her that had gotten under his skin.

There were limits, however, even for a man on a
mission.

"Here's what I suggest. I checked into the Marriott
down at the harbor. If you think there's a chance we
might share a mutual passion for pizza instead of corn
dogs, join me for dinner tonight. If you don't, I'll pack
up and fly home tomorrow. No harm, no foul."

OH, SURE. NO HARM, NO FOUL.

Easy for him to say.

Mia wasn't as certain. She could still feel remnants of
the excitement that had ripped through her when she'd
identified Brent in the peephole. If that wild, completely
unexpected thrill was any indication, she might not be
able to walk—or sail—away so easily this time.

She spent the rest of the afternoon debating whether
to have dinner with him. She hadn't forgotten that
moment outside his office when she'd caught him
cruising that damned Web site, but time, distance and
some serious rationalizing had put that in perspective.

After all, Brent was no different from the guys at her
office. They weren't perverts. Just healthy, curious males.
Better they should bookmark a Web site showing scantily

clad women than one with hard-core porn. Besides, Don Juan's site was down. Gone. Nothing but fuzz. Mia had put that embarrassing incident behind her. She refused to let it ruin her life.

That was her justification, anyway, for driving to down to the Harbor Place Marriott just after six. That, and a sneaking desire to find out if Brent Walker was as intriguing off the ice as he was on.

WHEN SATURDAY-NIGHT DINNER led to a Sunday-afternoon stroll along Newport's famous Cliff Walk, Mia had her answer. And when the Sunday stroll led to Monday, Wednesday and Thursday after-work get-togethers, the spark had most definitely rekindled.

Maybe it was Brent's deep, rich laugh. Or his gentle touch when he brushed a thumb over her cheek. Or his *very* obvious restraint every time he kissed her goodnight. Whatever the reason, Mia had made up her mind by the time Friday evening rolled around. She wanted more than a touch. More than a kiss. More than an evening of pizza and TV watching, which was what they'd decided to do.

A fifties' era, B-grade gangster movie flickered on the screen in front of them, but she barely noticed the stiff dialogue or atrocious acting. She sat curled loosely against Brent's side. She could feel the rise and fall of his chest under her palm, absorb the faint, leathery tang of his aftershave with every breath. When she angled her head, she could count the white squint lines carved into his deep tan. Yielding to a need she didn't even try to deny now, she leaned in and nuzzled the warm skin of his neck.

He went still for a moment. Only a moment. Then he curled a knuckle and nudged up her chin. His blue eyes telegraphed a warning Mia had no trouble translating.

They weren't constrained by overcrowded facilities and a complete lack of privacy this time. They were alone. On her comfy sofa. With no sisters or scientists likely to walk in on them.

"You sure about this?" he asked, giving her a last out.

She framed her reply in a smile and a soft, "Oh, yeah."

The heat flared as hot and as fast as it had at Palmer. One minute Mia was straining against his chest, eagerly taking in his taste and his texture. The next, they were stretched out hip to hip on the sofa cushions.

Brent didn't try to rein in his hunger. Neither did she. Their hands as eager as their mouths, they burrowed through assorted layers of clothing. Mia got his shirttails free of his belt and slid her hands under the hem of his T-shirt. She was down to her bra and panties, Brent to his slacks, when he rolled off the sofa and to his feet in one fluid move.

"I've been hoping for this moment for two extremely long months," he said as he scooped her up in his arms and strode toward the bedroom. "We're going to do it right."

Mia wasn't sure how he defined *right,* but what followed certainly fit *her* definition. Balancing her on one knee, he yanked down the spread and deposited her on the bed before shedding the rest of his clothing. His body was so well honed, so taut and finely muscled. She barely had time to admire a chest dusted with dark gold hair and a flat belly before his weight pressed hers into the mattress.

Mia thrilled to the feel of him. So sleek and smooth and warm. She ran her hands over his shoulders, down his back, tracing her fingertips along his spine, gliding her palms over his tight, trim rear.

Brent explored, too, using his hands and mouth with a skill that soon had Mia gasping. Her lips, her throat, her breasts and belly all got his personal and very precise attention. Her nipples were tight and aching when he finished with them. Her lower belly quivered with pleasure. And when he found her hot, wet center, she almost groaned aloud.

She felt him iron hard against her hip, felt the rough hair on the thigh he used to nudge hers apart. Her back arching, she opened for him then had to grit her teeth when he rolled away from her to grope in a pocket of the slacks he'd dropped beside the bed. Ripping open a condom, he sheathed himself and turned back to her.

The first thrust was slow and deliberate. The second, almost as deliberate but faster, deeper. By the third, Mia had hooked her calves around his and joined him in a mating ritual as old as time.

THEY MADE LOVE A SECOND TIME just after dawn.

Mia didn't intend to wake the slumbering beast. She drifted out of sleep and lay on her side, her head pillowed on her bent elbow, studying the face mere inches from her own. In the dim light of dawn she could see his lashes curving against cheeks just beginning to show a night's worth of golden bristles. Brent's phrase from the evening before circled in her mind.

Right. This was so right.

Driven by the need to imprint his feel indelibly in her memory, she feathered her fingers over his bristly chin. As light as her touch was, it brought him blinking awake.

"'Morning, gorgeous."

Gorgeous she wasn't. Her hair was in tangles and her face couldn't show a trace of color except maybe smudged mascara. But the lazy smile in his eyes made Mia's heart ping as hard and fast as the sleet that had danced off the roof of the BioLab.

"'Morning," she got out on a ridiculously breathless note. "Want me to put on some coffee?"

"Coffee would be good. Later." He hooked an arm over her waist and tugged her closer. "First…"

Uh-oh. Mia was trying to find a tactful way to avoid a kiss tainted by morning-mouth when Brent solved the problem. Easing her onto her other side, he tucked her against his chest. Her thighs rested on his, her bottom snuggled against his groin. Mia thought they would just lie together in the quiet of the dawn. The quick hardening beneath her thigh soon banished that notion.

A STRENUOUS HALF HOUR LATER she sprawled bonelessly amid the rumpled covers. Brent lay beside her, pillows doubled up under his head as he surveyed the pale green walls and bright chintz.

"This is nice," he told her lazily. "A big, wide bed. Soft sheets. Bright colors."

"And no cameras."

She didn't realize she'd muttered the words aloud until he turned his head and flashed her a grin.

"No cameras," he echoed. "And no Web site featuring

your face or features without your specific consent. John took care of that."

"John Who?"

"John Monroe. You met him at Palmer. He was the PhD from Stanford working a hydro-computational measurement experiment, remember?"

"Not really. What has he got to do with my face or features?"

"He scanned the picture Tiki took of you up on the glacier using face recognition software and fed the results into a special program he's developed."

Understanding burst like a Roman candle. Gasping, Mia propped herself up on one elbow.

"Which he then somehow used to take down Don Juan's site!"

"Yep."

"So that's… That's what you and this guy John were doing that day in your office? Right before Beth got hurt? Taking down the site?"

"I didn't know you'd seen us, but yes, that's what we were doing."

"Oh, God! I'm such an idiot."

Brent angled a bristly chin and gave her a considering look. "I think I'm finally getting the picture," he said slowly. "You spot me drooling over Number 112. Next thing I know, you're putting me in a deep freeze."

"I thought… That is, I…" She heaved a long sigh. "Like I said, I'm an idiot. Can you forgive me?"

"Might take a while."

A vise clamped around her throat and stayed there until Brent's mouth tipped into a wicked grin.

"Okay, you're forgiven. By the way," he added nonchalantly, "John was also able to trace the site back to your sleazoid attorney. Once we ID'd the bastard, I sent his firm an electronic report detailing their junior partner's extracurricular activities."

"You didn't!"

"Yeah, babe, I did."

"Oh, Brent." Mia scrambled into a sitting position and dragged the sheet around her. "I appreciate all this. I really do! But you may have laid yourself open to a huge lawsuit."

A wolfish glint came into his eyes.

"I don't think so. Before we shut down the site, the face recognition software matched Number 113 to an online photo of a high school cheerleader. Turns out the girl looks a whole lot older than her actual age. Don Juan's got more to worry about now than coming out of the closet."

Mia was still trying to absorb that stunning revelation when he dropped another on her. Reaching out, he hooked a loose tendril behind her ear. His eyes held hers as he made an unexpected confession.

"I told you we get some downtime between summer and wintering over. What I didn't tell you is that this will be my last winter in Antarctica."

Her pulse skipped a beat. She was pretty sure she knew the answer to the question that jumped into her head but had to ask it anyway.

"Why?"

"Now I know why you put me on ice, we need to make up for lost time. I want to spend the long, dark winter nights with you, Mia. The short summer ones, too. If you'll let me."

A smile lit up her heart.

"You bet I'll let you."

CHAPTER SEVEN

BEFORE BRENT DEPARTED Newport he helped Mia draft a proposal for the National Science Foundation's Antarctic Artists and Writers Program. She played with the submission for several days after he left, fine-tuning the details.

"You sure you want to send it in?" Beth asked during one of the sisters' frequent phone conversations. "We went down to Antarctica in summer and our ship hit an ice shelf. If NSF announces the grants in mid-June as advertised, you'll be returning to Palmer smack in the middle of their long, dark winter."

"I know."

"Better stock up on Dramamine. A winter crossing of the Drake Passage will be hell."

"I know," Mia said again, groaning.

"Personally, I think Brent's worth a few bouts of nausea. Just don't ask me to go with you. One trip to the ice is enough for me."

"It probably won't happen. With funding cuts and tight budgets, Brent says the grants are tough to come by."

Tough, but not impossible.

As advertised, the grants were announced in June.

Five weeks later Mia found herself aboard the *Laurence M. Gould* research ship along with two replacement cooks, a waste management specialist and a five-person research team from the Woods Hole Oceanographic Institution.

The deck rolled under her feet for almost the entire crossing. More than once during the stormy passage Mia seriously considered jettisoning her new career as freelance textbook editor and children's book author. The outside temperature never rose above zero and the sun appeared only a few hours each day. Added to that were some extremely nasty seas that got the best of the Dramamine patch she'd stuck behind her ear.

But when the *Gould* steamed around a rocky point and Palmer's handful of blue buildings came into view, anticipation zipped along every nerve ending. And when she spotted a certain tall, broad-shouldered individual in an orange parka on the dock, she knew the crossing had been worth every minute on her knees in the bathroom.

She waited eagerly alongside the others who'd made the crossing with her. The Woods Hole team had brought crates of equipment, which had to be unloaded by crane before the passengers could disembark. The crane was then used to hoist aboard several large Conex Containers packed with Palmer's waste for shipping back to the States. *Finally* the gangplank rattled down and the new arrivals went ashore.

Allen Barclay stood next to Palmer's station manager to welcome them. Mia knew from one of Brent's e-mails that the bearded meteorologist was the senior NSF rep for the winter-over. Although both men swore otherwise,

Mia suspected their personal endorsement of her proposal probably contributed to the speedy approval of her grant.

Allen grinned and waved at Palmer's new artist/writer in residence. Brent's greeting was more personal. Framing her face in gloved hands, he smiled down at her in the way that made her melt despite the subzero temperature.

"Welcome back."

"It's good to *be* back."

Very good, she decided as he delivered a kiss that promised to make this a winter she would *never* forget.

For Marsha, who is always a pleasure to work with

MELTING POINT
Cindi Myers

Dear Reader,

I'll confess I'm a sucker for a foreign accent. Give me a man who speaks perfect English with an exotic hint of foreign climes and I melt. Couple that accent with an outwardly strong but inwardly vulnerable hero and you have the perfect recipe for romance.

Confession number two: I'm a winter person. Summer flowers are nice, but give me snow and I'm truly in my element. Whether racing down a ski slope or snuggling by a blazing fire, winter is my favorite time of year, which is one reason I chose to live in the Colorado mountains, where winter lasts a long time.

So you can see why I enjoyed writing "Melting Point" so much. My hero, Kristjan, has a delightful accent, some hidden vulnerabilities and he lives in Iceland, a land of long winters and wild, romantic scenery. Who could resist him? Certainly not my heroine, Stacy, who hides her own insecurities behind her no-nonsense competence. Like all of us, Stacy longs for love, but she's afraid of being hurt. Kristjan and Iceland bring out the best in her. I hope you'll enjoy their story.

I love to hear from my readers. You can contact me via e-mail at Cindi@CindiMyers.com, or write me in care of Harlequin Enterprises, Ltd, 225 Duncan Mill Rd., Don Mills, Ontario, M3B 3K9 Canada.

Cindi Myers

CHAPTER ONE

"HE'S LATE. WHERE THE HELL is he?"

Stacy Bristol paced the dance floor of the Reykjavik nightclub, the stiletto heels of her boots striking the hard polymer surface with a sound like castanets. Lights beneath the floor pulsed in time to the trance music piped from overhead speakers. Around her in the nearly empty club, photographers, makeup artists, dressers and a trio of gorgeous blonde models leaned against the bar or half reclined in chairs, carefully composed expressions of boredom on their faces.

"He'll be here." Jakob, Stacy's assistant, fell into step beside her. "Perhaps he had to stop and sign some autographs."

"He's a skier." Stacy checked her watch again. They should have started this photo shoot half an hour ago. "How many people can recognize even one famous skier on the street, much less badger him for an autograph?"

"Yes, but Kristján Gunnarson is a national hero," Jakob said. "The first gold medalist for Iceland ever. Iceland is a small country compared to the United States, so people here do recognize him. They do in the States, too. Isn't that why you wanted him for this campaign?"

"Yes, but I wanted him on time. I—"

The door to the street swung open, emitting the sounds of traffic, the smell of diesel and a tall, broad-shouldered blond. "Is this the photo shoot for Troll's Treasure Sweaters?" asked a deep male voice, the perfect English made somehow more perfect by the crisp Icelandic accent.

"Yes, it is." Stacy strode toward him. "You're late." As she neared him, she stifled a groan. His longish blond hair was uncombed and his jaw hadn't seen a razor in a couple of days. "You didn't even shave," she said, stopping in front of him.

She realized her mistake as soon as his gaze met hers. In her agitation over his tardiness, she'd forgotten the number one reason she'd wanted Kristján Gunnarson as the spokesmodel for this new marketing campaign. The man was absolutely heart-stoppingly, drop-dead gorgeous, with the clearest, bluest, most mesmerizing eyes she'd ever seen.

Angry as she was, at this close range those eyes were doing a number on her. "Shave?" He dragged a hand across his jaw, the masculine, rasping sound setting off a mini-earthquake of tremors deep in her abdomen. "I thought women liked the sexy stubble." He spoke the *w* in women as a soft *v*, the sibilant esses a gentle purr.

Stacy curled her hands into fists and pressed her nails into her palms, determined not to fall under the spell he was trying to cast over her. If there was one species she knew how to handle, it was irresponsible men. "There's no time for you to shave now. We'll have to do the best we can."

She started to turn away but a hand caught and stopped her. His long fingers curled around her wrist in a grip that was warm but firm. "If we are going to be working together, I should know your name," he said.

She stared first at his hand around her, then at him. He got the message and released her, though her skin still burned where he'd touched her. She resisted the urge to rub her wrist. "I'm Stacy Bristol," she said. "Head of marketing for Eagle Mountain Sportswear. We're the exclusive distributors of Troll's Treasure Sweaters in the United States." The company had added the new line of haute couture Icelandic sweaters at Stacy's urgings, though the owner of the company—and Stacy's boss—Bryan Patterson was skeptical about the wisdom of such an addition in the current economic climate. All the more reason Stacy had to make this marketing campaign a success.

"It's good to meet you, Stacy. I'm sorry I'm late." Kristján had the audacity to smile at her. Then again, he probably knew the effect of that smile. It rocked her back on her heels.

She became aware that every other female in the room—from the top model to the canteen girl—had drawn closer, like butterflies lured by an exotic nectar.

"It doesn't matter now." She dismissed his apology with less grace than she usually managed. "Put on the first sweater and get ready for the shoot."

She turned away and started back across the dance floor when a rush of breath—the collective sigh of every woman in the room—froze her and made her turn around. Kristján had stripped off his faded blue sweatshirt and was reaching for the sweater an adoring dresser was handing him. Muscles knotted and bunched across his broad shoulders and sculpted biceps, and when he reached up to pull the sweater over his head, Stacy's knees weakened at the sight of six-pack abs and low-slung jeans. This was not good. Definitely not good.

"You have a dressing room!" she barked.

A last tug on the sweater and his head emerged from the opening, blue eyes sparkling with mirth. "Why would I want to waste time with a dressing room?" All those mispronounced *w*'s made her breathless. Damn the man. And damn her own ill-timed lust. It was such a cliché for a woman to go gaga over a foreign accent. She hated to think of herself as a cliché.

Thankfully, the photography crew moved in with lights and cables and tripods, momentarily screening a now-dressed Kristján from view and allowing Stacy to retreat to the bar with most of her dignity intact.

"What did I tell you?" Jakob slid onto the bar stool next to her. "Isn't he magnificent? Your customers will love him."

"Yes. Magnificent." Kristján was posing now, hands on the hips of one of the perfect blonde females—who also wore one of the intricately patterned sweaters. But the model could have been wearing a potato sack for all any other woman viewing the ad would care. All female eyes would be fixed on Kristján, a Viking in Icelandic wool instead of a bear skin, or whatever it was Vikings wore.

The image of Kristján, naked and reclining on a bearskin, flashed into her head. She pushed it away and reached for one of the bottles of water lined up along the bar. "He'll sell sweaters," she said.

That was what was important. She needed this campaign to be a success. She'd lobbied Bryan to take this gamble, and if it failed he'd put the blame on her. She might even lose her job, and she'd for sure lose face.

With so much at stake, she'd come to Iceland to personally oversee a series of photo shoots at iconic locations. This nightclub was the first, but they also planned to visit the Haukadalur geyser, a fjord she couldn't begin to pronounce the name of and the Blue Lagoon hot springs. She'd personally recruited a flock of sheep and a shepherd for the session at the fjord, had negotiated a private shoot at the hot springs and had a schedule of the geyser's eruptions so that photos could be timed for maximum affect. She was in charge of herding a photographer, videographer, three fashion models and a slew of assistants, wardrobe personnel, gophers, caterers and others all over this frozen island country. But she was smart, capable and determined, and she'd done this kind of thing before. So none of them worried her.

Kristján Gunnarson, the beautiful blond national hero with a disdain for schedules and—if the gossip rags were to be believed—a love of all manner of personal pleasures, was the wild card in her game plan. He was the one who could make or break everything. The one Stacy would have to keep an eye on.

But for today, all she had to worry about was completing this one photo shoot on time. Yes, they were running a little late, but now that everyone was here, things were progressing smoothly.

Or not. The nightclub door flew open again and a short, round-faced woman carrying a baby rushed in. "So sorry I'm late," Jóna Gunnarsdottir, owner, operator and chief designer for Troll's Treasure Sweaters, said. "The baby had a doctor's appointment."

"That's all right," Stacy said. "As you can see, we're getting some great shots." She motioned toward the raised dais where Kristján and the other models were set up.

Except Kristján wasn't there.

"Excuse me?" The photographer, Stefan, stood in the middle of the dais, hands on hips. "We're trying to conduct a photo shoot here."

"Time for a break," Kristján, already halfway across the dance floor, called over his shoulder. "Is the baby ill?" he asked as he reached Jóna and Stacy.

"He is fine," Jóna said. "It was just a checkup."

"That's good." Without asking for permission or waiting for an invitation, he unbuckled the straps on the carrier and lifted the child into his arms. The baby giggled and blew bubbles as Kristján grinned at him.

Stacy stared, goggle-eyed. She didn't know which amazed her most—that Jóna was letting this guy manhandle her baby, or that Mr. Gorgeous seemed so comfortable with an infant.

"Is something wrong?"

Kristján's question snapped Stacy back to reality, and the knowledge that he'd caught her staring. She struggled to look unconcerned. "He certainly seems to like you," she said.

"Babies like me," he said, and bent to blow a loud raspberry against the infant's round belly.

"Of course," Stacy said, her voice faint. She gripped the edge of the bar, just in case her weak knees decided to give out. Cute gurgling babies! Gorgeous men with sexy accents! Every female hormone in her body was on overdrive. Obviously, the universe had decided that this was the day to turn her into a walking, talking stereotype.

But if she was melting at the sight of Kristján cuddling a baby, so would thousands of other women. And a good many of them would be likely to rush out and purchase a Troll's Treasure sweater, in hopes of transforming the man in their life into something close to Kristján Gunnarson.

"Stefan!" She waved at the photographer, who was deep in conversation with one of the female models. He looked up from his contemplation of the model's chest, not bothering to mask his annoyed expression.

"I want photos of this." Stacy pointed at Kristján, who was still cooing over the baby.

Stefan knew a good shot when he saw it. He focused the camera and began clicking away.

When Kristján realized what was happening, he frowned, and handed the baby back to Jóna. "Did you ask my sister if she wants her baby used to advertise sweaters?" he asked.

"Your sister?" Stacy blinked at Jóna. Was there a resemblance there? Maybe… "Why didn't you tell me he was your brother?"

Jóna flushed strawberry pink. "I didn't think it mattered. When you asked if I could recommend a model for the ads, I knew he would be perfect."

"Do you think Mr. Perfect could get back over here so we can finish this shoot?" Stefan called.

Kristján frowned, but made his way back to the stage. When Stacy and Jóna were alone once more, Jóna leaned close and spoke in a low voice. "I didn't tell you Kristján was my brother because I wasn't sure I could convince him to take the job. He's not a professional model, after all."

"I wasn't looking for a professional model for this campaign," Stacy said. "I wanted a real person others could relate to. An athlete who's so associated with Iceland seemed ideal."

"I thought it would give him something to do," Jóna said. "Maybe even get him started on a new career."

"Why does he need a new career?" Stacy asked.

"He's thirty-four years old. He can't continue to compete forever. Already he is one of the oldest skiers."

"Then couldn't he teach or coach?"

Jóna sighed. "He doesn't know what he wants to do. That's the problem. It's not good for a grown man to be so aimless."

Both women focused their attention on the stage, where the man in question stood, his arms around two comely female models, grinning at the camera. He might have just stepped into the club after a day on the slopes, ready for a little après-ski partying. No worries. No cares. No goals.

Stacy had his number all right. She knew the type well, and she knew enough to steer clear of him.

CHAPTER TWO

WHILE THE ANNOYING STEFAN directed him to look that way or pose another way, Kristján distracted himself by focusing on Stacy. The petite, dark-haired American stood out in the room full of pale blondes and redheads. But it wasn't merely looks that set her apart. She had an inner fire and intensity the statuesque beauties around him couldn't hope to match.

She moved around the nightclub, setting up the next series of photographs. She issued orders with the calm authority of someone who knew exactly what she wanted—an assuredness he hadn't felt in months.

He'd spent more than twenty years working toward a single objective—winning Iceland's first medal in a Winter Olympics. Standing on the podium, accepting the gold medal while the Icelandic national anthem played had been the greatest moment of his life.

And then what? He'd been swept up in a wave of television appearances, newspaper and magazine interviews, and sponsorship contracts. But when the applause faded and the cameras were switched off, he was left with an aching emptiness and the burning question: *what am I going to do with my life now?*

"All right everyone, I think we're done here." Stacy clapped her hands to capture their attention and strode to the middle of the dance floor. "Thank you all for your hard work. I'll see you tomorrow in Haukadalur."

The models shrugged into jackets, the camera crew began disassembling their equipment, and with amazing speed everyone dispersed. Within a matter of minutes only Kristján, Stacy, Jóna and the baby were left.

"I really have to go," Jóna said, gathering her infant carrier, blankets, diaper bag and purse. "I have an appointment to go over some new designs."

"I'd better go, too," Stacy said. "I need to review the proofs from today."

"Surely they will not be ready for a while," Kristján said. He checked his watch and was surprised to discover it was nearly noon. "Let me buy you lunch." He wanted the chance to get to know her better.

"No, really, I'd better go." Avoiding his eyes, she tried to duck past him, but he blocked her.

"Please," he said, offering his most winning smile. "I owe you for being late this morning. And I could show you Reykjavik. It's a beautiful city."

"I don't know…" She glanced at Jóna, who smiled approvingly at him.

"I think that's a wonderful idea," Jóna said. "I'd come with you, but as I said…" She hefted the baby carrier and moved past them to the door. "I'll see you in a few days, at the Blue Lagoon. Call me if you need anything." But her eyes telegraphed a clear message to Kristján—she would call him, and she'd want all the details.

He turned to Stacy. "Shall we go?"

She straightened her shoulders, as if steeling herself for an ordeal. Was he that repugnant to her? "Sure. Thank you for the offer."

They walked to a bistro a few blocks from the night-club. For once it wasn't raining in Reykjavik and temperatures were mild for March. "Have you visited Iceland before?" he asked.

"No. This is my first time. I was expecting more, well, ice."

He laughed. "You will see plenty of ice in the countryside. We still get snow this time of year and, of course, the glaciers never melt."

They were shown to a table by a window in the nearly empty bistro. She started to shrug out of her jacket. "Allow me," he said, and slid it from her shoulders. She seemed taken aback. Was she offended because he'd insulted her independence, or merely shocked at such gentlemanly behavior? "I apologize again for my tardiness this morning," he said, when they'd ordered their food. "I overslept."

"That was obvious. Hard night partying?" The disdain in her voice was clear.

He had, in fact, been at a party last night, a large affair given by one of his Olympic sponsors. He'd spent the evening avoiding the advances of a minor movie starlet and dodging questions from other guests about what he planned to do now that he'd won his gold medal. It had been a miserable night and the memory of it had kept him awake long after he'd arrived home. He'd tossed and turned for hours before finally falling asleep, only to awake to the realization that he was late for the modeling assignment he'd foolishly allowed Jóna to talk him into.

"Or maybe you were late because you didn't want to do this in the first place," Stacy said.

"I see you are a psychoanalyst as well as a marketing director," he said.

She flushed, an attractive pink staining her cheeks, but the wounded look in her eyes made him regret his sharp tongue.

"You are right," he said. "I did not want the job. I am an athlete, not a model."

"But you're also a celebrity. The hero of the hour. You should enjoy it while you can. If you play your cards right, you won't have to get a real job for months, even years."

It was his turn to flush. "Is that what you think? That I'm using my fame for my own gain?"

"Aren't you?"

The arrival of their food prevented him from answering immediately. Just as well, or he might have said something he'd regret.

"What is this?" Stacy poked a fork at her plate.

"Lamb sausage," he said. "It's very good. The pink sauce is remoulade."

"No mustard?" She wrinkled her nose.

"Try it. It is good."

"What are you having?" She peered at his plate.

"Reindeer." He cut into the steak. "Would you like to try some?"

"No, thanks."

They began to eat, but the accusations she'd made earlier still hung between them. Kristján laid down his fork. "Obviously, I did not make a good first impression," he said. "But I am not what you think I am. I agreed to this job as a favor to my sister. My other public appearances have been obligations to my sponsors or to my country. I am not a man who seeks the limelight." Other than his brief time on World Cup and Olympic podiums, he preferred the anonymity of his sport. Unlike soccer or hockey, few people followed downhill skiing.

"I'm sorry." Stacy's eyes met his, the soft brown of turned earth, full of contrition. "I have a nasty tongue when I'm stressed. But that's no excuse. I apologize."

"Apology accepted." He picked up his knife and fork and focused on his plate once more. Either that or continue to stare into her beautiful eyes and reveal his powerful and quite unexpected attraction to her. "What are you stressed about? Surely the shoot this morning went well."

"Yes, I think it did. But a lot depends on the success of this campaign. My boss thought adding this line was a risky move in this economy, but I persuaded him to take the chance. Now I want to prove to him I was right."

"And you think my picture will persuade people to buy my sister's sweaters?" he asked.

"I think any awake, breathing woman who sees you in one of those sweaters will want her man to have one—if only so she can indulge in fantasies of Vikings and Norse gods."

He laughed, out of surprise and embarrassment more than mirth, but Stacy didn't join in his laughter. "Don't pretend you don't know what you look like," she said. "I imagine your looks have been getting you what you want all your life."

And what do you want, Stacy? he wondered. Did her fantasies have anything at all to do with Vikings or Norse gods—or Icelandic skiers? "My looks did not win me an Olympic medal," he said.

"Obviously, you're talented and athletically gifted. I didn't mean to insult you."

"I'm not insulted. And it would be foolish for me to pretend I'm not flattered that you think I'm good-looking."

She flushed and looked away. Ah! So Ms. Always-in-Charge could be shaken up a little. "Tell me about your job," he said. *Tell me about yourself.* "Do you enjoy the work?"

"Yes, I do." She spoke briskly, back to business. "Our company, Eagle Mountain Sportswear, has shops in all the major ski resorts in the United States and Canada, so I get to travel to beautiful places and work with the store managers, as well as design national marketing campaigns."

"And do you ski?"

"Oh, yes. I learned to ski almost as soon as I could walk." Her expression sobered. "My father wouldn't have had it any other way."

"Did you ever try ski racing?"

She shook her head. "I was never that good or that brave."

"Some call it foolish, flying down an icy slope, always on the edge of hurtling out of control."

"Not as dangerous if you're any good," she said. "I'm purely a recreational skier. No daredevil stuff for me. A lot of times I'm so busy at the stores that I don't even get out on the snow."

"How did you come to have this job?" he asked. "Does your father or mother also do this kind of work?"

"Oh, no. My mother is a teacher."

"And your father?" he prompted, when she didn't volunteer more.

"He's a ski instructor. My parents divorced when I was eleven."

"I am sorry to hear that."

"It was for the best, really. My dad wasn't cut out to have responsibilities." She gave him a forced smile and pointedly changed the subject. "So, have you ever been hurt skiing?" she asked.

"Not too seriously." He knocked on the table. "I have been lucky." *And who has hurt you?* he wondered. There was a sadness about her that touched him and made him want to comfort her, though he had no right.

Tell me your secrets, Stacy, he thought. *And maybe I will tell you mine.*

WHETHER HIS MODESTY WAS genuine or merely practiced, Stacy had to admit she was charmed. Kristján was clearly not the dumb blond jock she had expected.

After lunch, he suggested they walk to the waterfront and she agreed. If she was only going to be in the country two weeks, she should see as much of it as possible.

Reykjavik might have been built in the past year, everything was so clean and modern; even obviously older buildings looked scrubbed and shiny. "Did you grow up here?" she asked as they waited to cross a busy street. "In Reykjavik?"

"No. My family lives in Húsavik, on the Northern Coast. My father is a teacher of Icelandic history." He slanted a look at her. "Vikings and Norse gods."

Touché. She suppressed the urge to giggle and hurried to keep up with his long strides as they crossed the street. She could smell the sea now, the salt and fish tang cutting through the odors of diesel and concrete. Ahead, in the middle of a large concrete plaza, rose what looked like giant…bones.

"The *Sólfar.*" Kristján nodded toward the plaza. "It means *Sun Voyager.* The sculpture represents the skeleton of a Viking ship."

Now that she had a clear view, Stacy recognized a ship's ribs and prow. It wasn't an actual ship, but a sculpture of a wreck, what would have been left of an ancient vessel ravaged by time and the elements.

"This land was first discovered and settled by Vikings—Naddod, from Norway, and later Gardar Svavarsson from Sweden, who lived for a time in my part of the country, Húsavik. Another Viking, Raven-Floki from Norway, gave the country its name, Iceland."

Vikings again. Explorers. Conquerors. Adventurers. How did that kind of bloodline produce a man who didn't know what he wanted to do with his life? Maybe Jóna was wrong about her brother.

Or maybe Stacy only wanted her to be wrong.

As they made their way around the massive sculpture of the Viking ship, two little girls rushed forward, talking rapidly in Icelandic. Kristján smiled, and obligingly signed the notebook they handed him. He was still smiling as they skipped away and Stacy joined him.

"More adoring fans?" she asked.

His smile faded and he shoved his hands into the pockets of his jeans. "When I was training for the

Olympics, I thought only of winning a medal," he said. "I didn't think of what my life would be like after I won. I couldn't have imagined this."

"It's not that bad, is it?" she asked. "You're a national hero. Didn't you win some kind of big award?"

"The Order of the Falcon. Iceland's highest honor." His voice grew rough. "It is true that at the Olympics, I represented my country. But I don't think any person thinks of himself as a national symbol. I won the medal for Iceland, but when I was competing in that race, I was competing for myself and my family. I wasn't thinking of my countrymen—these strangers—who felt a part of the race, too."

"And overnight you went from being a private citizen to a national symbol. I suppose that does feel strange." Disorienting. She'd only been thinking of the glamour of celebrity, not the difficulties like loss of privacy, or even loss of self.

"In a few months, most people will have forgotten," he said. "I will go back to being anonymous."

"Then what will you do?" she asked. "Will you start training for the next Olympics?"

He shook his head. "I am tired of that life. I don't know what I'll do." He smiled, the self-deprecating charm of a boy in the body of a handsome man. She felt the attraction of such a man even as she fought to resist. "Maybe I'll become a ski bum," he said. "I'd be good at it, don't you think?"

Wrong answer. Stacy's stomach felt as if she'd swallowed a rock. The last thing she wanted in her life was another ski bum. Growing up with one had been enough.

CHAPTER THREE

STACY TOLD HERSELF a good night's sleep would restore her to the practical, sensible woman she was. She dealt with good-looking, athletic men every day of her life and none of them made her all dreamy-eyed the way Kristján had. The strain of travel must have something to do with her reaction to him—though this was one symptom of jet lag she'd never encountered before.

She didn't see Kristján the next morning as she boarded the van for the trip to Haukadalur, which both relieved and worried her. She was grateful she didn't have to spend several hours in close quarters with him, yet she was worried his absence meant he wasn't going to show up at all.

"Kristján said he's taking his own car and he'll meet us there," Jakob said, sliding into a seat across from Stacy.

"Let's hope he's on time today."

"If he's not, we'll have more time to enjoy the scenery."

Stacy refrained from reminding Jakob that they weren't here to enjoy the scenery. She knew how uptight that sounded. And it wasn't as if she couldn't enjoy the beauty of the country; she simply knew her priorities. Get the work out of the way and there'd be plenty of time for pleasure later.

For the moment, however, she had little else to do but enjoy the passing countryside. As soon as they left Reykjavik they entered an otherworldly landscape of towering cliffs, ice-blue lakes and jagged lava fields, a world of water, ice and rock that resembled a lunar landscape. Stacy recalled reading that the astronauts who had landed on the moon had trained here; now she could see why. The terrain was cold and forbidding, yet fascinating and romantic, also, with a wild beauty unlike any she'd ever known.

Their schedule called for filming first at Geysir, the hot water spout from which all others derived their name, then moving on to nearby Gullfoss, the Golden Falls.

As the crew unloaded their equipment, a red Porsche slid into the parking space next to the van. Stacy's heart sped up as Kristján emerged from the driver's side. She couldn't help it; he was so perfectly tall, blond and tan, designer shades shielding his sea-blue eyes. He scanned the crowd until he found her, and smiled. She smiled back, her insides as warm and goopy as hot fudge.

Not good. Not good.

He strode toward her, long legs quickly covering the distance between them. "Did you enjoy your trip along the Golden Circle?" he asked.

"Yes. It was beautiful." She turned away from him; it was either that or get caught staring into his eyes, as mesmerized as a mouse by a cat. *Get a grip,* she told herself. *He's just a guy, and definitely not one you want to be involved with.*

"Let's set up in front of the Geysir," she said. "Are the models ready?"

Kristján fell into step beside her as she started across the parking lot. "You'll get better pictures if you photograph by Strokkur, the Churn," he said. "It's more spectacular than Geysir, and more predictable, erupting approximately every five minutes."

She was tempted to remind him that she was in charge and she'd decide where to film, but really, there was no point in being stubborn for the sake of misplaced pride. And she could see no reason for Kristján to mislead her. "All right," she said. "Thank you."

She directed the crew to relocate to Strokkur. They were breaking down the equipment when a battered Mercedes sped into the lot and a short man in a red down coat tumbled out of the driver's seat. He aimed a camera at them and began clicking away as he hurried toward them.

Stacy stared, sure the man would collide with a car or fall into a hole, but he sidestepped every obstacle, taking picture after picture as he drew closer.

"Hello, ma'am." He offered Stacy a gap-toothed smile. "What is your name?"

"She isn't going to tell you." Kristján stepped between Stacy and the photographer. "I told you to leave me alone."

The photographer's grin didn't waver. "It's a public place. You're a public figure. A man has a right to make a living, and the tabloids will pay good money for shots of you and your new girlfriend."

"Girlfriend?" Stacy peered from around Kristján's broad back. "I am not his girlfriend."

"The tabloids don't care about that." He snapped another photograph.

"You'd better leave. Now." Kristján took a step toward the photographer, his expression grim.

"I was just leaving." The man sprinted to his car, pausing to snap one more picture before he climbed inside and roared away.

"Who was that?" Stacy asked as she stared at the fading exhaust plume left by the rattletrap car.

"His name is Lang Kerr. He makes his living photographing celebrities and selling the pictures to Web sites and tabloids."

"A paparazzo." She laughed. "I never knew anyone who was pursued by paparazzi before."

He put a hand to her back and steered her down the path toward Strokkur. "You won't think it's so amusing when you see a picture of yourself identified as the newest mystery woman in my life."

Stacy sobered. "No, that wouldn't be funny."

"I'm sorry," Kristján said. "One day interest in me will die down and there will no longer be a market for the photos, but for now, I can't do much to stop him."

His concern for her was touching. "It's all right," she said. "No wonder you were reluctant to take this job— to willingly be photographed."

His smile was rueful. "I have a hard time saying no to Jóna. Besides, if I hadn't agreed to do this, I wouldn't have met you, and that would be a shame."

They reached the end of the path just as the waterspout shot into the air in a jet of steam and hot water. But the spectacle was dulled for Stacy by the impact of Kristján's last words. Was he flirting with her? Or was the sentiment more serious?

"The eruptions vary in size," Kristján continued, as if nothing of particular importance had passed between them. He was flirting, then. She suppressed her disappointment.

"Some are much more forceful," he continued, "so don't stand too close."

Unlike in the United States, there were few warning signs and no roped-off areas keeping visitors away from the steaming geysers, bubbling hot pots and other dangers.

Stefan, mindful of his cameras, set up well away from the water and arranged Kristján and the female models for the first shoot.

The scenery was truly spectacular, and the people in it were equally awe-inspiring. The three female models were Scandinavian Graces, long-legged and blonde, with perfect cheekbones. Kristján stood among them like a conquering warrior, all broad shoulders, narrow hips and masculine beauty. There was nothing androgynous or effeminate in his good looks and as usual a crowd of women had gathered to watch.

But as Stacy observed his staged interaction with the models, she remembered how he'd looked in the Reyjavik nightclub, with Jóna and her baby. The Warrior at Home, she might have labeled the picture. Was it only wishful thinking that made her believe that was a truer picture of Kristján than this fantasy among the geysers?

"I suppose that will have to do," Stefan said at last, with his usual coolness, as if expressing enthusiasm to his subjects might spoil them. "Let's break down the equipment and move on to the waterfall."

While the crew was reloading the van, Kristján approached Stacy. "Let me take you to Gullfoss in my car," he said.

"All right." She saw no reason to refuse. Besides, there was no reason she and Kristján couldn't be friends. He was a nice guy, just not her type. He probably felt the same way about her. For all she knew, he was dating a fellow Olympian, or had a girlfriend back home in Husavik. After all, how likely was it that a man as gorgeous as this one would be unattached? The thought did little to cheer her.

"Nice car," she said as he held the passenger door open for her.

"A gift from an admirer," he said.

"What does your girlfriend think of all this public adulation?" she asked. Not the most subtle question, but she'd never been much for coyness.

The engine roared to life. Kristján glanced at her. "No girlfriend," he said.

"No?" Her heart refused to settle into a steady rhythm. "Does this mean all the pictures I've seen of you with other women are like the ones Lang Kerr took of me today? Misrepresentations?"

"My lifestyle these past few years has made relationships difficult," he said. "Too much traveling, long hours training." He shook his head. "I thought it was better to focus all my energy on skiing."

"What about now?" She remembered him cuddling the baby and her heart did a crazy tap dance. At that moment he'd been the picture of a man who was ready to settle down.

"Maybe." He shifted gears. "If I find the right woman. What about you? Do you have some rich American lover?"

She wondered at his choice of words—lover instead of boyfriend. Was he being deliberately provocative? "I'm not dating anyone in particular," she said. Not dating anyone at all, actually. Her friends said she was too picky. She saw it as simply not wanting to waste her time on someone unsuitable.

"I am surprised," Kristján said. "You are a beautiful woman. The kind many men would be attracted to."

It was definitely too warm in this car; she resisted the urge to roll down a window. "I guess I just haven't found the right man," she said.

"You believe there is only one?"

The question startled her into looking directly at him again. "I…I don't know. Isn't that what everyone thinks? I mean, except for polygamists."

He laughed. "I think one wife would be enough. I wouldn't want to be at the mercy of two or more."

She had a hard time picturing him at the mercy of any woman, but then again, under the right circumstances…. She forced her mind away from that particular fantasy. "Maybe there is more than one right person," she said. "But I'd be happy to find just one."

"I imagine your parents' divorce has made you cautious about relationships," he said.

"Not any more cautious than anyone else," she said. "I mean, I would like to avoid making a mistake, if I could." She'd always thought if she was careful enough, if she took her time and chose wisely, she could have a real "happily ever after." But here she was, almost thirty, and she hadn't even come close to finding "the one." Maybe her friends were right and her standards were impossibly high.

She was surprised to find the van waiting for them in the parking lot at Gullfoss. For a man with a fancy sports car, Kristján didn't drive very fast. Or had he prolonged the trip on purpose? Could it be she wasn't the only one who felt the attraction between them?

KRISTJÁN COULD THINK of worse jobs than posing with a trio of beautiful women, but it wasn't how he wanted to spend the rest of his life. Balancing on jagged rocks in the icy mist from the waterfall that roared behind them wasn't very comfortable or exciting. And the arrogant photographer, Stefan, annoyed him with his constant instructions to "move there, stand there, raise your arm there, look there." If not for Jóna, Kristján would have walked off the set long ago.

And Stacy. He stayed because of her, also. Because she intrigued him. And because the thought of disappointing her made him feel small and ugly.

So he tuned out Stefan's badgering and thought of Stacy. Surely she was aware of the attraction between them. Alone in his car, the air had simmered. She'd definitely warmed to him, but he'd sensed she was holding back.

As if she was deliberately erecting a barrier between them. Why was she trying to keep him away? Or maybe she was only protecting herself. If she didn't let him close, she didn't have to worry about the consequences.

He recognized the tactic. It was one he'd used himself,

not to keep away women, but to keep out fear and anxiety before a race. He refused to think or talk about the possibility of injury. He avoided passing by the first aid station or medical tent. If another skier was injured he refused to look, and pretended it had never happened. Such indifference, and at times even delusional thinking, had been a matter of survival.

In denying her attraction to him, was Stacy doing the same thing? Or was he the one who was arrogant now, in thinking that after a few hours' acquaintance, he could be such a threat to her peace of mind?

"All right. We're done here." Stefan clapped his hands, dismissing them. The female models hurried away, muttering complaints about the damp and cold and what the weather was doing to their hair. Kristján headed toward Stacy.

"Ride back to Reykjavik with me," he said.

She zipped her leather coat, then shoved her hands deep into the pockets. "I should go back in the van with the others," she said. "Stefan and I need to discuss tomorrow's shoot."

"You will talk, but will he listen? He strikes me as the type who most enjoys the sound of his own voice."

A smile tugged at the corner of her mouth, but she suppressed it. "I also need to make some calls to confirm the arrangements for tomorrow."

"You can telephone from my car." He put his arm around her. "Come on. It is too cold to stand out here arguing. You should have a warmer coat."

His solicitude threw her further off guard. "I really don't think—"

"What is it about me that makes you so nervous?" he asked.

She met his gaze, her eyes sparking with anger. He almost smiled, pleased to have aroused any emotion in her. "I'm not nervous," she said. "But I do have a job to do."

"I won't stop you from doing your job. I only want to know why you are friendly to me one moment and freeze me out the next."

She looked away again. "You're imagining things."

He leaned closer, his voice low, his lips almost brushing her ear. "I wasn't imagining the heat between us in my car before. Don't tell me you didn't feel it, too."

Her lips parted, and he steeled himself for her denial. He was aware of her shallow breathing, and of his own pounding heart.

"I… There may be some…some *physical* attraction between us," she said. "But there's no point in taking things further. I'm only going to be in Iceland another week or so and as I said, I have work to do, so a relationship would really be impossible…."

Her feeble protests told him all he needed to know. He touched her cheek, and when she tilted her head slightly in response, he covered her lips with his own.

CHAPTER FOUR

STACY HADN'T LET HERSELF acknowledge how much she'd wanted Kristján to kiss her until his lips touched hers. She'd tried to dismiss her attraction to him as a normal appreciation of his good looks, or the influence of their exotic and romantic surroundings.

But he proved what a poor liar she was when his mouth slanted over hers and she leaned into him without even a token protest.

Kristján, too, gave no indication that he had ever doubted her response to him. He claimed her lips with a confidence that bordered on arrogance, his boldness fueling her ardor. Her life offered few opportunities to surrender control; the sensation was as intoxicating as expensive champagne.

She arched her body to his and parted her lips, inviting him in. He deepened the kiss, arms encircling her, tongue caressing, leaving her dizzy and breathless and thoroughly delighted.

Too often she'd been disappointed by men who devoted little effort to the art of kissing. They approached this meeting of lips as a preliminary activity to be gotten out of the way quickly, or they stuck firmly to the approach of overeager adolescents, mashing too-moist lips to hers and trying to force their tongues down her throat.

Kristján was either naturally gifted, or he had devoted some time and effort to perfecting his technique. His mouth on hers was firm and coaxing, teasing her with butterfly kisses, moving on to more intimate caresses, exploring and exciting, letting the intensity build slowly, savoring the sensation of lips meeting lips.

Obviously, he had not concerned himself only with skiing. If a local charity ever wanted to raise money, they could do worse than an old-fashioned kissing booth with national hero Kristján Gunnarson doing the honors. Of course, Stacy would go broke trying to keep all other women away.

When at last he broke the kiss and raised his head, she bit back a sigh of regret. "That was very nice," he said. "Do you still think a relationship between us is impossible?"

His words were like a slap, bringing her back to her senses. What was she thinking, standing here in a crowded parking lot, kissing a man who was so obviously wrong for her? Was she so starved for affection she'd allowed good looks and a talent for kissing to overrule her hard-won common sense?

She shoved out of his arms and took a step back, struggling to regain her composure. "Mr. Gunnarson, we work together," she said. "There is no relationship."

"That kiss proves there could be." He looked amused, which only made her angrier.

"No, there could never be," she said. "You may be accustomed to women swooning over you because you're a handsome celebrity, but I could never be interested in a man who cares only about skiing and himself."

She turned and hurried toward the waiting van, prepared to turn a deaf ear to his protests, but he made none. She was grateful, too, that he didn't try to follow her. She boarded the bus and moved to a seat at the back, ignoring the questioning looks from her coworkers.

She settled into the last seat on the right side and stared out at the parking lot, the cars and people there blurring into a kaleidoscope of colored dots.

Was this her father's legacy? Did her love for him doom her to always being attracted to irresponsible, unsuitable men? Yes, Kristján was handsome and kind and intelligent and charming—and a man who had no idea what he wanted to do with his life, as aimless as she was driven. The combination was a recipe for heartache, as she'd seen played out in her parents' marriage and her own early relationships with similar charming and irresponsible men. It was so easy to like them, and then to fall in love with them. Her father had been the first hero in her life, and a part of her would always adore him. But his type couldn't be depended upon; they always disappointed, and when they did, the hurt was that much harder to bear.

NOTHING LIKE BEING passionately kissed by a woman, then being made to feel as if *you* were the one out of line, Kristján thought as he watched the van, with Stacy on board, pull out of the Gullfoss parking lot. A stranger might have thought Kristján had said or done something terribly insulting, the way Stacy stalked away from him.

By the time he reached his car, both his anger and his libido had cooled enough to allow him to think more clearly. Stacy didn't strike him as a tease, and she'd clearly enjoyed the kiss. So what was going on?

He had plenty of time to puzzle over this question on the drive back to Reykjavik. Time to remember and replay that amazing kiss.

Stacy kissed the way she did everything else, with fervor and determination and a clear idea of what she wanted. Hers was no passive surrender, but a passionate participation in which she gave as much pleasure as she received.

He smoothed his palms along the leather-wrapped steering wheel, wishing he was touching Stacy instead. So much for thinking he'd cooled down. That kiss—or more likely, their first exchange of glances in the Reykjavik nightclub—had started a fire in him no amount of snow and ice would put out.

Was it merely that after so many years of putting aside his desires in pursuit of his Olympic goals, he was primed to find an outlet for all those suppressed feelings? He shook his head. If that was the case, he'd had plenty of opportunities in the weeks before he walked into that nightclub. Something about Stacy herself drew him, as if he'd not only been waiting for the right time to begin a relationship, but he'd been waiting for *her*.

I could never be interested in a man who cares only about skiing and himself. The words stung. True, he'd been focused on training and racing for much of his life. But those days had passed. He was giving up competition so that he could devote his energy to other things.

The fact that he didn't yet know what those things would be didn't mean he was lazy or aimless.

As for the other—where had she gotten the idea he thought only of himself? Hadn't he won a medal for his country? And he'd taken this job as a favor to Jóna.

Or was she thinking of another man when she made those accusations? One whose actions had led her to believe another relationship was impossible?

THE NEXT DAY'S SHOOT WAS scheduled on the beach near the fishing village of Akranes. The beach fronted a fjord, the name of which Stacy could not begin to pronounce, much less spell. But it was convenient to Reykjavik and reputed to be a beautiful spot. Her plan was to arrive just as shooting was scheduled to begin, let Stefan and the models do their thing, then leave before there was an opportunity for any more awkward conversations—much less unforgettable kisses—between her and Kristján.

She blamed herself for handling things badly yesterday. She never should have let down her guard around him—and she really shouldn't have said what she did when they parted. He wasn't the kind of man she wanted to be with, but he probably didn't deserve the accusation she'd hurled at him.

So the goal was to get through this day with as little friction as possible. To that end, she'd hired a driver to take her to Akranes a half hour behind the van that carried the rest of the crew. She expected everything would be set up by the time she arrived.

Instead, she found Stefan and the three women standing on the rocky beach, surrounded by a dozen or so bawling and butting sheep. Kristján was nowhere in sight.

"Tell me again why we have to have sheep." Stefan scowled at the animals. These weren't the fluffy white lambs Stacy had envisioned. They were big, gray, unruly creatures. And they smelled bad.

"The sweaters are made of one hundred percent Icelandic wool," she said. "And I thought some shots with them would be pastoral and picturesque."

"I suppose you think this freezing, desolate rock in the middle of nowhere is picturesque, too?" Stefan demanded.

"It's a fjord. Iceland has dozens of them." She looked out across the crashing waves to towering cliffs in the distance. From this vantage point no other person or sign of human habitation could be seen—only miles of foaming gray sea and rocky white cliffs, birds screaming and wheeling overhead. It was a setting that had changed little in thousands of years, and it stirred something primal in her. "It's wild and rugged and—"

"It's freezing cold!" Stefan pulled his coat tighter around him and stalked away. The models huddled together, looking frozen and miserable.

Stacy spotted an older man in rough trousers and a heavy coat, and picked her way across the rocks to him. "Are you the shepherd?" she asked.

He said something in a language she couldn't understand. Icelandic, she supposed. "Do you speak English?" she asked. "Are you in charge of the sheep?" She gestured toward the milling animals.

"Neitun Englendingar." He shook his head.

Stacy groaned. An icy wind whistled through her thin leather coat. This was not going well at all.

"What do you want to say to him? I'll translate."

Like a knight appearing out of the mist, Kristján strode toward her across the rocky beach. Dressed in a long shearling coat, blond hair tousled by the wind, he looked like the hero of some romantic movie, come to rescue the damsel in distress.

She refused to think of herself as a damsel, but she wouldn't say no to a little help right now. "Ask him if he doesn't have any pretty sheep," she said. "Lambs, or some that aren't so…so dirty." She steeled herself for Kristján's laughter. She wouldn't blame him if he did laugh—the situation was ridiculous.

But he addressed the shepherd with a straight face. The man nodded and turned away, the sheep stumbling after him.

"Where is he going?" Stacy asked.

"To find pretty sheep."

Was he making fun of her? She followed him across the beach, stumbling on the uneven ground. "How could anyone live in this frozen wilderness?" she asked. She pulled her coat tighter, trying to shut out the cutting wind.

"You grow accustomed to it. We pride ourselves on being immune to the weather." He began picking up driftwood, piling it in his arms.

"What are you doing?" she asked.

"I'm building a fire." Within a few minutes, he had a roaring bonfire going. The models, all smiles now, hurried over to huddle in the warmth of the blaze, though Stefan remained in the van, probably sulking.

"Thank you for the fire," Stacy said. "And for your help with the shepherd. I…I'm sorry for what I said to you yesterday. That was uncalled-for."

"There are many more things I care about outside of skiing," he said. "And many more people I care about other than myself."

For a brief moment, standing next to him on this wild beach in the warmth of the fire he had built, she wished more than anything that she was one of the people he cared about. "I know," she said softly. "And I am sorry."

"I am not sorry we kissed," he said.

When she was truthful with herself, had she really regretted that kiss? She'd wished it never happened, but only because she hated that she'd been so weak, unable to resist an attraction that was wrong on several levels. But the kiss itself…how could she regret having experienced those wonderful few moments in Kristján's arms? "It would be better if it didn't happen again," she said.

"As you wish. But if you change your mind…"

A loud whistle cut through the air and they looked up to see the shepherd striding toward them. He carried a trio of fluffy white lambs in his arms. Behind him trailed a single large, dirty ewe, who wore a crown of primroses on her wooly head. "See?" Kristján said. "Pretty sheep."

Stacy tried to hold back her laughter, but it was impossible. Kristján joined in, then they went to meet the shepherd.

Stefan was persuaded to emerge from the van, and the female models cuddled the lambs while the ewe looked on unhappily. Kristján posed with the women, and by himself on the edge of the water, wind whipping through his hair as he gazed across the fjord, a solitary sailor thinking of his return to the sea.

Stacy watched him from a seat by the fire. He had surprised her today, with his willingness to help even after she'd insulted him. But then, he had defied her expectations from the very first, morphing from unkempt playboy to doting uncle right before her eyes.

She thought again of the kiss they'd shared, of the skill and passion and surprising tenderness of those moments in his arms. That unexpected sensitivity got to her the most. She prided herself on being an independent woman who was too smart to get involved with a man who didn't have his life as together as she did her own.

Yet this kind, confusing man who seemed to want to take care of her wrecked that resolve with one glance, one touch, one kiss.

CHAPTER FIVE

THE ICELAND TOURIST BOARD, which had helped Stacy arrange the various location shoots, hosted a dinner for her and her crew at a trendy Reykjavik restaurant that evening. From his seat at one end of the long table, Kristján smiled and joked and answered questions about his Olympic experience. But part of him was always aware of Stacy. She sat at the opposite end of the table, holding court with the Director of Tourism and a man from the Icelandic Film Commission. The day on the windswept beach had heightened the color in her cheeks and she wore her hair loose about her shoulders. She might have been an exotic Siren, emerged from the forest to taunt a group of sailors, her dark beauty in sharp contrast to the paleness of those around her.

What was it about her that made it impossible for him to turn away? Was it the age-old story of wanting what he couldn't have? Did the same disdain for danger that made him want to hurtle down icy slopes at speeds in excess of sixty miles an hour compel him to seek out a woman who was determined to reject him?

Or was something else at work here, something more primal and important to his happiness? For longer than he cared to admit, he'd been searching for something to make him happier and more fulfilled. He'd thought the answer lay in winning the Olympic medal, but that momentary triumph had left him feeling emptier than ever.

Could it be that the answer lay not in something, but in some*one?*

Stacy laughed at something one of her admirers said, her head thrown back, the ivory column of her throat exposed. Kristján stared at that delicate skin, thinking of how it might feel to kiss her there. One of the men poured more wine into her glass and leaned forward to whisper in her ear. She laughed more and only sheer force of will kept Kristján from leaping from his seat and pulling her away.

"If you keep glaring down at the other end of the table, holding your knife like that, people are going to get the wrong idea."

Kristján blinked and stared at Jakob, the young production assistant who sat on his right. "What did you say?"

"The knife." Jakob nodded at the utensil, which Kristján had used earlier to slice into a reindeer steak, now clutched in his fist, as if he was ready to strike out at any moment.

Kristján opened his hand and let the knife fall to the table. It landed on the heavy linen cloth with a muffled thud.

"So, is it Stacy or the Director of Tourism you want to get rid of?" Jakob asked. "Or the other guy?"

He'd prefer both men leave the party now, and never come back. "I have nothing against any of them," he said, forcing himself to relax and feign an interest in casual conversation. "Have you known Stacy long?" he asked.

"Stacy?" Jakob frowned. "I only met her when she came for this shoot. She hired me over the phone to work with her while she's in Iceland."

"What is she like to work with?"

"You've seen her. One of these hard-driving American women. Everything has to be done her way." His lip curled in a sneer. "God forbid she surrender even a little bit of control to anyone else."

Yes, Stacy wanted to remain in control—of her surroundings, of other people and maybe also of her emotions. Feelings were messy things when allowed to reign free. Racers were taught to control their excitement and fear before a race, to prevent adrenaline from taking over.

But Stacy wasn't a racer, and allowing herself to admit she was attracted to him wouldn't result in disaster—but maybe past experience told her it would.

"There you go again, spacing out on me," Jakob chided.

Kristján shook his head. "I was thinking of something else."

"Yeah, well, what man doesn't think about *that?*" Jakob grinned and took a long drink of wine. He'd already had most of a bottle, and his eyes were beginning to lose their focus. "Nothing like a little unrequited love to fuel our fantasies," he continued.

The way Jakob looked at him made Kristján uncomfortable. "Excuse me," he said, and stood.

Stacy looked up at his approach. Her eyes brightened and she even started to smile, but the welcoming expression quickly vanished, replaced by studied indifference.

Did she spend her whole life disguising her true feelings this way—or was it only her feelings for him she was reluctant to reveal?

"May I join you?" He indicated the chair the Director of Tourism had recently vacated.

"Jens is sitting there," she said.

"I'm sure he won't mind." Kristján sat. And if Jens did mind, he was too much of a diplomat to make a fuss. There were advantages to being a national hero that Kristján usually ignored, but wasn't there a saying about all being fair in love and war?

STACY HATED THAT KRISTJÁN had such a talent for unsettling her. All evening she'd successfully avoided staring at his end of the table, only occasionally glancing over at his handsome face as he laughed or talked with one of the other members of the crew or one of the government guests. Yes, he was a handsome man. And yes, he had a talent for kissing. But he didn't really mean anything to her, and she was convinced that to the outside observer, the two of them were no more than casual acquaintances.

Her two dinner companions had certainly never suspected she was interested in anyone but them, and she tried now to regather the thread of conversation they'd been enjoying before Kristján interrupted. "Lars was telling me about the Clint Eastwood movie that was filmed here a few years ago," she said. "I had no idea so many movies were shot in Iceland."

"Directors like our dramatic scenery and unspoiled countryside," Lars said.

"And our rocky shores and beautiful sheep," Kristján said, his expression very solemn.

Lars looked puzzled, while Stacy bit her lip, trying not to laugh. She could resist good looks, macho posturing and even sexy flirtation—but a man who could make her laugh could also make her melt.

Jens returned, a fresh drink in hand. "Kristján," he said. "So good of you to join us." Though his expression said it was anything but.

"I wanted to talk to Stacy," Kristján said, with the attitude of a king dismissing a subject.

The other two men exchanged looks. "I guess we'd better be going," Jens said.

"You don't need to do that," Stacy protested.

"We really should go," Lars said.

When the two left, Stacy turned on Kristján. "That was very rude," she said.

"I only told the truth. I didn't ask them to leave."

"No, but you were sending that message, in that way guys do."

"In what way guys do?"

"You were sending signals. Like…like a bull moose claiming a female for his harem." And she had no desire to be compared to a cow, even if only subconsciously.

He laughed. "Didn't we already discuss this? One woman at a time is fine with me." He leaned toward her. "And speaking of signals, the ones you're sending me are definitely mixed."

"We've definitely discussed this already."

"Then let's try a new topic of conversation. The night is young. It's raining outside and we have a late start in the morning, so we have plenty of time to talk." He made the possibility sound so inviting, as if nothing could be better than learning more about each other. And here, with him close enough for her to see the golden glint of stubble along his jaw, she could think of nothing she would like better than to sit into the waning hours, the velvet murmur of his voice wrapping around her like a caress.

She swallowed and steeled herself against that seductive image. "What do you want to talk about?" she asked.

"Whatever you like. You may have your way with me."

She knew he was being deliberately provocative, but still she couldn't keep the heat from rising to her cheeks. She sipped her wine and quickly regained her composure. "All right," she said. "Tell me about yourself. Did you grow up wanting to be an Olympic skier?"

"Surely you read all that in my press kit. Or saw one of my interviews."

She'd read the press kit, and seen some of the interviews. In them he was charming, witty and suitably modest. But she always felt his story was a tad too well rehearsed. As if he was deliberately leaving out certain details. She leaned forward, chin in hand. "I want to hear it from you. The real version."

He blinked, clearly caught off guard. "You think the press kit and interviews are lies?"

"Not lies. But they're only part of the story—the pretty, concise one that sells well to the media. There's always more."

The official story was that he'd skied as a child, joined

the Junior Olympics team at fourteen and steadily climbed through the ranks, failing to qualify for the Olympics in 1998, qualifying but placing out of medal contention in 2002 and 2006, and finally triumphing this year at thirty-four, when many had thought him past his prime.

Stacy continued to hold his gaze, waiting for him to elaborate on these basic and well-known facts. "My brother was the one who was supposed to go to the Olympics," he said after a moment. "I skied to be with him, but he was always the star."

"Did the two of you compete against each other?" she asked. "A friendly rivalry?"

He nodded. "Though not so friendly at times. We were close in most ways, but when it came to skiing, Arni showed no mercy. He would berate me whenever I lost a race, and brag about his own growing collection of medals and trophies." He fell silent, as if remembering that painful rivalry.

"What happened?" Stacy asked. "Why didn't he go to the Olympics?"

"He quit racing in high school. I continued and I began to think that I would be the one to win a medal."

"Your brother must be very proud of you," she said.

He hesitated. "He has never said so, and I would never ask."

And didn't that say a lot about the family dynamic? Jóna certainly wasn't shy about singing her brother's praises—though she, too, had never mentioned her other brother, Arni. Such family dynamics fascinated Stacy, an only child.

"Now you have your medal—what next?" she asked.

"I don't know. Pursuing a goal like the Olympics is very single-minded," he said. "It doesn't leave room in life for anything else. And once that goal is reached…" He held out his hands, palms up. "I won't miss the grueling schedule of training, traveling and competition, but it frustrates me to no longer have a goal and purpose."

"You don't have to do anything," she said. "You could live off your celebrity for some time to come."

He shook his head. "That is not for me."

Then what *was* for him? At thirty-four, shouldn't he know by now? He must have given the future *some* consideration. Or was this an Icelandic trait to which her Puritan-work-ethic-indoctrinated self couldn't relate? "Have you spent much time in the United States?" she asked. "Besides the visit to Utah in 2002?"

"The World Cup races are at Vail each year, but other than that, I haven't seen much of your country."

"My father worked at Vail for a while when I was growing up," she said. "I remember watching the World Cup races with him when I was a teenager." She'd been staying with her father for a week over a school break; it had been a good visit, one in which he'd kept all his promises, including taking her to see the World Cup races. She'd been among the hundreds of people, many of them teenagers like herself, who had stood on the sidelines to cheer the men who flew down the treacherous Birds of Prey course. Had she watched Kristján race without even realizing it? She was so aware of him now it was hard to imagine a time when she would have been indifferent.

"You said your father is a ski instructor?" he asked.

"He works for the Adaptive Sports Center in Crested Butte, Colorado."

"What is the Adaptive Sports Center?"

"It's a nationally recognized program that teaches people with all kinds of disabilities to ski. My dad has worked with veterans who lost limbs in the war, blind children, people in wheelchairs—all kinds of people." She said the words with some pride. After so many years of aimlessness her father finally seemed to be settling down and doing something useful.

"And they are all able to ski?"

She nodded. "Some of them skied before an injury or illness and want to get back to it, while others have never skied before. But with the help of adaptive equipment, they're all able to get back on the snow."

"I've met some of the Paralympic skiers," he said. "They amaze me. It's difficult enough to race down a course on two legs, yet they compete with only one leg, or none."

"My dad has trained some Paralympians. But mostly he's just helping regular people get out and enjoy themselves." She smiled. "For a long time I thought my dad had wasted his life skiing, but now I'm proud that he's making a difference in people's lives." It had taken her a long time to get to the point where she could say that and mean it.

"I suppose some people, like your father, take more time searching for the work they are meant to do," he said.

"I don't know how hard my dad was searching all

those years of bumming around to different ski resorts," she said. "I think he was just having a good time and stumbled into this."

"Is something less worthy because one 'stumbles into it,' as you say? Is it so horrible to think one might find the right job—or the right romantic partner—by chance?"

Why was he bringing romance into a discussion about jobs and work? "I didn't say he wasn't doing good work," she said. "But it would have been easier on me and my mom if he'd become responsible and settled down earlier." Those first few years after her parents split had been bleak ones. Stacy had waited months, hoping her dad would come back—that he would love her more than he loved skiing.

"So you learned from him and became responsible and settled very early."

"You make me sound boring and…and uptight," she said.

"I would never call you boring." He leaned closer, his voice a low murmur only she could hear. "And when you kissed me the other day you definitely weren't uptight."

Heat curled through her abdomen at his words. "You're never going to let me forget that kiss, are you?"

He touched a finger to her lips and felt them tremble. "Do you *want* to forget it?"

She leaned back, away from him, refusing to look him in the eye. She couldn't think clearly when she stared into that stormy blue. "What I want and what's right and smart aren't always the same thing," she said.

"I don't think you give yourself enough credit. I think

we don't often go wrong when we follow our instincts. And my instincts tell me we should explore this attraction between us."

She laughed, hoping to sound scornful. But the sound came out high and pinched. "Now that's a line I haven't heard before," she said. "I give you points for originality."

"It's not a line. Look at me, Stacy."

Reluctantly, she met his gaze.

"Not every man is out to take advantage of you," he said. "All I want is for you to stop running from me and pushing me away. I won't take anything you don't want to give."

What would he say if she told him he'd already taken a little piece of her heart? If she'd believed theirs would be nothing more than an amusing, shallow fling between two people who were unlikely to see each other again after this week, she wouldn't have hesitated to throw her arms around him right now, kiss him soundly and drag him off to her room at the hotel.

But her feelings for Kristján were anything but shallow. Being with him stirred her deep inside in a way that no other man had—a way that made her feel too uncertain and out of control. So why couldn't she be honest and tell him that? "I really do like you," she said. "And I'm sure we'd have a wonderful time together. But I'm not good at casual relationships. And I don't like being hurt, even if the damage is unintentional."

Something flared in his eyes, some passion or depth of feeling she was unable to read before he smothered it. "I understand," he said. "I, too, am afraid that with you I might not guard my feelings as carefully as I should. But I can't help but regret what might have been."

They might have been a wonderful couple for the few weeks or months romance and passion outweighed more practical concerns. But real life and practicality always intruded eventually and, just as her parents had discovered they could not live on love alone, she and Kristján would learn the same thing.

She blinked. What was she doing, thinking about *love* with Kristján? She hardly knew him. Oh shaking legs, she stood. Time to put some physical distance between the two of them, before the lateness of the hour and the wine she'd drunk and the pull of desire got the better of her. "Good night," she said. "I'm glad we cleared the air between us. We can be friends now."

"Friends." His smile was forced, and he leaned toward her. At first she feared a repeat of the scene in the Gullfoss parking lot, but instead of her mouth, his lips brushed her cheek with a feather-touch that nevertheless sent warmth pooling between her legs.

"Good night," she said again, and turned and fled the room, before lust and longing trampled what remained of her better judgment.

CHAPTER SIX

THE TOURIST BOARD had convinced Stacy that she owed it to herself and her crew to spend two full days at Iceland's famous Blue Lagoon. They would shoot the final series of ads at the spa and hot springs and enjoy some well-deserved rest and relaxation before Stacy returned to the States.

The thought of leaving Iceland so soon—of leaving Kristján—set up a dull pain in Stacy's gut. The pain further annoyed her because she did not see herself as the type of woman who would moon over a man.

But for some reason this man—this handsome, witty, surprising, impossible athlete—got to her. With a look or a touch or a word he laid bare her every insecurity, probed every secret and made her question so much of what she thought she knew about herself.

When she was with him she felt too vulnerable and uncertain—yet also more feminine and desirable and cherished—than she had in all her adult life. Kristján wanted to take care of her—and the fact that she wanted to let him do so frightened her enough to convince her she should get on the next plane back to Colorado.

But first she had to finish the shoot. And hope that the

healing waters of the Blue Lagoon would help clear her confused thoughts and snap her out of the lust-induced haze that was the only explanation she could come up with for her strange behavior around Kristján.

A van transported the crew to the Blue Lagoon the next morning, though their photography session would not begin until late afternoon, when Stefan hoped to take advantage of the sunset for some dramatic photos. Stacy checked into the hotel, then changed into a bikini, grabbed a towel and headed for the pools.

Like almost everything else in Iceland, the Blue Lagoon seemed transported from another planet or a pre-historic landscape. Milky-blue water lapped at obsidian lava formations, steam rising gently from the water's surface or shooting from vents in the rock. Bathers floated in the salty water, or smeared themselves with the white mineral-rich mud that could be scooped from the bottom of the pools, or from buckets that attendants filled daily and placed around the pool.

As Stacy stood on the boardwalk taking in this surreal scene, she heard someone shout her name, and turned to see Jóna waving from the water. The designer wore a frilly pink swim cap and held her laughing, naked little boy as he dangled his feet in the water.

Stacy waded to them. "Nice cap," she said, eyeing the headgear, which up close resembled something out of *Swan Lake*—the psychedelic version.

Jóna laughed. "The minerals in the water are very hard on the hair," she explained. "Some women use conditioner to protect their hair, but I prefer to keep mine covered."

"The baby is enjoying himself." Stacy smiled at the little boy, who grinned back at her, and she felt the familiar tug at her heart that happened more and more these days around small children.

"He loves the warm water." Jóna settled the boy into an infant's swim ring. "There. He can float safely and you and I can visit." She scooped a handful of mud from a pail and began slathering it on her arms. "Would you like some? It's very good for your skin."

When in Rome… "Sure." Stacy accepted a handful of mud and copied Jóna, covering her arms, shoulders and face with the warm, gritty substance. It felt surprisingly soothing, though she was sure she looked as ridiculous as she felt.

"How is the shooting going?" Jóna asked.

"It's going well," Stacy said. "I think the ads will be beautiful and hopefully effective."

"Kristján seems to be enjoying himself more than he thought he would."

Stacy's heart beat faster at the mention of Kristján, and she looked around them, as if expecting him to rise from the water like Poseidon.

"He's in the sauna, I think," Jóna said, answering the question Stacy hadn't asked. "Hiding out from that photographer."

"Lang Kerr? Is he here?" Stacy searched the area, half expecting to see a short man in a down coat, camera in hand.

"Kristján thought he saw him earlier, so he persuaded Arni to go to the sauna with him."

"Arni? Your other brother is here?"

"Yes. He loves the Blue Lagoon, so we decided to make a family reunion of this trip."

"Where does Arni live?"

"In Husavik, with our parents."

Arni was even older than Kristján and he still lived at home? But maybe he took care of his parents. "What kind of work does Arni do?"

"Computer drafting. He's very good at it, though I'll admit I don't understand it. He's always trying to convince me to draw my sweater designs on the computer, but I prefer pen and paper." She gave her son's floaty a little shove and he drifted to Stacy, who clasped his little hands in hers and grinned.

"You should consider extending your visit," Jóna said. "You could come to Husavik and meet my parents. The scenery on the coast is magnificent—we're known for the whales that gather there. You can even take a tour out to see them. And we have interesting museums, including the World Phallology Exhibit."

Stacy looked up from her game of peekaboo with the baby. "The what?"

Jóna laughed. "The world's largest collection of penises. There's one from a whale that's four and a half feet long."

"That sounds like it would give me nightmares. I think I'll pass."

"I'm only trying to point out all the reasons Husavik should not be missed."

"Maybe some other time," Stacy said. "I should be going home."

"Don't you have vacation you could use?" Jóna asked.

Stacy did have several weeks of accumulated vacation time. She seldom bothered to use it all. "Why are you so interested in having me stay?" she asked.

"I like you and I want to show off my country." She hesitated, then added, "And Kristján likes you."

"He said that?" Stacy was grateful for the mud mask that hid much of her expression.

"He didn't have to. I hear it in his voice when he talks about you. He hasn't been this happy since winning the Olympics."

"I can't take credit for that," she protested.

"I think you can. Before he met you, whenever we talked on the phone Kristján was so focused on himself— how hard it was to know what to do with his life, how tired he was of traveling, how he had nothing to look forward to. You've got him thinking outside of himself, taking an interest in other people, talking about the future as something positive, something he looks forward to."

"You're the one responsible for that. You persuaded him to take this job. Maybe all he needed was work and being around new people."

"That might be part of it, but I think most of it is due to you. You've sparked something in him I don't think he'd even try to explain, but I see it."

Stacy looked away. She couldn't very well deny that Kristján had sparked something in her as well.

"Don't tell him I said anything. He'd be furious with me for meddling," Jóna said. "And you're both certainly old enough to manage your affairs without my input. I just wanted you to know that you are welcome to stay if you like and…and I think my brother could make you happy, though I might be a little bit prejudiced."

Stacy nodded, too moved to speak. The picture Jóna had painted of a depressed, confused Kristján was such a contrast to the strong, confident man she knew. Had Jóna exaggerated to garner sympathy for her brother? Or had Stacy really made such a difference in his life?

She knew danger lay in expecting another person to fill the holes in one's life. But was it possible that the right partner—the person, even, that you were *meant* to be with—could help you find ways to fill those holes yourself?

She thought of the holes in her own life—the spaces that should have been filled with family and children and the love of a good man. Was Kristján the one who would help her fill those holes?

BY THE TIME KRISTJÁN reached the sauna, Arni was already waiting for him. Kristján was sure his brother had planned this. Though the accident that had left him paralyzed from the waist down had happened almost twenty years ago, Arni avoided calling attention to his disability, especially around Kristján.

"From Olympic medalist to sweater model running from the papparazzi," Arni said when the brothers had exchanged greetings. He shook his head. "How the mighty have fallen."

"I'm doing this as a favor for Jóna," Kristján said, refusing to rise to Arni's bait.

"Sure. And I suppose it has its perks." He stretched his arms over his head, the powerful muscles of his shoulders and chest knotting, in sharp contrast to his withered lower body. "So which one of the models are you sleeping with?" he asked.

"None of them. Why would you think that?"

"If it was me, I'd be taking advantage of the situation." He grinned. "According to the papers, you're a real playboy these days."

"You should know better than to believe everything you read in the papers."

"Ah, but they always have pictures—photographs of you and the most attractive starlets and socialites. When you're tired of them, you should send a few of those beauties my way."

Kristján remained silent, remembering a time when their roles had been reversed—when Arni had been the brother all the women flocked to and Kristján the silent onlooker.

Arni must have been thinking similar thoughts. "Do you remember the time you had a crush on that girl on the ski team, the one who wore the long braids?" he asked. "What was her name?"

"Greta." She'd been sixteen, he seventeen, and so much in love he could scarcely sleep or eat.

"She kept coming over to the house and you thought it was because she was crazy about you, when all along it was me she wanted." Arni laughed. "I was in a wheelchair and she still preferred me to you."

Kristján nodded; the old hurt long since healed, replaced by a different kind of pain when he thought of his brother. Before Arni's accident, the two had been close; Kristján longed to find a way past Arni's bitterness, to rekindle the friendship that had meant so much to him. He leaned forward and ladled water onto the stones in the center of the sauna, and steam rose between them, obscuring their vision. For a moment the only sound was the hissing of steam, and the creak of the wood benches as they shifted their bodies. Then Arni's voice penetrated the fog. "Don't tell me you're making it with the American—that little director or whatever she is."

Kristján stiffened, but he kept his voice even. "Stacy is the marketing director for the company that plans to sell the sweaters."

"You always did like the dark ones. So, are you sleeping with her?"

"No." Though not for want of trying.

"What is wrong with you? All these women ready to give it up for you and you aren't taking advantage."

He couldn't tell his brother that he was at the point in his life where he wanted more than sex from a woman. For too long almost everything in his life had been transient and temporary, from his address to his relationships. He was ready to stop, to put down roots. He no longer wanted only to go to bed with someone; he wanted to love them and stay with them. Maybe forever.

"How is Clara?" he asked. Clara was the woman who had stuck by Arni the longest, calming his mood swings and teasing him out of his ill temper.

"Clara is fine." All trace of sarcasm and bitterness had vanished from Arni's voice. "She wants to get married."

"You should marry her. She loves you."

"And you know all about that, right, Mr. Playboy?"

"I would marry if I found the right woman. Now that I'm retired from racing, I hope that I will."

"You won't retire. After all these years, racing's in your blood. I'll bet you a thousand kronur that when the season starts you'll be waxing your skis and heading back out there."

"No bets," Kristján said. "I don't intend to race again."

"One medal and you're done? I don't believe you. Don't you know the whole country expects you to go back in four years and do it again? You can't let them down. You can't let *me* down."

The words were a knife, sawing at an old, familiar wound. "In four years I'll be thirty-eight," he said. "Too old to compete with the teenagers and twenty-year-olds."

"That's just an excuse. People said you were too old this time, too, and you proved them wrong."

"I'm tired of that life. I'm ready for something different."

"I'm tired," Arni mimicked in a high-pitched whine. The wood creaked as he dragged himself over on the bench, until he was next to Kristján. "If you don't care about your countrymen, then think about me. You should go out there and win a medal for me, since I can't win one for myself."

The words sent a mixture of nausea, rage and despair swirling through Kristján. He gripped the edge of the wooden bench until his knuckles ached. "I won my medal for you," he said. "I told you that when I gave it to you." The heavy gold medal in its fancy presentation case was somewhere in the house Arni shared with their parents— if Arni hadn't hurled it into the sea during one of his rages.

"I'm surprised you didn't tell the press that. 'I won this medal for my crippled brother.' They would have eaten that up. Women would have been throwing themselves at you even worse than they do now. They'd have been begging to sleep with you."

"Shut up." Kristján didn't raise his voice, but the coldness in the two words cut through the heavy atmosphere inside the sauna.

"Who are you to tell me to shut up? I taught you everything you know about skiing and racing. I showed you everything that would have made me great, if I'd only had the chance."

Kristján stood, so weary that even that simple movement took great effort. "I'm done here," he said. "Do you need help getting back into your chair?"

"No, I don't need your help!" Arni snapped.

Kristján exited the sauna, but returned seconds later, pushing the lightweight racing chair—a gift he'd sent last year—over to the edge of the bench.

Arni swore, but hoisted himself into the chair, jerking out of Kristján's reach. "Leave me alone," he ordered, and rolled away.

Kristján stared after his brother's hunched figure, watching the muscles of his shoulders and arms flex and strain as he powered the wheelchair over the rough walkway.

When they were children, Kristján had idolized his older brother. Arni had been the fastest, the smartest, the most handsome boy in their neighborhood. Early on, he'd been lauded as one of the best young Icelandic skiers, and had been groomed as a future Olympian. Kristján, not as gifted, had been accepted as part of the team because his brother was there, but Arni drew the lion's share of attention, winning more races, receiving more praise. Kristján was proud of his brother, and was never happier than once when Arni had won a gold medal at a junior competition, and Kristján had claimed the silver.

He still had that photograph somewhere: two young

teenagers in ski gear, heads close together, medals held aloft. At the time, Kristján had thought it would always be that way, the two of them together, a team that couldn't be beaten.

Then the accident had happened, when Arni was seventeen, Kristján fifteen. Not a skiing accident, as everyone might have expected, but an automobile accident. A car in which Arni was riding plunged off a cliff. The driver, a boy from their neighborhood, was killed, while Arni's spine was crushed. He lived, but he would never race again.

Now he had to sit on the sidelines and cheer as Kristján won the medals. He had to build a different kind of life than the one he'd planned.

For a long time Kristján had believed he could help his brother. He could allow Arni to live vicariously through him. Even at the Olympics, he had tried to share the experience with his brother, telling Arni that he was racing for both of them. When he'd presented his medal to his brother, they had both wept, and Kristján had told himself it was enough.

But now he saw it would never be enough. He could not erase Arni's bitterness and anger over what had happened to him. All his love and goodwill would never make up for the accident and the end of Arni's dreams. Kristján had to stop trying to live for his brother. He had to start living for himself.

CHAPTER SEVEN

A SECLUDED SECTION OF the pools had been roped off for the photo shoot late that afternoon, closed to the public, including nosy photographers like Lang Kerr. Stacy had seen no sign of the annoying little man, but she was glad the Tourism Commission had arranged for them to have this privacy.

The orange and gold light of sunset tinted the mists rising from the pools, deepening the blue of the opalescent water. Stefan first shot Kristján and the female models at the edge of the water, posed among the black lava formations. Next, he stood them in water to their waists. Finally, he had them immerse themselves in the water and clicked off a series of shots as they rose, water streaming from their bodies, a god and goddesses rising from the sea.

"Now I know why Jóna didn't want to watch. All that heat and salt water is ruining her expensive creations."

Stacy turned and was startled to see a handsome young man in a wheelchair rolling toward her. There was something very familiar about the man, though she would have sworn they'd never met. "I'm Arni Gunnarson." He offered his hand and she shook it, trying hard not to show her surprise at this unexpected meeting.

"I'm Stacy Bristol," she said.

"I know. Kristján and Jóna have both mentioned you."

And what did Kristján have to say about me? she wondered. "It's nice to meet you," she said. "I'm glad you were able to join your brother and sister at this beautiful place."

"They didn't tell you about the wheelchair, did they?" Arni's tone of voice told her he'd correctly read her surprised expression. "They always leave out that little detail, as if maybe no one will notice."

She didn't know how to respond to this, so she remained silent.

Stefan directed Kristján to raise his hands over his head, as if reaching to pluck the dying sun from the sky, while the women draped themselves on either side.

"Kristján's done a lot of crazy things in his life, but this has to be the craziest," Arni said.

Stacy stiffened at this implied criticism of Kristján. "I believe your sister talked him into modeling as a favor to her," she said. "He's actually very good." Modeling required more than outstanding looks. It required patience, a willingness to follow directions and most of all, a presence in front of the camera. Kristján had all of those, and a knack for looking past the camera lens, as if confronting the viewer herself.

"Jóna worries Kristján has become a lazy playboy who will only get into trouble," Arni said. "I told her not to worry. As soon as the next racing season begins he'll be too busy to get into trouble."

"I thought he was giving up racing."

Arni shook his head. "He says that now, but I know

him. Skiing is in his blood. Besides, what else can he do? He doesn't have any other talents or education."

Stacy could think of a few talents Kristján had demonstrated, though she supposed a killer smile and great kissing technique weren't in demand in the job market. Still, she thought Arni underestimated his younger brother—and was that a touch of jealousy she detected? "Jóna tells me you're a computer draftsman," she said.

"I won an industry award for my designs last year. But I can't take any special credit. Design comes naturally for me."

"You're too modest, I'm sure." She might have said more, but she was distracted by the sight of a soaked Kristján peeling a wet sweater off his torso, revealing rippling abs and a sculpted chest. He was pure male perfection. Even the models, who were used to seeing exceptional men, stopped to stare.

Kristján seemed oblivious, ducking himself beneath the surface and rising up, raking his hair back, water cascading through his fingers.

"You should have seen him as a kid," Arni said. "He was so skinny the other racers called him toothpick. Of course, being a lightweight is a handicap in racing. Heavier racers have gravity in their favor. No one who knew him then ever expected him to have the success he's had."

"Some people have to grow into their talent, I suppose." She appreciated the glimpse of Kristján as an awkward youth—it made the man he was now less intimidating, though she was sure that wasn't Arni's intention.

Like Kristján, Arni was handsome and charming. But his charm had a hard edge to it that made her uncomfortable. She turned to him. "It was nice meeting you, Mr. Gunnarson," she said. "I really need to confer with my photographer now."

"Don't let me keep you." He flashed a smile, showing off gleaming teeth. "Maybe I can buy you a drink later."

"Thank you." She hurried away, after the retreating figure of Stefan.

But before she could catch up with Stefan, Kristján approached. He was still shirtless, the wet denim of his soaked jeans clinging to his muscular thighs like a second skin. "I need to talk to you," he said.

"I really have to speak with Stefan," she protested.

"Then later. I'm having dinner with my family, but can you meet me here about eight o'clock?"

"Here? At the pools?"

"Why not? The pools are very relaxing at night. The darkness and mist—very sexy."

The last thing she needed was to be alone in the dark with this man she found so difficult to resist. But as the days passed she was finding it more and more difficult to justify her resistance. So he wasn't a man she could spend the rest of her life with. Did that mean it was wrong for her to enjoy a few moments of pleasure with him? Would leaving him later really hurt as much as denying herself now?

"All right," she said. "I'll meet you at eight. But I really do have to go now."

"I'll look forward to it. And, Stacy?"

"Yes?"

"You don't have anything to be afraid of from me."

She started to argue that she knew that. But she merely shook her head and moved on. Of all the emotions she experienced when she was with Kristján, fear did not figure into the picture. Maybe a little uneasiness about the changes a man like him could bring to her life, but that wasn't the same as fear. She was cautious, but she certainly wasn't a coward.

AT ONE TIME, THE POOLS of the Blue Lagoon had been as familiar to Kristján as the rooms in the house he'd grown up in. The summer after Arni's accident, the brothers had spent weeks here, Kristján pushing Arni's chair along the boardwalk, helping him in and out of the water, and trying in every way possible to ease his brother's suffering and assuage his own guilt. Arni hadn't yet decided to blame Kristján for his troubles and those weeks here had drawn them even closer. Did Arni even remember that now?

Arni was the gifted brother, the Olympic hopeful who was supposed to be Iceland's first medalist. He was supposed to shine while Kristján remained content in his shadow.

But Kristján wasn't content. That was his ugly secret and the source of his guilt. The life he lived now was Arni's dream, and a constant source of friction between the brothers.

"Kristján, is that you?" Stacy's voice, soft and questioning, interrupted his thoughts.

"I'm here," he said, and held his hand out to her.

She ignored the gesture and lowered herself into the pool beside him. "How was dinner?" she asked.

Dinner had been uncomfortable—Arni communicating in terse sentences only when necessary and Jóna trying to keep the conversation light. "Jóna was in a good mood. She's delighted with your ideas for advertising her sweaters."

"Your brother doesn't seem very happy."

"Arni has his moods."

"Is he in pain?"

"I don't know. He doesn't talk about it."

He took a step toward her and she deftly moved away. "Why did you want to see me?" she asked.

"First, tell me what my brother said to you this afternoon."

"He didn't say anything in particular. He was just making conversation."

Maybe Arni saved his bitterness for Kristján. Certainly Arni was capable of being most charming, especially to beautiful women. "Did he flirt with you?"

"Why? Are you jealous?"

"Yes."

His honesty seemed to surprise her. She looked away.

Kristján decided it was time to change the subject. "The moon is almost full tonight," he said, looking up at the pale orb that flooded the pools with silvery light.

"It's beautiful." Water lapped against him as she moved closer. "What is wrong with Arni?" she asked. "Why is he in a wheelchair?"

"He was thrown from a car in which he was a passenger when he was seventeen." All their lives had changed that summer. "He had just made the Olympic ski team. People were already talking of him winning a medal for Iceland."

"How awful for him. And for you."

That she would see his suffering in this touched him. "He can't forgive that I can still ski and he can't."

"But he can. Ski, I mean. My father teaches people in wheelchairs to ski all the time. Some of them have even competed in the Paralympics."

If Arni could ski again, would he let go of some of his anger at Kristján—and at himself? "I don't know if he would do it."

"Call my father and talk to him. He may know of a program in Europe, if Arni doesn't want to come to the States."

"All right. I'll do that." Anything, if it would help bring back the old Arni—the brother he loved.

"Now tell me why you wanted to see me tonight."

"I went to the sauna this afternoon with Arni."

"Jóna told me. What does that have to do with my being here tonight?"

"It has everything to do with my wanting to see you."

Her expression told him she didn't see the connection and was quickly losing patience with him. He forged on. "Arni doesn't want me to give up racing," he said.

"When he spoke with me, he seemed convinced you wouldn't give it up."

"He said I had won a medal for myself, now I had to win one for him."

"Oh."

"For most of my life I have been living for my brother, always asking myself, 'What would Arni do?' When I won the gold medal, I presented it to him. I told myself that finally I had done enough."

"And was it enough?" she asked quietly.

"No. And I realized today it never will be. I have to stop trying to live for my brother and pursue the things I want." He closed the gap between them and looked into her eyes, daring her to move away or to deny the pull of desire between them. "Tonight I want you. Not because it's practical or wise or a good plan for the future, but because I feel things for you I have never felt for any other woman. And I can't let you leave without exploring those things." He took her by the shoulders and pulled her to him, his lips silencing any protests she might have made, letting her know with his lips and tongue and body how much he meant the words he said.

She didn't resist, but returned the kiss with all the fervor he'd hoped for. When they broke apart at last, breathless and a little dazed, she looked into his eyes. "All right," she said. "I'll stay with you tonight. We won't think beyond that."

STACY FOLLOWED KRISTJÁN along dimly lit paths, past mist-shrouded pools bathed in silvered moonlight. It was a scene out of a fantasy or a dream and the fact that Kristján was with her only added to the dreamlike quality.

His honesty tonight made her want to be honest, as well. She'd avoided him because she was so afraid of making a mistake. But maybe the larger mistake lay in not enjoying the gift he offered for even the little time it might last.

Sex was a dance whose steps she thought she knew, but once again, Kristján surprised her. When she moved into his arms, he backed away. "I want to look at you," he said, and undid the tie at the neck of her bikini top.

As he peeled the swimsuit from her, she fought the urge to cover herself. She hated feeling this vulnerable, as if he had removed more than her clothing. She forced herself to focus on him, stripped of his swim trunks now and standing before her in all his perfection.

Except she could see now that he wasn't perfect. He had scars around both his knees and another up the inside of his wrist. She traced the jagged line of paler flesh with one finger. "What is this?" she asked.

"Broken wrist. They put a metal bar and seven screws to hold it together." He indicated another, smaller scar at his shoulder. "There is more metal here, and new tendons in both knees."

He would laugh if he knew how much she had complained the summer she stepped off a curb wrong and had to wear a walking boot for a month. "Is all the pain worth it?" she asked.

"Yes. To stand on the Olympic podium was worth it, but also, every time I step into a pair of skis and feel the snow slide beneath my feet it is worth it."

"But why? It's just a sport." So many times she had wanted to ask her father that question.

Kristján pressed his lips together, his gaze focused inward. Was he trying to find words to describe something she couldn't hope to understand? "Our lives are shaped by expectations," he said. "When we are children, we must live up to the expectations of our parents and teachers. Later, our bosses and neighbors and lovers and even our friends expect us to act in certain ways. Even the most independent person can't escape that. On the snow, I leave all that behind for a while. Even when I'm racing, with coaches and judges and teammates all judging my performance, I can forget them. To race well takes such a connection between my body and the skis and the snow, there isn't room for anything or anyone else in my head. For the few minutes of a race or even a casual run down the slopes, I am really free."

She nodded, not completely understanding, but envious that he had found this escape from the pressures of every day. She seldom struggled with the expectations of others, but she often put pressure on herself to live up to some imagined ideal.

"Pretend you are skiing now," she said, sliding her palms along the perfect plane of his shoulders. "No expectations, only the freedom to enjoy this moment."

She felt his lips curve in a smile as he trailed a path of kisses along her jaw, and she answered with a smile of her own as she arched her body to his. When his mouth covered hers she felt herself melting into him, the last hard edge of resistance disappearing in the heat of his kiss.

Her skin warmed at his touch, and her body hummed with an awareness of him—of the tautness of his waist and the long line of his thigh, of the heaviness of his hand on her hip and the way her breasts compressed against the wall of his chest, and of the insistent nudge of his erection against her stomach, and her own growing need to feel him inside her.

When at last they broke the kiss, she started to tell him how much she wanted him, but he silenced her words by sweeping her into his arms and carrying her to the bed.

She giggled. She didn't mean to, but she couldn't help it.

"What is so funny?" he asked, eyebrows arched in mock outrage.

"It's such a romance-movie moment," she said. "The Viking warrior sweeping the woman off her feet and carrying her to bed."

"Do you have something against Viking warriors?" He opened his arms and dropped her—gently—onto the bed.

"I think they're wonderful." She held her arms out to him. "I think *you're* wonderful." Though she might never admit it out loud, maybe what she'd needed all along was for a man to sweep her off her feet, to battle past the walls of her logical objections and practical behavior to give her what she really wanted, which was to be loved solely for and in spite of herself.

They lay side by side in the narrow bed, letting the tension build. He smoothed his hand along the indentation of her waist and up the curve of her hip. "You're perfect," he said.

"And I think I'm glad to discover a few of your imperfections," she said, touching the scar on his shoulder.

He laughed. "I have plenty of flaws."

"But not in bed, I don't think." She rolled onto her back, bringing him with her. He knelt between her legs and kissed his way down her body, teasing her nipples to swollen, aching peaks, feathering kisses across her belly. She moaned as his mouth closed over her sex, arching to him as his tongue swept over her, shuddering with desire and need.

Then he was kneeling over her, sheathing himself in a condom, burying himself in her with a guttural cry that spoke to some ancient, primitive part of her. He was indeed a warrior home from battle, and she was his sanctuary.

Love was such a loaded, powerful word, but she knew no other way to describe what passed between her and Kristján that night. As much as she might have wanted to fool herself, this was about more than sex. They were two people who had formed a connection almost from the moment they met. They needed each other, though how much and for how long was too soon to tell.

But as she lay in the darkness when their desire was spent, reveling in the feel of his arms around her and the sound of his deep, even breathing soothing her to sleep, she wanted more than anything for this feeling to last. All the failed relationships of her past had surely taught her lessons she could use to make this one work. If she had to change Kristján, or change herself, she would find a way to hold on to these feelings between them.

CHAPTER EIGHT

KRISTJÁN SLIPPED OUT of the room while Stacy slept. He made his way along the deserted boardwalk by the pools, his steps muffled on the damp wood. The muted light of dawn struggled to pierce the mist, reminding him of mornings when he was a boy, rising early to go out with his uncles on their fishing boat.

He was on a mission of a different sort this dawn. His fingers in his jacket pocket curled around the slip of paper on which Stacy had written her father's number. She thought her father could help Arni; if Kristján could arrange for the two of them to meet, he thought he could persuade Arni to take this chance.

He left the pools and emerged in a sheltered picnic and concession area. He bought a cup of coffee, then sat at a wooden table and pulled out his phone. It would be about two o'clock in Colorado; he hoped that was a good time to call.

On the fourth ring a hearty, friendly voice answered. "Hello?"

"Hello. My name is Kristján Gunnarson. I am trying to reach Ed Bristol."

"You got him. What can I do for you?"

"Your daughter gave me your number. I understand you teach skiing to the handicapped."

"Stacy gave you my number?" Ed's voice brightened. "How is she doing?"

"She's great. She's here in Iceland supervising the photography for some advertisements." Shouldn't he know this already? Had Stacy not told him?

"Iceland? How about that? Hey—Kristján Gunnarson! Aren't you the guy who won the gold in men's downhill in Vancouver?"

"Yes."

"And you know Stacy?"

"I'm part of the ad campaign she's working on." That was better than saying *I slept with her last night. Oh, and I love her.*

"I watched that race on television. You were great. A big moment for you and for your country."

"Yes, it was." Even after months of such praise, the attention made Kristján uncomfortable. "I really wanted to find out more about your job," he said.

"Sure. I teach for the Adaptive Sports Center at Crested Butte Mountain Resort. We try to find a way to help almost anyone who wants to ski to get on the mountain and have a good time. We work with kids and adults—a lot of veterans these days. Had a veteran in here this morning, a double amputee. After a couple of hours we had him making runs by himself. He was thrilled. I was, too. That's the great thing about this job—I get to help change people's lives. I get back as much happiness as I give."

Kristján felt a rising excitement, not unlike what he

experienced before an important race. "Stacy said you'd worked with some Paralympians."

"You bet. We've had several Paralympians train here."

"Do you think someone who skied professionally—at an Olympic level—before an injury put them in a wheelchair, could learn to ski again? To maybe compete again?"

"Absolutely. They'd be ahead of the game because they'd be familiar with the dynamics of skiing and racing. As long as their upper-body strength and balance were reasonably good, we'd put them in a mono-ski and away they'd go. Hey—you haven't been in some kind of accident have you?"

"No, no, I'm asking for a friend." He hesitated. "For my brother. He was injured nineteen years ago, but he used to be a very good skier."

"Bring him to see me and I'll get him set up. The exercise would help him physically, but I think the biggest benefit is mental. I see it all the time. This gives people back some of their independence. It gives them back an activity they love."

"How long have you been teaching?" Kristján asked.

"Ten years now. I love coming to work every day."

"What did you do before?"

Ed laughed. "I guess you'd say I was a ski bum. I taught able-bodied skiers, worked in lift operations, did some bartending—whatever it took to earn a lift ticket and time on the snow. I'm surprised Stacy didn't tell you that. She and her mom never thought much of my priorities. They didn't understand I wasn't happy with a conventional job and a conventional life."

"Stacy's very proud of what you're doing now."

"She told you that?" His voice was rough.

"Yes."

Ed cleared his throat. "So what are you doing now that the Olympics are over? Have you started training for the next one yet?"

"I'm retiring."

"Really? Well, why not? Go out on top."

"I would like to visit you," he said. "And bring my brother."

"Anytime. I'd love to meet you and your brother."

"I'll be in touch. Thank you."

"Thank you. And say hello to Stacy for me."

"I'll do that."

He hung up the phone and sat with his now-cold coffee, watching the sun climb in the sky and burn away the mist. The prerace excitement and the anticipation that something big was about to happen stayed with him. He had thought when he retired from racing, he would leave skiing behind, but what if he did something like Stacy's father? What if he used his skills to help others?

He felt a new urgency to make this trip. He wanted to help Arni, but it might be that he would help himself, as well. Here was a way for him to do what he knew best—skiing—without the grind of travel and constant pressure of competition. Here was a way for him to help other people—people like Arni. The darkness that had shadowed him since his decision to quit the Olympic team lifted at the thought.

STACY WAS SURPRISED to find herself alone when she awoke. Even as she'd fallen asleep last night, she'd looked forward to waking with Kristján this morning. Instead, she had to settle for a note he'd left on the dresser.

Good morning, sleeping beauty. I have things I must do this morning and didn't want to wake you. Have a good day and I will see you later. Love, Kristján.

The word *love* was wobbly and faint, as if he'd hesitated over writing it. But he had put it down all the same, and those four simple letters made her feel like shouting with joy and excitement and, yes, a little bit of fear.

Part of her wanted to find him and go to him and tell him how happy she was. But the other part of her told her it would be good to spend a few hours apart from him, thinking about what she really wanted to do.

She needed to call her boss in the States and let him know she planned to take a couple of weeks' vacation. Kristján could show her his home country and they'd have time alone to get to know each other better. Then maybe he'd agree to come to the States with her. Her mother would absolutely love him.

And what about her father? Her father wouldn't miss the irony of having his daughter fall for a skier—an Olympic medalist, at that. As a teenager, especially, she'd been so vocal in her objections to his lifestyle.

She sighed. Maybe it was past time she apologized to her dad for some of the things she'd said. She still didn't agree with all the choices he'd made in his life, but maybe it was time to let go of some of those grudges. She could remember the good times they'd spent together and try to overlook his faults—just as he must have to overlook hers.

Smiling to herself as she pondered all the possibilities for her future, she quickly showered, then headed for the spa, where she'd previously scheduled a day of pampering: facial, body scrub and massage and manicure and pedicure. When she saw Kristján again she'd be a new woman, inside and out.

KRISTJÁN FOUND ARNI in his room and told him they'd been invited to visit the Adaptive Sports Center at Crested Butte Mountain Resort in Colorado. While he'd anticipated some reluctance on Arni's part, he wasn't prepared for his brother's anger.

"Aren't you the generous one, arranging all this without bothering to consult me?" Arni's voice dripped with contempt.

"I haven't arranged anything," Kristján said. "And I am consulting you now. Don't you want to ski again?"

"Sitting in a chair while someone pushes me over the snow is not skiing."

"This isn't like that and you know it. You could ski on your own—independently. You could even race again."

Arni looked away, lips pressed so tightly together all color was blanched out of them.

"Maybe it's not the idea that bothers you so much, but that I am proposing it," Kristján said. "Would you deny yourself something you want solely to spite me?"

"You have no idea what it's like for me."

"Then tell me." He moved around so that Arni was forced to look at him. "Help me understand why you hate me so much. I'm not the one who put you in that chair."

Arni swallowed, his Adam's apple prominent with the

effort. "If we go to America, I know exactly how it will be," he said. "Everyone will be looking at you. Everyone will be talking to you. I'll be the poor crippled brother in the wheelchair—isn't Kristján wonderful for taking such good care of him?"

The pain and truth of Arni's words cut deep. If the media tracked down the story of the Olympic gold medalist helping his wheelchair-bound brother to learn to ski again they would make the most of it. Once again Kristján would be the hero, Arni in his shadow. "The press won't find out," he said.

"Oh, no? They follow you everywhere." Arni snatched a magazine from the table by his chair and tossed it at Kristján. Kristján stared at the color photograph that took up most of the front page of the tabloid. It showed Stacy leaning from around Kristján, her hands at his waist, his hand protectively on her shoulder. *American mystery woman latest conquest for Olympic playboy* read the caption.

Had Stacy seen this? Would she be upset that she was on display like this, or would she laugh it off now that she and Kristján really were lovers? He folded the paper and laid it back on the table. "We'll leave before they know we're gone," he said. "The press won't find us in Colorado the way they can here."

"You make it sound so easy," Arni said. "It isn't for me."

"You were never a coward before," Kristján said.

"Who are you calling a coward?" Arni's gaze burned into him.

"You just admitted you're afraid of what other people

think of you." Kristján grasped the arms of the wheelchair and leaned down, his face inches from his brother's. "Why do you give a damn about what anyone else thinks? What do *you* want?"

"I...want to be able to ski again. To race."

"Then don't pass up this opportunity."

The lines around Arni's eyes deepened. "What if it's too late? It's been so long..."

"You won't know if you don't try."

"And you'll be there with me?"

Kristján's throat tightened as he recognized the anxiety behind Arni's plea. Arni really did want Kristján with him now. They would be a team again, facing this together. "I'll stay until you ask me to leave," he said. Not even then, if he didn't think Arni meant it.

"I won't ask you to leave." Arni gripped Kristján's hand. "I can't do this without you. Watching you all these years doing the things I wanted to do—it's kept me going. Maybe for the wrong reasons sometimes, but it got me through some tough times."

"We'll get through this together, too."

"Yeah." Arni blinked rapidly, his eyes shiny. "Yeah, we will."

CHAPTER NINE

BY THE TIME STACY EMERGED from the spa she was massaged, buffed, polished and perfumed as she had never been before. She practically floated out the door, her head filled with fantasies of seeing Kristján again, and having the most fantastic, stress-free sex of her life.

She quickly came back to earth when she saw Jóna waiting for her outside her room. "Have you seen Kristján?" Jóna asked, worry lines making furrows between her brows.

"No. I mean, not recently." Not since she'd fallen asleep in his arms last night.

"I can't find him or Arni anywhere. They've both checked out of the hotel, and they aren't in any of the pools or the sauna."

Stacy put one hand to the wall to steady herself. "They're gone?"

"Arni and I were supposed to have lunch together, but when I went by his room, he was gone. The front desk told me he'd checked out earlier, and so had Kristján. No one knows where they've gone. I was hoping they were with you."

Stacy shook her head. "I've been at the spa all morning."

She stared at Jóna. "They left? Without saying goodbye?" After all Kristján's tender words last night—his sweet note this morning—had he really just abandoned her?

She closed her eyes, remembering a morning when she was eleven. She'd awakened early and gone into the kitchen to make a bowl of cereal. There, on the kitchen table, was a note from her father. He was sorry, but he had to leave, and he wouldn't be coming back. It had been months before she'd seen him again, longer than that before she could think of him without crying.

But there was no reason for Kristján to leave this way. Surely she couldn't have misjudged him so badly. "Maybe there was an emergency," she said. "Something with Arni…"

"They would have contacted *me*." Jóna searched Stacy's face. "I thought maybe…did the two of you have an argument? Something that would have made Kristján want to leave?"

"No! Not an argument."

"I thought maybe you were upset about this." Jóna reached into her purse and withdrew a folded newspaper and handed it to Stacy.

Stacy stared at the large color photo of her standing with Kristján, that day at Gullfoss. She blinked back sudden tears. Maybe the photographer had recognized something between her and Kristján that she hadn't been willing to recognize yet herself: the two of them looked right together. Like two people in love.

"I hadn't seen it," she said, handing the paper back to Jóna. "But I'm not upset about it. Kristján and I…we spent the night together. It was wonderful." The last words were a whisper, squeezed out past a threatening flood of tears.

Jóna put her arm around her. "Then something must have happened. Kristján wouldn't leave without speaking to you. He loves you."

"He told you that?"

"He didn't have to tell me. I saw it in his face every time he looked at you. Do you love him?"

"Yes." She took a deep breath, pushing back the fear. "Yes, I do."

"Then we'd better find him. And Arni, too. It isn't like him to leave. He doesn't like to be out in public."

"Have you tried Kristján's cell?" Stacy asked.

"I did, but he's not answering—at least he's not answering me. Why don't you try?"

Stacy dug her phone from her purse and turned it on. "I had it off while I was in the spa," she said, waiting impatiently for the signal to register. Her heart skipped a beat when the message icon appeared. "I have a message. Maybe it's from Kristján."

She could have wept for joy when his voice filled her ear. "Arni and I are flying to Crested Butte this afternoon," he said. "Don't tell anyone except Jóna. We're trying to avoid reporters. Your father has agreed to meet us there. I hope you will meet us, too. I have some very important things to say to you."

She listened to the message twice, elation warring with confusion. "They've gone to Crested Butte, Colorado," she told Jóna.

"Colorado? Why? And why leave so suddenly?"

"The message said something about wanting to avoid

reporters." She shoved the phone back in her purse. "My father is in Crested Butte. He works with the Adaptive Sports Center. I think Kristján persuaded Arni to go there, to learn to ski again."

Jóna's eyes widened. "I think Arni would give anything to learn to ski again."

"I still don't understand the rush. Why did they have to leave right away?"

"Kristján was probably afraid Arni would change his mind," Jóna said. "And the more quickly they acted, the less likely that reporters would learn of the trip. Here in Iceland, Kristján really has no privacy."

Stacy nodded, thinking of Lang Kerr. "I can understand them not wanting the press to learn of their plans." But couldn't he have taken the time to stop and say goodbye?

"Do you live very far from Crested Butte?" Jóna asked.

"Only a few hours away. Kristján asked me to join them there."

"Will you?"

"I don't know." Everything was happening so fast. She needed time to think....

"Don't talk yourself out of this if it's what you really want," Jóna said. "Sometimes it's good to follow your heart instead of your head."

LEGS STRAPPED TOGETHER, modified ski poles tipped with short skis grasped in either hand, Kristján strained to keep the mono-ski upright, and to tilt his body while shifting his weight the right amount to accomplish a turn.

His arms and shoulders ached already and this was only his second run. He felt the mono-ski shift beneath him and struggled to regain control, but felt himself tipping, sliding on his side to a stop.

Ed skied to a stop beside him. "You all right?" he asked.

"Only my pride is injured," Kristján said, shoving himself upright once more.

"It's a lot harder than it looks," Ed said. "Wait until they have you skiing on one leg, or blindfolded."

"I feel like I'm learning to ski all over again."

"You don't have to do this."

"No. I want to." He looked up at Stacy's father. In the three days he'd been in Colorado, the two men were fast becoming friends. One day of watching him work with Arni had been enough to convince Kristján that this was what he wanted to do with his life. "I want to help others, the way you are helping Arni." His brother was happier than Kristján had seen him in years. No longer so angry, he was the brother Kristján had missed having in his life. To make that kind of difference in others' lives would mean more than a whole drawerful of gold medals.

"I've been talking to some people in the front office," Ed said. "You know, some resorts pay a celebrity skier to be their spokesperson, so you could do something like that and teach."

Kristján nodded. While he'd kept a low profile so far, it was probably unrealistic to think he could leave his fame behind forever at a ski resort. And perhaps his name and face could raise the profile of the Adaptive Sports Center.

What would Stacy think of his decision? Would she be happy that he'd decided on a career helping others? She seemed proud of her father now, but she clearly resented the skiing lifestyle he'd lived when she was younger.

Would she only see her father in Kristján—a man who had put skiing above his family? Kristján's heart twisted at the thought. Would he have to choose between skiing and the woman he loved?

"Come on," Ed said. "You've still got a lot of work to do before you're ready to teach."

Kristján grunted as he struggled to keep the mono-ski upright. "I may never graduate from this contraption," he said.

"Knowing what it's like for your students will really help you as an instructor," Ed said. "Don't get too discouraged. You'll soon be a lot better at it."

"I'm not discouraged. It's exciting to learn new things. It makes the sport brand-new again."

"I saw Arni this morning," Ed said. "He's doing a lot better than you are."

"Skiing always came easier for him than it did me," Kristján said. "It's one reason why being in a wheelchair has been so hard for him."

"He's doing great. He'll be racing you down the slopes in no time."

"If I know Arni, he will win."

They reached the bottom of the run, and Ed helped Kristján remove the bindings from his legs and climb out of the mono-ski. The bullet-nosed pod mounted on a single long ski looked like something out of a science fiction movie—some ultramodern means of transport. Coupled with the ski pole outriggers, the mono-ski allowed a seated person to maneuver down the slopes with surprising dexterity.

"Kristján!"

At first he thought he was dreaming. Or maybe when he'd fallen he'd hit his head. But no, Stacy really was walking toward him, smiling—as if it hadn't been four days since he'd seen her or spoken to her.

STACY KEPT HER SMILE IN PLACE as she walked toward Kristján and her father, though her stomach did backflips and her legs felt unsteady. In the four days since he'd left Iceland she'd purposely avoided talking to him—not because she didn't want to hear his voice, but because she'd needed the time apart to clear her head. She had to convince herself that she loved Kristján enough to stay with him, even if he didn't have a steady job or a definite idea of what he wanted to do with his life. Her heart told her yes, though her brain was still having trouble accepting the situation.

She had left a single message on his voice mail, assuring him she would talk to him soon, but asking him not to call her in the meantime. She doubted he understood, but they would have plenty of time for explanations later.

"Sweetheart!" Her father greeted her with open arms. "It's great to see you again. You look more beautiful every time I see you."

"Thanks, Dad. It's good to see you, too." But she looked at Kristján as she spoke. His eyes locked to hers, filled with questions, and a sharp desire that made her heart race.

"Hello, Stacy," he said, his voice calm. Cool, even.

"How are you doing?" her father asked. "When did you leave Iceland?"

"I left three days ago. I had some things I had to take care of at home before I came here." She looked at the mono-ski, then at Kristján. "Were you skiing in that?" she asked.

"It's part of the training for new instructors," her father explained. "We want them to experience things from the client's point of view."

"Instructor? I don't understand."

"I've decided I want to work with the Adaptive Sports Center," Kristján said. "I want to use my experience skiing to help others like Arni."

"You've decided to work here? Really?" She looked to her father for confirmation.

He nodded. "I think he saw what a blast his brother was having and didn't want to miss out."

She felt torn between laughter and tears. She'd spent days worrying about how she'd cope with Kristján's lack of a focus for his life, and he'd solved the problem on his own—with the help of her father, no less!

She looked away, trying to compose herself. "How is Arni?" she asked.

"He's well," her father said. "He's enjoying the resort and being out on the snow again."

"That's good."

"We'd better get this back to the office." Kristján spoke—though he addressed himself to Ed, not Stacy.

"You go on," she said. "I need to talk to Dad for a minute."

The two men exchanged questioning looks. "We'll catch up with you in a minute," Ed said. "Leave the mono-ski. We'll get it."

Kristján hesitated, then left them, shoulders set in a stiff line, telegraphing his displeasure.

Ed turned to Stacy. "It's good to see you," he said.

"It's good to see you, too, Dad."

He shoved his hands in the pockets of his ski jacket. "So what did you want to talk to me about?"

This was the hard part, but she was determined to go through with it. "I wanted to apologize. I…I know I was really hard on you, especially when I was a teen. I said some things I realize now were really hurtful, and I'm sorry for that."

"Don't worry about it. Teenagers say a lot of things they don't mean."

"Still, it was wrong of me to judge you."

He cleared his throat. "When I was younger, I know I let you and your mom down. I didn't want to hurt you, but…well, I guess it took me a long time to grow up."

"Maybe I needed to get older to understand some things, too, Dad." Such as how following a dream wasn't always a bad thing, and how taking time to discover what you really wanted in life could be years well spent.

When she'd first met Kristján, she'd been so afraid he was just another self-centered, irresponsible ski bum—one more man she couldn't count on to be there for her. But she'd been wrong about him, and maybe she'd been wrong about her father, too. Whatever mistakes he'd made in the past, he loved her, and he was here for her now.

"Kristján said you told him you were proud of me," he said.

The vulnerability behind those words brought a lump to her throat. "I am proud of you," she said. "You do wonderful work, and I know you've helped a lot of people." Meeting Arni had opened her eyes to how important something as simple as skiing could be, especially to a person who had had so many things taken away from him. To give that measure of independence and freedom back must mean a great deal.

"It meant a lot to me to hear that."

"I should have told you, Dad. I'm sorry."

He patted her shoulder. "I love you, sweetheart. And I like Kristján, too. He's a great guy."

"Yes, he is."

"So, is he someone special to you? More than just a friend?"

Her cheeks felt hot. "What makes you say that?"

"The way he talks about you. The way the two of you looked at each other just now."

Kristján had looked angry with her just now. Had her father mistaken that for passion? Or were the two emotions not that far apart? "Kristján and I are good friends," she said. "Maybe more."

"None of my business, I know. But I'm still your old man. I have to ask."

"It's okay, Dad." His concern was touching, really. "I'll let you know."

"Do you still ski?"

She laughed. With her father, it would always come back to skiing. She could accept that now, and even embrace it. "Yes, I do."

"I know some terrific stashes I can take you to. We'll have a blast while you're here."

"That'll be great." It had been years since they'd spent much time together. It would be good to rebuild the closer relationship they'd once enjoyed.

He leaned down and grasped one side of the mono-ski. "Help me carry this back to the center."

She took up her half of the burden and they began moving through the crowd at the base of the lift. She couldn't stop smiling, savoring this new connection with her father. Right now she felt closer to him than she had in years.

She felt closer to Kristján too. He had broken down barriers no man had breached before. She'd thought she was being smart, protecting herself from being hurt, but he'd shown her the rewards of taking risks. She hadn't won an Olympic medal, but love was an even bigger reward—one she was beginning to hope would be hers.

KRISTJÁN PACED THE Adaptive Sports Center office, which was a confusion of wheelchairs, crutches and one seeing-eye dog who waited patiently in a corner. What did Stacy mean, showing up out of the blue, then ignoring him?

Granted, she was talking to her father, but she'd scarcely looked at him, even when Ed had spilled the news about his decision to teach at the Adaptive Sports Center. Was she so disappointed that he was following in her father's footsteps?

The door opened and he looked up as father and

daughter entered, the mono-ski supported between them. Ed moved behind the desk to answer the phone, and Stacy made her way to Kristján. "How are you doing?" she asked.

"I'm fine." His eyes searched hers, trying hard to read her emotions. "I expected to hear from you before now."

"I know. I...I had some things I needed to sort out." She looked away from him, at the equipment scattered around the room. "You really want to teach here?"

"Yes." Unable to stand the suspense any longer, he took her hand and pulled her into a small side office, and shut the door behind them. He had things he needed to say to her, but not in front of an audience. "Skiing is what I know and what I love. I know you don't understand that, but it's part of who I am. This is a way to still ski, but to help others and do something meaningful."

"I understand." She squeezed his hand, and looked at him once more, her eyes shining. "While you've been here, deciding what you really wanted to do with your life, I've been thinking about my life, as well."

He stiffened. Was this the point where she told him they couldn't be together? Did she think he would let her go without a fight? "What did you decide?"

"That I need to make some changes. I need to spend time on things other than work. I need to stop judging people on the basis of what they do, and look instead at who they really are. And I need to think about myself the same way."

That told him all about her. But where did that leave *them?* "One of the things I admired about you when we first met was that you had such a strong sense of purpose," he said. "You knew exactly what you wanted and what to do to get it, while I felt so aimless and unfocused."

She smiled. "I guess I am like that. But you made me see that sometimes I've wanted the wrong things." Her eyes filled with tears again.

He could stand it no longer, and gathered her in his arms. She didn't resist, but leaned into him, her head on his shoulder. "Why are you crying?" he asked. "You are too hard on yourself."

"I'm not sad, I promise." She sniffed, and raised her head to look up at him. "I'm just so happy. Seeing you again, hearing you talk about your work—it makes me see how much I love you. How *right* being with you feels."

The fear and pain that had squeezed his heart vanished, and he felt like shouting for joy. He settled instead for holding her closer. "I love you, Stacy," he said. "Please don't leave me again."

"I won't. I want to stay with you. And I want to spend time getting to know my father better, too. That's why, when I was in Denver, I made arrangements to transfer here, to Crested Butte. So that I can be with both of you."

"You're moving here?"

She nodded. "I've made all the arrangements."

"What if I can't extend my visa and must return to Iceland?"

"Businesses there need marketing directors. Or I can freelance." The determination that had impressed him that first day returned to her eyes. "I'm not going to worry about that now. I've wasted too much time already preparing for bad things that never came to pass. I want to enjoy the life I have right now. With you."

He kissed the top of her head and hugged her tight.

"You'd follow me even to the 'frozen wilderness' as you called it?"

"Yes." She snuggled closer, a refugee who had found her true home in his arms. "Wherever I am with you, I know I'll be warm."

* * * * *